My Sister's Keeper

A Hood River Valley Mystery

Lana M. Fox

Contents

Other books by Lana M. Fox:
The Truth Will Set You Free

This book is dedicated to one of the strongest women
I know, my mom, Beatrice Hubbell Goss. You were an
amazing mother and friend!
And to all of the other strong women in my life. You
inspire me!

Prologue

Two weeks earlier

George Scott sat in his chair with a cup of tea on the table beside him. It was plain tea, none of that flavored stuff for George, and he liked it extra hot with two spoons of sugar. The doctor had told him he probably should cut back on sugar, but at age seventy-seven, George thought he should be able to eat and drink whatever he wanted.

Bailey, his hundred-pound yellow lab, laid on the rug beside him. George bent and patted her head, and she looked up at him in adoration. He smiled, rubbed her ears, then picked up the latest Longmire book and settled in to read a while before bed.

Rain plummeted the picture window next to him. Bailey whined. She hated the rain. George thought it was because she wanted to go for a walk, and they didn't walk in the rain. She got up and stood with her nose pointed to the window next to his chair. George looked up. "What is it, girl? Is there a stray cat out there?"

The dog looked at him and gave a soft, whoof. Then she paced back and forth with her hackles raised.

George patted her head. "It's okay. That mean old cat can't get inside tonight."

A low rumble came from Bailey's throat. George put his book down and stood. "Okay, I'll turn on the yard light and make sure there isn't anything going on out there. Will that make you feel better?"

He walked over to the lightswitch by the outside door and flipped it on. He looked out the window. "I don't see any cats." He unlocked the door and opened it. Nothing stirred on the lawn except the rain. "I think we're okay." He shut the door, turned off the light and went back to his chair and his book. Bailey followed him and lay at his feet with a sigh.

He was just getting into the story when his phone rang. He picked it up and saw his old friend, Murray's, name. "Hey Murray."

"George. I just got your voicemail. Sorry, my phone died, and I turned it off and plugged it in. So, you heard from Rose?"

"Yeah, she's finally leaving the cult." At least he hoped she was, and this wasn't a bid for money to keep the cult going. Rose, his oldest daughter, had tried getting money out of him before. There was no way he was funding that crazy Jeremiah Swanson and his cult. But Rose had said she was leaving. She hadn't asked for money. He'd volunteered it.

"Good. About gul-durned time," Murray said. "Does Liz know?"

George thought about his younger daughter. "No, and we both know she doesn't want me to give Rose money. But if there's any chance of getting Rose out..."

"Yeah, I hear you."

"I left an envelope in the glove compartment of your pickup. If Rose comes looking for it, I need you to give it to her."

"Course I will. Sorry, I missed you. Probably ran home for dinner and fell asleep in front of the TV."

George smiled. That wouldn't be a surprise. Murray did it every evening. Then he'd go back to his shop and work well into the night. "No problem. I appreciate you doing this."

"If she's leaving that place, isn't she coming home?"

"No, she said it isn't safe right now. I told her to come on home, that I could protect her, but she insisted on hiding out somewhere for a while."

"No tellin' what those crazies would do," Murray said. "If she comes by, I'll give her the envelope."

"Thanks. And Murray, let me know if she shows up, okay?"

"Course I will."

George said goodbye and turned off his phone. He picked up his tea and noticed it had cooled, so he got up and went into the kitchen to warm it. He set the cup in the microwave and turned it on.

A noise in the back of the house caught his attention. It sounded like a window being forced open. George felt his heart pound and headed towards the hall. Bailey came from behind him, barking her head off and running toward his bedroom.

Dread curdled in his stomach. Someone was breaking in, and his gun, a .38 revolver was under his mattress. What if he couldn't get to it in time? He hurried down the hall behind Bailey, hoping the burglar would hear the dog and change his mind.

The door to his bedroom was open and Bailey lunged towards the windows, barking and growling. George's heartbeat tripled. Where was his phone? He should call Liz or Mitch. He tried to think but couldn't remember where he'd left the phone. Bailey's barking was giving him a headache. George rubbed a hand across his forehead and felt perspiration run down his face.

Suddenly, he remembered talking to Murray just a few minutes before. He grabbed the gun from under his mattress and headed back to the living room to call his son-in-law, the sheriff. Bailey quit barking, turned to him, and whined.

"What is it, girl? Did the bad guys go away? We should probably call Mitch anyway. Liz will be mad at me if I don't."

He headed back into the living room and picked up his phone from off the end table. The picture window behind him shattered into a million pieces and before George could react, a sharp pain hit his head, taking him to his knees, then to the floor.

Chapter 1

The day after my dad's funeral, while my husband drove our daughter back to college in Corvallis, I went looking for my sister. She had joined The Bread of Life cult ten years earlier, removing herself from our lives. When I'd reached out to let her know about our father's murder, Rose hadn't responded.

Mitch had wanted me to wait for him to get back. We had words.

"We'll drive up and check it out tomorrow," he'd said, with a frown. As sheriff of Oregon's Hood River County, Mitch was used to giving orders.

As his wife, even though I was also one of his detectives, I was used to ignoring them. "No, I'm going today. I can't put this off any longer." I slipped on my rain jacket. The late April rains were soaking everything. So typical of spring in the valley.

"Don't be stupid, Liz. You know better than to go alone." He put his Oregon State Beavers hat on and grabbed his jacket from off the hook by the kitchen door.

I bristled at his words, hating the derogatory tone in his voice. "I'm not stupid. This is something I need to do. I want to find out why Rose didn't show up for Dad's funeral." Our daughter stood next to us, her suitcases already in the truck. I pulled her into my arms. "Call me when you get there, okay?"

She nodded and held onto me longer than usual. "I hate to leave. Will you be, okay?" she whispered.

I smiled and said, "yes, of course." Then I hugged her tight and let her go.

Mitch ignored our exchange. "Why can't you listen to me for once?" he yelled. "I don't want you going up there alone. Who knows what those crazy people might do? At least take a deputy with you."

"I don't need to take anyone with me, I can take care of myself."

He looked down on me from his ten-inch height advantage. "One day, Liz. It won't hurt you to wait one more day."

"No." I wasn't about to back down.

Mitch shook his head and stormed out the door. Bella's eyes were huge, and I hugged her again. "Have fun at school. Study hard." I smiled, kissed her cheek, and watched her walk out to Mitch's truck and jump in. She waved, as they drove off. Mitch stared straight ahead.

I locked the kitchen door and ran through the rain to my Jeep Cherokee, thinking about Bella. It always upset her when Mitch and I had words in front of her. I'd have to call her later and let her know everything was all right. I hoped it was. Mitch had been acting weird lately. He'd been angry and depressed. I thought he was going through a mid-life crisis. He'd be turning fifty soon, and

I assumed that was bothering him even though he said not.

I put Mitch and his bad moods out of my head and headed south on Hwy 35 towards Mt. Hood. The rain, which had eased off earlier in the day, had returned with a flourish. My window wipers couldn't keep up with the amount of water coming down.

The directions I'd gotten off my google app took me about twenty minutes out of Hood River, just past the small community of Parkdale. Soon I was in the national forest and the trees rose on each side of the highway. The mountain, which reigned over this part of Oregon, was hiding in the clouds. I kept an eye out and soon there was a sign on the right stating, Bread of Life, and an arrow pointing down a dirt road. It was a hand-made sign and looked like it hadn't been there long.

My Jeep Cherokee bumped along the road as I tried to avoid potholes. I didn't know much about the cult except it had been started by a man named, Jeremiah Swanson and his wife, Priscilla. Because my husband and I both worked for the county sheriff's office, we could've kept a closer eye on the cult, but there hadn't been a reason to. Then, about a month before my father's death we'd gotten information saying there were some things going on at the cult that had brought it to the attention of the FBI. If they'd found anything in their investigation, we hadn't heard.

As I drove, I thought back ten years earlier to when Rose had told us that she was quitting her job as a nurse and joining the cult. Dad and I had been horrified. We tried our best to talk her out of it.

"You don't understand," she'd told me. "It isn't a cult, it's a way of life. We grow our own fruits and vegetables and raise our own meat in a calm spiritual atmosphere." Her eyes had glowed. "Can you imagine how wonderful the food is for you when it's grown with no stress in an atmosphere of love? Jeremiah says we can live forever if we live stress free and eat food that is grown without chemicals and tended with love. It will be wonderful, Liz. I wish my whole family would join." Her soft blue eyes had been filled with awe and a reverent smile had curled her lips. I wanted to throw up.

"It's a cult, Rose. Swanson separates people from their families and directs their lives. Why would you want to join something like that? You'll never be able to make your own decisions."

"You don't understand," she'd said, and she was right. No matter how hard Dad and I tried, we couldn't talk her out of leaving and joining the Bread of Life.

Now my heart was heavy as I drove along the muddy road into the compound. I knew if Rose had been told about our father's murder, she would have been in touch. Rose had adored our father. Why hadn't she come home or called when she heard about his death? Was she not allowed? Did she know anything about his murder? Over the years she'd asked Dad for money. As far as I knew he'd never given her any, not wanting to support the cult. Had someone from the Bread of Life taken matters into their own hands and tried to force my father into giving them money?

Anger burned inside of me. If they had, I would take their compound apart, stone by stone, brick by brick until I found the person responsible, even if it was my sister.

As I drove into the parking area of the compound, I noticed how well kept it was. It consisted of a large building in the center, surrounded on both sides with smaller structures. Even though everything was soaked, I could tell the grounds were kept clean and neat. The buildings were all painted white and there were flowerbeds with the first spring flowers—daffodils and tulips-- doing their best to rise from the damp earth.

I pulled up to the main building and looked around before I got out of my car. I didn't see any vehicles parked nearby and wondered if they parked them away from the compound. I knew Jeremiah Swanson drove a Mercedes, because he and Priscilla had picked Rose up when she moved in with them. At least they had back then.

The main building looked like a remodeled barn from the outside. I wondered what it looked like on the inside, but I wasn't prepared for what I saw when I got out of my car and climbed the steps up to the front door. Where had they gotten the money for this place? It was certainly different from where they'd started. When Rose joined them, they'd been living in Washington State in dilapidated cabins on an acre of land owned by Priscilla's family.

I knocked and the door was opened immediately by a woman wearing a long purple dress. She stepped forward and held the door partially closed behind her like she didn't want me seeing what was going on inside. "May I help you?"

"Yes, I'm looking for my sister, Rose Scott."

"Rose doesn't live here any longer." She started to step back in and close the door, but I grabbed it and held it open. Rain dripped down my arm inside my coat sleeve.

"What do you mean? Where is she?"

The woman shrugged. She had straight blonde hair that fell to her shoulders, dark blue eyes, a small straight nose, and a determined jaw. "I don't know."

She tried again to shut the door and I held on tight, not about to let her shut it in my face. "I'm her sister. When did she leave?"

The rain had come back with a vengeance, and I was getting soaked. I held the hood of my raincoat over my hair, but water splashed into my eyes. A man, who I recognized as Jeremiah Swanson, came to the door. "Lydia, please allow the lady to come in out of the rain."

His voice was strong and soothing, and I could see why women were drawn to him. He was tall and handsome with black hair and piercing dark eyes. He wore white linen pants and a white shirt with a yellow sweater thrown over his shoulders. He took the door from Lydia's hand and opened it wide. "Please come in and tell us why you're here."

Lydia stepped back with a look of distain and let me inside. What I saw took my breath away. There was a large entryway, which led into a cavernous room that had several over-sized leather couches and recliners in front of a massive rock fireplace. A fire glowed brightly in the grate.

Along one wall were two long rows of tables and chairs, all made of mahogany, all beautifully carved. Each table held a tapestry runner in golds, blues, and burgundy, with bronze candlesticks sitting in the middle of it. There were two more fireplaces, one on each side wall. To the left of the room was a grand piano with several chairs situated around it.

Jeremiah Swanson made his way over to the main fireplace and stood in front of it. "Lydia, please get a towel for Miss..." He looked at me expectantly.

"Detective Ellisen." I wasn't in uniform, but I carried my badge, so I took it out of my bag and showed it to him.

He looked at it with interest then handed it back to me. "Detective Ellisen. Please come closer to the fire. What brings you to our home today? I certainly hope you don't think one of my family has broken the law. We are peaceful people." He said it like I should have known that.

I walked over and stood by the massive fireplace as Lydia slipped from the room. "I'm looking for my sister, Rose Scott."

He looked disconcerted for a moment before he pulled his smiling, congenial mask back in place. "Ah, Rose Sarai. I'm afraid she has left us."

Rose Sarai was the name Jeremiah had given Rose when she joined his family. Sarai was the name of Abraham of the Bible's wife before God changed it to Sarah. I'd asked Rose why he thought it was necessary to change her name. Her answer was surprising, "Jeremiah gives the women in his family names of strong women of the Bible, so we'll always feel strong like they were."

I'd laughed. "More like he wants to use the Bible to get you to do what he wants."

Rose had huffed and turned away and I'd seethed.

Now, I looked at Jeremiah, trying to keep my face neutral and not show how I felt about him and his lifestyle. I hoped my revulsion didn't show in my eyes. "When did she leave?"

Lydia came back into the room and handed me a large fluffy white towel. I nodded my thanks and rubbed the water from my face and patted down my hair, which I was sure was flattened to my scalp.

"I hate to tell you this, but Rose Sarai left us a few days ago." Jeremiah gave me a sad smile.

"Do you know where she went?" I tried to fluff my hair, but knew it was a lost cause. I rubbed the towel against the front of my coat, not wanting to get water on the expensive Italian rug at my feet.

He motioned for me to sit on one of the sofas and he took a seat on the matching recliner. "I don't. It was a shock to find she'd packed her things and left in the middle of the night."

"Did she get the message our father was killed?" I watched him closely for any reaction, but his face remained passive. "Do you know if she was on her way home?" I stood by the sofa, not wanting to sit. The warmth of the fire was seeping through my wet coat.

Jeremiah looked down at his clasped hands, then up at me. "I'm sorry about your father. Rose didn't say anything before she left."

"He was murdered." I said, my voice cold and harsh. I wanted to see his reaction.

"Murdered? Do you know why?" His look was one of interest, but not the reaction I was looking for.

"No, do you?"

He blinked, took off his glasses and rubbed his eyes. "How would I know? I don't know your father."

"Rose never talked about him?" I didn't believe him for a second.

"No. Of course I knew Rose Sarai had a birth father, but when people join my family, they leave their birth families behind. I understand that is hard for their birth families to accept, but we are a family unit. Birth families cease to exist in our world." He stared at me as if he were daring me to disagree.

If he said birth family one more time, I was afraid I'd deck him. "I'm pretty sure Rose kept in contact with our dad." I wasn't at all sure of that, but I wanted to see what he'd say.

"I don't know how. We only have one telephone here and it's in Lydia's office." He glanced up at the woman standing in front of the fire. "We don't encourage contact with the outside world, do we, Sister Lydia?"

She shook her head. "I keep my office locked. No one uses the phone without me knowing."

"Well, she contacted him somehow." *Liar.*

Jeremiah shook his head, but he looked a little hot under the collar. "I don't know what to tell you. Rose disappeared a couple days ago. We've been looking for her, but so far, we haven't found her." He held out his hands with his palms up. "I don't have any idea why she'd take off like she did."

Lydia had moved closer to the fire and stood with her back to it facing us. I looked at her. She didn't look stressed. In fact, there was no emotion written on her marble smooth skin. "Were you the one who took my phone call?"

She stared at me. "What phone call?"

"I called to let Rose know about our dad. Whoever answered the phone said she'd give her the message and have her call me back, but she didn't call. I kept calling, every day for a week, but no one answered after my first phone call." My voice shook and I gritted my teeth. My heart ached for my dad, but I made myself stand tall and not let them see my feelings.

Lydia shook her head. "We often have trouble with the phone here. We are so far out the phone often doesn't work."

"It is as I have told you, Rose Sarai has left us." Jeremiah looked like he might cry. "Look around you, Detective. I have provided a safe haven, a little bit of heaven here in this place and Rose Sarai chose to walk away. It's inconceivable what went through her mind. I thought she was happy here."

I stared at the fire and felt its heat seeping into my clothes. I hoped with all my heart that Rose had decided to leave the cult and was out there somewhere hiding from Jeremiah. I moved my gaze back to him. "Something must've happened. Was she having trouble with anyone?"

"Not that I know of." He looked up at Lydia. "Sister?"

Lydia moved and I glanced up at her. Had I seen a look of triumph on her face for an instant? Jeremiah looked at her, and her expression changed to one of concern. "No, of course not. Everyone gets along as you know, Father."

"Someone here knows where she is."

"She must've found another family to live with," Jeremiah said, not taking his eyes off Lydia. Was he giving her a warning look, telling her without words to be careful what she said?

She nodded. "Rose had become bored, I'm afraid. She wanted more responsibilities, but we all have our jobs, and we all work together."

Jeremiah nodded. "I don't know why Rose Sarai would leave. She seemed happy and then a couple days ago she was gone." He looked down at his hands which were clasped between his knees. "We are despondent."

"I would like to talk to some of the other members of your family." I leaned towards Jeremiah trying to soften my expression, knowing this man was all ego.

He smiled the smile of a man who knows he's attractive to members of the opposite sex. "Believe me, we've talked to our family. No one knows where she went."

"Someone has to know something, Mr. Swanson," I said, leaning closer and looking into his mesmerizing brown eyes.

"He told you we talked to them all, Detective. They have nothing to give you." Lydia stood by the fireplace, her voice sharp and her body stiff and condescending.

I knew I was upsetting her just by being there. Good. I looked at her. "I can come back with a warrant and look over your property." I made my voice as stern as possible. "But I'd rather not do that if I don't have to."

"Why would you look over our property? We have done nothing wrong." Jeremiah looked perplexed.

"My sister is missing, Mr. Swanson. Our father was murdered. What if someone has killed her too?"

Jeremiah put a hand against his chest. "I never thought of that."

I hadn't either until that moment, but I realized it was a possibility. "I want her found. If she's been missing for several days, we need all the help we can get to find her."

He stood up. "Lydia, bring the sisters who were close to Rose Sarai. We need to help Detective Ellisen find our little Rose." He sounded worried and I wondered why.

Lydia didn't like it, but she left to find her "sisters."

I watched Jeremiah pace back and forth in front of the fire. "Has there been anything unusual happening around here? Something that would upset Rose?" I hoped she'd left of her own accord, but a small niggling doubt nagged at me.

He shook his head. "Not that I'm aware of. Lydia oversees the ladies. If she says everything is like always, I'm certain it is."

I nodded. "May I see Priscilla?"

Jeremiah stood in front of me like a statue, his face carved into stone. "My wife?"

I nodded. "Yes, I'm sure Rose told me your wife was the one who talked her into joining your...ah...family." Rose had found an immediate connection to Priscilla Swanson. She'd told me Priscilla was everything she'd always longed to be, so centered and content with her life.

To my surprise Jeremiah's eyes filled with tears. "I'm afraid my wife is no longer with us."

Chapter 2

"She's dead?" Was that the reason Rose had left? Was she so upset about Priscilla's passing she had to get away from the other members of the cult? I couldn't wait to tell Mitch about this.

"We don't know. She disappeared the same day as Rose Sarai." He took off his frameless glasses, blinked and ran his fingers under his eyes to wipe away the tears.

"Did you report them missing?" Something didn't feel right about this. Why would Priscilla disappear?

"It is not our way." Jeremiah looked up and put his glasses back on as Lydia came back into the room followed by a procession of silent females. They filed in as though they were stepping into a courtroom. "Ah, here are my ladies," Jeremiah said.

I cringed. Had he won them over with his gentle talk and handsome face? What else had he promised them? Was it the allure of a home without the stresses of the outside world, as Priscilla had promised Rose? Or did they give each woman what they thought they wanted most. Did it differ for each of them?

Lydia introduced the women to me in a brusque voice and so fast, I hoped I wouldn't have to repeat their names. There were ten of them. All were beautiful and I thought ranged in age from early twenties to early forties. None were as old as Rose, but Rose had never looked her age and I had a feeling looks were a big thing for Jeremiah when he wooed women into his cult.

I smiled at the women, who smiled back as though I were a special guest instead of a detective with the sheriff's office. I asked Jeremiah for a room so I could talk to them one at a time and he agreed, although I knew he didn't want to.

"I will sit in on your interviews, Detective Ellisen," Lydia said, looking at Jeremiah, not at me.

He inclined his head. "Yes, that would be good, Sister Lydia. It will make the ladies feel more comfortable." He gave them a sweeping beatific smile and you could almost see them swoon.

Lydia led us into a hallway which had doors on both sides. She stopped at one whose door was open, and we all went into a conference room. It was big enough for a large table with twelve chairs around it. Off to one side was a coffee cart with a huge coffee pot, sugar bowl, cream pitcher, and a stack of spoons inside an old-fashioned crystal spoon rest.

I felt my eyes widen. There was no expense spared when they refurbished the old barn. Everything was natural woods, and the furniture was high-end and shined with furniture polish. The smell of lemon permeated the air. Lydia offered me a seat at the table. She introduced me to Sister Ruth, named after another strong woman of the Bible, and she and Ruth sat across from me.

"Ruth, I'm Rose's sister. I understand she and Priscilla went missing a few days ago. Did you talk to them before they left? Do you know where they went?"

Ruth was an extremely slender woman with long dark hair she wore in a ponytail high on her head. Her eyes were a dark brown and she had delicate features. She glanced at Lydia, giving her a confused look, before she answered me. "I talked to Rose the morning she left."

"What did you talk about?

Ruth shrugged. "What we talk about every day. How the work is going, what needs to be done. Rose Sarai was a lead sister."

Lydia made a sharp movement, and I held up my hand to stop her from interrupting. "What does a lead sister do?"

The younger woman looked at Lydia for guidance. Lydia gave a quick, short shake of her head. Ruth looked back at me. "She's in charge of what to plant in the garden and greenhouse. I help her with the vegetables."

I could tell from the blush that stained her cheeks she'd been about to say something else, but no matter how hard I tried, I couldn't pry any information out of her. I knew I'd stand a better chance without Lydia sitting there.

"What about Priscilla? Are you worried about her?"

A frown creased Ruth's forehead. "Mother Priscilla? She isn't missing. She went to spend time with her mother. Right?" She looked at Lydia.

Lydia nodded. "I don't know where you got the idea she was missing."

I frowned, trying to remember what Jeremiah had said about her. "Jeremiah said she went missing the same day Rose did."

Both women shook their heads. "He must've meant she left the same day," Lydia challenged.

"That's not what he said."

Neither woman replied. Hmm, I thought. Interesting. Apparently, Jeremiah was keeping it from the rest of his family.

The rest of the interviews were much the same. The women were afraid to say anything that wasn't scripted by the propaganda of the cult. It was lovely, a wonderful environment to raise children, and they all loved it there. They missed Rose Sarai and wished she hadn't left. None of them knew why she left. They all thought Mother Priscilla had gone to visit her birth mother in Washington.

After I'd talked to all of them, I turned to Lydia. "Have you told everyone here that Priscilla has gone to visit her mother, so they won't be upset she's not here. Are you trying to hide the truth from them?"

"Mother Priscilla will be back." Lydia stood and headed for the door.

"That's not what Jeremiah said." I stood and followed her.

"I'm sure it's what he meant." She turned back to me. "Father Jeremiah is upset Mother Priscilla left. He wanted her to wait until we found out if Rose Sar was coming back. Mother Priscilla had things she needed to do, so she left anyway."

Yeah right. "I thought Jeremiah was the supreme ruler of the family."

Lydia's shoulders stiffened and I could tell by the closed expression on her face she wouldn't tell me anything more. I asked her to show me where Rose lived.

Lydia walked ahead of me back into the main room. There she stopped to look back at me. "She lived here with the rest of us."

"Yes, but did she have a house, or did she share with some of the other women? Where did she sleep and keep her things?" I had visions of dormitories or large bedrooms with many people sleeping in them.

"We do not encourage our family to have "things." We all share of what Father Jeremiah provides for us." Her voice was stiff with anger.

"I get it you don't want me nosing around, Lydia, but my sister is missing. How would you feel if it were your sister?"

"I have many sisters. I would be worried, but Rose Sarai is in God's hands. She left on her own. We didn't ask her to leave."

I'd been a cop for over twenty years, and I thought I was a good judge of character. From what I read in Lydia's posture and her clipped answers, I knew she didn't want me there, didn't want me asking questions, but that wasn't all going through her head. There was something else. Something I couldn't put my finger on. She knew something, either about Rose or about Jeremiah Swanson that she was determined not to let me find out. And I got the sense she didn't particularly want Rose back. Jealousy, maybe?

Lydia led me back to where Jeremiah sat talking to another man. He stood up when we entered. "Ah, Detective, I see you've conducted your interviews. Have you found out anything besides what we've already told you?"

"No, it's funny none of the ladies I talked to seem to know anything about Rose's disappearance." I looked at Lydia, letting him know having her sit in on the interviews was the reason I hadn't found out anything. If I had to go back, I'd make sure she wasn't around when I talked to the "sisters".

The man with Jeremiah stood and Jeremiah introduced us. "This is my brother, Ezekiel."

I walked over and held out my hand. "Detective Ellisen from the Hood River County Sheriff's office."

He took my hand in his and shook it, his grip warm and hard. He looked somewhat like Jeremiah, and I wondered if they were brothers, but Ezekiel was younger and more outdoorsy. He wore blue jeans and a flannel shirt, a contrast to Swanson's white slacks and white shirt. Ezekiel was taller and his muscles bulged against the arms of his shirt.

"Detective." He let go of my hand and walked around me to the front door, letting himself out.

I turned back to Jeremiah. "Mr. Swanson, I'd like your permission to look at Rose's room before I go."

Jeremiah raised his eyebrows and glanced at Lydia. "Is Rose Sarai's home presentable, Sister Lydia?"

"I'll go see." She hurried out of the room.

As I watched her go, I wondered just what they were afraid of me seeing or finding in Rose's room. I knew if they had their way, I'd find nothing and give up. They didn't know me very well.

"Rose Sarai had a house instead of sleeping in one of the dorm rooms. She was a trusted member of the family."

"Does that mean you don't trust the rest of the family?" I asked.

Jeremiah shook his head. "It doesn't mean that at all. Perhaps I should've said, Rose Sarai was a senior member of the family. All members who have been with us for a long time have their own houses. The new members stay in the dorms."

A few minutes later, Lydia came back for me. She motioned for me to follow her, and we went out the main door and crossed to the houses on the left. I put up my hood as we hurried to the one farthest away from us. "I don't understand why you are nosing around our homes," Lydia said as she marched through the rain towards a group of smaller houses.

"I'm searching for anything that might give me a clue to Rose's disappearance."

She rolled her eyes.

The house looked just like the others on the outside. It was a small bungalow with a front door, a window on each side of the door and a sidewalk leading up to the porch. As Lydia let us in, I looked around for clues my sister had been there.

Nothing jumped out at me. There were no clothes lying around, no makeup or toiletries in the bathroom, no clothes in the closet. I frowned at Lydia. "Did she take everything with her? I assume she had clothes and shoes, maybe even some toiletries?"

"She took everything she brought with her, which wasn't much. The clothes Father Jeremiah gave her have been cleaned and are in storage in case she comes back."

I went through each of the rooms. It was a nice little place, with a bedroom, bathroom and a kitchen and living room combination. Comfortable looking furniture sat in the living area and the table and chairs in the kitchen matched the cabinets and doors. Everything I'd seen was so perfect. It made my skin crawl.

I wondered if Rose had found peace there. I stood and looked out the kitchen window, thinking about her. Where had she gone? Why had she left? Was she okay? She was my sister, but I didn't have a deep connection to her. We'd never been close. Now I wished I'd tried harder, maybe I would know where to look for her.

"I need to use the bathroom," I said to Lydia, and she nodded as I let myself into the small room. I didn't have to go. I wanted to look around. Rose had to know I'd come looking for her. If she wanted to leave me a clue to where she was, she would know the only place I'd be left alone was in the bathroom.

I looked through every drawer, the tiny cupboard above the toilet, the small cupboard under the sink. I even went through the package of toilet paper. I didn't find anything, so I flushed the toilet and ran the water so Lydia would think I had gone in to use the bathroom.

When I came out of the door, Lydia was gone and one of the sisters had taken her place. I looked around. "Where's Lydia?"

"She had a phone call. Father Jeremiah sent me to tell her and stay with you while you finish looking at Rose's house."

I didn't recognize this girl from the ones I'd interviewed. She seemed timid and I tried to put her at ease. "I'm Liz, what's your name?"

"Dorcas." She smiled and gave me her hand.

I took her hand in mine and she placed a piece of paper in it. She looked at me with big brown eyes begging me to not say a word.

"What does a lead sister do?" I asked her.

Her eyes got bigger. "Who told you about that?" She stepped away from me as if to distance herself from the question.

"One of the other girls I talked to mentioned that Rose was a lead sister."

She shook her head. "She shouldn't have said anything. Father wouldn't like it." Her big dark eyes looked haunted.

"Why not?"

She held up her hand, palm out towards me. "Because we are told not to let outsiders know what goes on here."

"But Dorcas, Rose was my sister and she's missing. Please, if you know anything you've got to tell me."

Again, she shook her head. Then in a voice so low I could barely hear, she whispered. "Later."

"Are you finished here?"

"Yes, I think I am," I said, slipping the paper she'd given me into my pocket.

We walked out of the bungalow together and headed to the main building. When we were out of the house, away from possible cameras or bugging devices, I asked her, "Were you friends with Rose?"

"Yes, I was." She stared at me, and I felt like she was trying to tell me something without saying it. Then she said, "Rose didn't leave because she suddenly wanted to. She left because Priscilla was leaving for good, and she was afraid they'd try and blame her."

Chapter 3---Rose

Two weeks earlier

The night had gotten darker, and the rain pelted against her back as Rose pulled up her hood, drew her cloak closer and crouched under an oak tree by the side of Hwy 35. She didn't want anyone to spot her, so every time a car came up the highway, she'd hurry into the trees and hunker down. It felt like she'd been walking for hours, and her feet were killing her, but she had to keep moving. She didn't have a choice in case she was being followed.

It had gotten dark over an hour ago and still she hadn't found the place Mother Priscilla had told her about. If she didn't find it soon, Mother Priscilla might not be there. Part of her wanted to turn around and go home, but she knew it wasn't safe there anymore. The rain made it impossible to see. All she had was a small flashlight.

Pain tugged at her heart. She'd been so happy at the compound for so many years. Why did things have to change? Why did people have to be so greedy? Rose mourned the loss of the life she'd found with the Swanson's. Tears poured down her cheeks.

Mother Priscilla had told her that morning to leave the compound after it had been discovered Rose knew more than she should about some of Father Jeremiah's business dealings. "You must leave, Rose. Jeremiah is getting out of control. I'm afraid for you." She handed Rose a cashier's check for forty thousand dollars. "Put this somewhere safe. We'll need it later."

Mother had tears in her eyes while she whispered the warning to Rose. Rose had stared at the older woman, wondering why she'd told her Father Jeremiah was getting into shady dealings if it was going to put her in danger. Father would not be pleased if he found out.

But Mother Priscilla had been acting odd lately.

For the first few years after Rose joined the family, she'd lived peacefully and more happily than anyone had a right to, or so she thought. Not that she'd had it bad at home. But she'd been tired of living by herself. Liz was married and had a daughter. She was busy with her career as a deputy sheriff. Their father was happy in his life as a farmer.

Rose had fallen in love and when it didn't work out, she'd decided she had to make some changes. At first, she thought she'd move to a different state and start over.

Then she met Priscilla who'd told her about a life Rose had only dreamed of before. Living off the land, growing her own fruits and vegetables, no worries or stress, it sounded heavenly, so she decided to join them. But then things had changed.

Every time money became tight in the family, Father Jeremiah asked them all to talk to their families, explain how important their work was and beg for more money. Rose didn't understand why her birth father had never given them a penny. She'd gone through all the money she had saved when she joined the cult.

She wondered sometimes if she was less of an asset to the family since she was out of money. She knew it wasn't what Father Jeremiah said, but she'd felt a subtle shift in his attitude towards her. It was a good thing Mother Priscilla was on her side.

She thought again of the forty thousand dollars Mother Priscilla had asked her to hide for her. "Just in case," Mother had explained. "I can trust you to not tell Father, can't I Rose?"

Rose had assured her she could and one of the trips into Hood River to recruit, she'd snuck away and given the money to her dad to put in the bank. She knew he'd never tell anyone where it came from.

Sometimes Rose wondered what her life would have been like if she hadn't joined the family. Would she have married by now? Had a family? She'd never found a man who interested her enough to be his wife, except Dan. There'd been a few other men over the years, of course, but they all let her down in one way or another. She often wondered if her standards were too high. Maybe she could have found someone if she'd been able to accept a less perfect man.

Then she'd found the man who could make her forget all her stupid standards. He was perfect for her in every way, except one. He didn't feel it was necessary to be faithful to one woman. That's the way all the men in the Swanson family, including Father Jeremiah, felt.

Rose was repulsed, even though she followed all of Father Jeremiah's teachings, she couldn't bring herself to have sex whenever or wherever one of the men wanted. She was afraid of being forced, but Mother Priscilla had demanded Rose be left alone. Surprisingly, Father Jeremiah hadn't fought her on it. He knew his wife and Rose had a close friendship and he let her alone to grow her vegetables and in return, Rose turned a blind eye to the sexual activities within the family, just as Priscilla did. She also knew that the men all favored the younger women, and she was close to fifty.

She'd become a sort of maiden aunt no one touched, which was fine with her. She was important to the family because she was the head gardener and Father Jeremiah demanded their vegetables and fruit be grown on their land. Rose knew he would have gotten rid of her long ago if it hadn't been for her knowledge about growing food. She had her birth father to thank for that.

Headlights swept over the place where Rose was crouched, and she shrunk inside the cloak, hoping it wasn't one of the men coming for her. Had they found out she'd left? She held her breath as the car slowed down. A powerful light shone over the ground not two feet from where Rose huddled.

The car stopped and two men got out. Rose could hear their voices and knew it was two of the men out looking for her. She didn't dare move.

"She couldn't have gotten this far without help," one of the men said. "We'll never find her in this rain."

Rose couldn't tell who was talking, Brother Luke or Brother Ezekiel.

The men walked into the forest and stopped. Twin beams of light shined on the ground at their feet and then through the trees. "We'll never find her in here tonight," the other man said. "I don't think we should trudge through the underbrush looking for her, do you? She'd never stay out in this downpour. She has probably found a ride and is miles away."

Rose recognized his voice as belonging to Brother Luke. She squeezed her eyes shut and willed the men to turn around and leave.

The powerful beam of a flashlight lit up the ground for fifty feet. Rose held her breath, and crouched behind the tree, only peeking around when she could no longer hear them talking.

"She's got to be around here somewhere. She couldn't have gotten far." The voice belonged to Brother Ezekiel.

Rose prayed Brother Luke would talk him out of searching further. God must've been listening because soon he said, "she could be anywhere. Maybe someone came along and picked her up. We might as well get out of this rain. I hope she's somewhere dry."

"Swanson will not be happy if we go back without her." Brother Ezekiel started through the brush, shining his light on the ground.

"Since when did you start worrying about Swanson being unhappy? If he wants to crawl around in the forest in a rainstorm, let him come out here and look for her."

"Yeah, right."

Rose could hear the crunch of their boots against the brush. She eased around the tree, wondering if she could go in the opposite direction without them hearing her. She stepped back and her foot found a hole. She turned and twisted it. "Eiiyee," she cried before she could stop herself. She clamped a hand to her mouth and stood still.

The men stopped. "Did you hear that?" Brother Ezekiel asked. "Sounded like an animal of some kind. Maybe a bobcat?"

"Or a cougar. I've heard there are cougars out here. You know they can grab you and break your neck before you ever see them coming."

Rose's eyes widened at his words. She glanced around. Were there cougars watching her? What was more dangerous, the cougars or the men hunting her? She was so tempted to call out and let them know she was there. They'd take her home and she could get dry and warm. Then she remembered Mother Priscilla's warning and she stayed quiet.

Brother Luke flashed his light around in the tops of the trees. "Maybe we should head back. We can look again when it gets light. How far can one little woman go?" He brought his flashlight back down to the ground and shined it in the trees. It came to rest on her, and she knew she'd been caught. She froze, afraid of what they'd do, but he only held it on her for a couple of heartbeats, then moved on.

Her heart pounded. Had he seen her? If he had, he wasn't letting on to Brother Ezekiel. The two men walked back to their vehicle, talking softly. Rose couldn't hear what they were saying.

She lifted her head just enough to peek at them and watched them climb in the car and head back towards the compound. With a breath of relief, Rose started to stand, but the car suddenly skidded to a stop, made a U-turn, and headed back her way.

Chapter 4-Liz

Present day

"Please keep your head down and keep walking," Dorcas whispered when my steps faltered.

I nodded, not wanting to spook her. "Do you know why Priscilla was leaving? Were she and Jeremiah having trouble?"

"No, I don't know. Mother Priscilla announced at dinner one night she was leaving. Father Jeremiah didn't say anything, but I could tell he was upset. I don't think anyone saw it coming. We all thought she'd be back in a few days. She's never stayed away long, but it has been a couple weeks." She shook her head. "There's something bad going on here. Rose said she'd found out something, but she wouldn't tell me what."

"Do you think she knew why Priscilla decided to leave?"

"Maybe. They were close and Jeremiah didn't like that. He demanded Priscilla's time and attention to be on him."

"Did he have other women?"

"Yes." She kept her gaze straight ahead. "I know Mother Priscilla hated it. I saw the look on her face when

Father zeroed in on another one of the women here." She sounded sad. Then she shook her head and glanced over at me. "I came here looking for peace. My personal life was a mess and I needed time to regroup. They promised me I'd find it here, but it didn't last long. They make demands. They prey on the misfits and the lonely."

"You can't just walk away?"

Dorcas shook her head.

"What is a lead sister?"

"That's the title Mother Priscilla gave Rose. She wasn't to be touched."

"By the men? Jeremiah?"

She started to speak, but a male voice calling her name, stopped her.

A tall man in a dark green trench coat hurried up to us. "Sister Dorcas, you need to be in the classroom. I'll escort Detective Ellisen back to the hall."

Dorcas didn't say anything as she turned away. I watched her scurry down the sidewalk. I looked up at the man. The rain had slowed down for a few minutes, and we stood on the sidewalk, staring at each other.

He was nice-looking, with a dark brown stubbled beard and bright blue eyes. Rain glistened in his coffee-colored hair, and his smile was a little crooked. "Sorry about that. Sister Dorcas teaches the younger kids, and they are finished with their break. She needs to be there with them."

I nodded, wondering how I could get Dorcas away from there. I knew I had to try. What did she mean by saying Rose wasn't to be touched? Had Priscilla put a ring of protection around Rose? Why?

"Father Jeremiah is waiting to tell you goodbye." The man motioned to the door with a sweep of his hand.

I followed him up the stairs and into the main room. Jeremiah waited for me by the fireplace. I thanked him for letting me see Rose's room.

"Did you find anything?" He looked at me over the top of his glasses. Was that a smirk on his face?

I shook my head. "No." I pulled one of my cards out of my bag and handed it to him. "If you hear anything or if Rose comes back, will you please call me?"

"Of course. I'm sorry about our little Rose. I'm saddened she felt she had to leave so suddenly. I feel she will find her way home. Please let us know if you talk to her." He gave me a smile that while I think he meant it to be charming came across as slimy.

I told him I would, and the man who had escorted me back into the building, escorted me out. Were they afraid I wouldn't leave? I couldn't get out of there fast enough. There was something not right and chilling about that place. Dorcas didn't feel like she could leave. Where was Rose? Was Priscilla visiting her mother like they wanted me to believe?

All these questions swirled through my brain as I got into my car and headed back up their driveway to the main road.

I needed to talk to Mitch. I called his cell phone, but he didn't pick up. I left a message. "Mitch, there's something I need to talk to you about. Call me." As I headed home, I wondered why Mitch wasn't picking up his calls. He'd been acting weird lately. He was angry all the time and I didn't know how to deal with him. I kept telling myself it was a mid-life crisis and he'd get over it. He'd better. I didn't know how much more I could take.

As I drove down Hwy 35 towards Hood River, the rain came back in full force, and I thought about Rose and what I should do next. What had my sister seen that drove her away from the Bread of Life compound? She'd been there ten years. Had she left of her own free will? Was she still alive? Had Priscilla been afraid of Jeremiah? Had he decided to replace her?

Or did Rose find out our father was killed and ran because she assumed someone from the cult, did it? Had they killed our dad? I had to find Rose and see what she knew.

My first stop coming down from the Mt. Hood area was at my dad's place in Odell. Odell was about five miles from where I lived in Hood River. It was a small area with orchards and a few businesses.

After Dad was killed, I kept hoping Rose would show up at his house, so I went there to check and see if she had been there. As far as I could tell, she hadn't.

I thought about my dad and the orchard where he grew pears and apples. He'd lived in the farmhouse where he raised us girls. He had remodeled it a few years before and had them take out walls and opened it up so there weren't small, dark rooms. Now, the kitchen was bigger and brighter, and the living room and family room had been made into one big room. I loved Dad's house. It had always felt like home. What would we do with it now with Dad gone? I wondered. I couldn't imagine selling it.

Tears pooled in my eyes as I drove down his driveway into the farm. I couldn't believe he wasn't there, waiting for me with a cup of coffee. Dad loved his coffee and always had a pot going. I pulled up and stopped next to the house and sat there for a few minutes before I went in, thinking about dad and Rose.

Finally, I made myself get out of the car and walk inside. I'd been there since Dad died, but either Mitch, Bella or my friend, Jenn, had come with me. I hadn't been there alone. I took the key out of my bag and unlocked the door and let myself in. Everything was just like he'd left it. Dad was always clean and neat. The house wasn't showy, but it was comfortable. It was home.

I flipped on the kitchen lights because the rain and gray skies had made it dark in there. My heart hurt as I made a pot of coffee and sat at the table while it brewed. I kept expecting Dad to walk in from the other room and demand I find Rose.

"I'll find her, Dad, I promise," I said into the empty room.

As soon as the coffee was made, I poured myself a cup and taking Half & Half out of the fridge, I poured some into my cup. Dad had always teased me about needing the cream. "Real cops drink it black," he'd told me, grinning.

"I guess I'm not a real cop, then," I'd replied, and we'd laughed.

After I stirred cream in, I headed down the hall to Dad's office. Mitch and I had gone through it after Dad was killed, but I knew if there was anything in the house that might lead me to Rose, it would be in his office. That's where he and Bailey had spent most of their time.

Bailey was Dad's hundred-pound yellow lab. She now lived with me. I missed hearing her nails click on the tile floor as she scrambled down the hall to greet me. But she'd be there when I went home later.

My phone rang as I stepped into Dad's office, and I took it out of my back pocket. It was Mitch. "Hey, are you headed home?"

"Yeah, I dropped Bella off and gave her some money. It's what I do now, hand her money all the time. We need one of those bumper stickers that say, my child and my money go to OSU."

I smiled and some of the tension eased a little. Mitch had always known how to make me smile. "I know, but she appreciates it, and she does try to be careful about how she spends it."

"Yeah, she's a good girl. We're pretty lucky."

I knew he'd give her everything in the world if he could. "Yes, we are. Mitch, I have something I need to talk to you about. Will you be home soon?"

"I should be there in a couple hours. How are you doing?"

I was surprised he asked. "I'm doing okay. I went to the Bread of Life compound and talked to Jeremiah Swanson about Rose. He says she disappeared a few nights ago and they don't know where she is. I asked him if I could talk to his wife, and he said she left a couple days ago. One of the girls who lives there told me she left because Swanson chose another woman."

"That doesn't surprise me. Isn't free sex what these cults are all about?"

"A big part of it, I'm sure." I looked down at my dad's desk and moved a paperclip around. "I think we should look for her."

"Did Swanson say he wanted us to? Was he going to report her as missing?"

"I don't think so, but Mitch, Rose may be with her. Swanson got teary eyed when he told me she left, but he didn't say he wanted us to investigate her disappearance."

"Which he wouldn't if he had anything to do with it."

"Exactly."

He sighed into the phone. "Let's talk about it when I get home. You know I'll help you look for Rose. We'll find her."

My voice clogged with tears. "Mitch, I'm worried she had something to do with Dad's murder."

"I know you are. Listen, honey, just hang on until I get home. Are you back at the house?"

"No, I'm at Dad's." I swiped at the tears. "I'm going to look around here and see if I can find anything. I didn't have a chance to ask Dad if Rose had called him in the last few days. Maybe there's something here."

"Okay. Do you want me to come to your dad's house or do you think you'll be home when I get back into town?"

"I'll probably be home. Why don't you call before you hit town?"

"Okay. Hang in there Liz. We'll find Rose."

I said goodbye and hit the stop button on my phone. Mitch sounded like his old self, and I breathed a sigh of relief. I was tired of feeling like I had to be careful what I said around him for fear he'd yell. I hoped he was going to start acting like himself again.

Then I remembered the note Dorcas gave me when she met me in Rose's house, and I took it out of my pocket and opened it.

It was a phone number, but nothing indicating whose it was. My heart pounded. Who did Dorcas want me to call? Was it a number for Rose?

Chapter 5

My hands shook and I almost dropped my phone. I dialed the number. Would Rose answer? I sat in my dad's office chair, my eyes glued to the phone as I listened to it ring and ring and ring.

No one answered and I hit the red button to end the call. I stared at the phone, frustrated. Why had Dorcas given me this number? Who did she want me to talk to? Maybe it wasn't Rose. Maybe it was her mother or an old boyfriend, or someone who would help her get out of the Bread of Life cult.

But my gut said it had something to do with Rose. I put my phone down, thinking I'd try again later.

Everything on my dad's desk was organized. I thought of my own desk at home where I threw the mail and any other papers I needed to look at. I was sure there was at least one coffee cup and probably a half-filled can of Pepsi sitting there too. Dad had a picture of Rose and me when we were little girls, a desk pad with a few notes about when to spray, and a couple phone numbers I didn't recognize. When I pulled out the middle desk drawer, I found just what I expected; two pens, a pencil, paperclips, and a couple small notebooks.

Mitch and I had gone through Dad's desk after he was killed, looking for a motive, and found nothing, but I wanted to look again. Maybe we'd missed something.

The drawer on the right held bank statements stapled together by year for the last five years. There was quite a bit of money in his accounts. We'd found his will a couple days before and everything he owned had been left equally to Rose and me, but Rose's half of the money was to be put in a trust she couldn't draw from without my approval. I knew why Dad did that. He didn't want Rose giving his hard-earned money to Jeremiah Swanson, and I didn't blame him, but I hated to be the go between because I knew it could cause trouble between my sister and me.

I heard the doorbell ring and wondered who in the world would drop by. Probably Jehovah's Witnesses or a real estate agent who wanted to sell the place for me. It was hard to believe Dad had only been gone a couple weeks and I'd already had several phone calls from either real estate agents or neighbors offering to buy Dad's place. I told them all the same thing; it wasn't for sale. The doorbell rang again before I could get there, and I hurried into the kitchen and down the hall to the front door.

When I opened the door, my dad's neighbor, Travis Knight, stood there looking down at me. I couldn't help but smile. Travis was seriously handsome, With his coffee-colored dark brown eyes and soft black hair. I felt myself catch a quick breath and laughed. I'd known Travis since he was born. He'd grown up on the farm next to us, and we'd been friends forever. He was five years younger than me, but we'd played together as children. I babysat him when he was ten and I was fifteen.

"Hey Travis." I opened the door to let him in and told my heart to just stop its crazy pounding. Travis had dumped his longtime girlfriend a few months earlier and Mitch and I had been there for him just like he'd been there for me when my dad was murdered.

I don't know when I'd started noticing how handsome he was. He was my friend, not some hunk, but lately I had noticed and felt guilty for my thoughts.

"Liz."

Even the way he said my name sent a thrill through me. He had a deep, soft voice and a way of looking at me that made me feel like I was the only woman on earth. Something Mitch had stopped doing years ago. "Come on in." I waved him into the house. "What are you doing today?"

He followed me down the hallway into the kitchen. "I stopped by to see if you were here. I thought you might be."

"Sit down." I motioned to the table and chairs near the windows. "Would you like a cup of coffee?"

Travis nodded and sat on one of the chairs. He stretched out his long legs and smiled. "I wanted to see how you're doing. I didn't get to talk to you much at the funeral."

I took a mug out of the cupboard and poured him a cup of the hot brew, then set it next to him. Instead of taking the time to go back to the office to get my cup, I took another one out of the cupboard and poured myself a cup also. Then I sat down across from him.

"I'm so angry, Travis. Who would do this to my dad? It was such a shock."

He reached out and took my hand. "It was. I can't imagine who would do it. Not to George."

"Me, either. Did he ever mention having trouble with anyone? Maybe one of the workers?"

Travis shook his head. "No, I can't think of anyone. He was such a good man and fair to his crew."

He squeezed my hand and let it go. I fought back tears. I hated feeling so vulnerable.

"What can I do to help you, Liz? You know I'll do whatever I can."

"I know, and I love you for it, but right now I'm concentrating on finding Rose. If I let myself think about Dad, I'm afraid I'll never..." My breath caught and more tears welled up in my eyes, spilling down my cheeks.

Travis stood and pulled me into his arms. "I'm sorry, Lizzie," he whispered against my hair.

I nodded and held onto him for a minute, loving the smell of the orchard, fresh air, and rain. I took a deep breath then I pushed out of his arms and sat down, rubbing the moisture from my face. "Sorry."

"Don't ever be sorry. You can cry on my shoulder anytime." He gave me a tender smile, then sat down again.

"I went to the compound where Rose has been staying this morning, but they said she left a few days ago." I shook my head, thinking about where she might have gone. "I hoped she'd come here, but I don't see any sign of it."

He frowned. "Did Mitch go with you?"

"No, he took Bella back to school."

Travis took a sip of coffee. He put the cup down and his dark eyes bore into mine. "You went alone?"

"Yeah, I wanted to see if they'd heard from her and talk to some of the people there."

"I wish you would've had someone go with you." Travis sat his cup on the table, a frown forming across his forehead.

"Travis, I'm a cop. I can handle myself in difficult situations." Geez, what was with the men in my life? Travis and Mitch both seemed to forget I'd been a sheriff's deputy and then a detective for the last ten years.

He looked down at his coffee, moving his thumb around the rim of the cup. "I know, but I worry about you."

For the first time since my dad died, I felt a warmth steal over me. I reached over and took his hand. "I know you do, but you don't need to."

He looked at our clasped hands for a minute. Did I imagine the regret that crossed his features? Or was it worry? What was going on with my friend? He let go and changed the subject. "Would you like me to take care of the orchard for a while? Just until you decide what to do with it?"

I groaned. "I hadn't given it a thought. I'm sure there are things that need to get done soon. I hate to ask it of you, but it would help a lot if you could. I know Jose will help with whatever needs done. You and Jose probably have a much better idea of what that is than I do." Jose Barrera was my dad's foreman and had been with him for over twenty years.

"Consider it done. I'll go talk to Jose as soon as I leave here." He drained his coffee cup. "Is there anything else I can do for you, Liz?" he asked as he stood up.

I stood and looked up at him. Travis was at least an inch or two taller than Mitch. "No, unless you hear something about Dad. I'm sure there are rumors flying around the valley. If there's anything helpful, you'll let me know?"

"Of course." His eyes looked deep into mine. He had suffered from my dad's murder too. They'd been friends and neighbors for a long time.

I moved towards him, thinking he was heading for the door, but he didn't move, and I found myself close enough to smell his clean outdoors smell again. He smelled of the earth after the rain, coffee, and a hint of mint. I wanted to lean into him but caught myself just in time before I embarrassed myself to death. What was wrong with me?

Travis reached out and put his arms around me, drawing me into his embrace and my heart hammered in my chest. Could he feel it? I hugged him back, then tried to step away, but he wouldn't let me go. Instead, he held me closer and whispered, "if you need me for anything, just call, okay Liz?"

I smiled up at him, trying my best to pretend his nearness wasn't affecting me. Travis and I had been friends for so long it wasn't unusual for him to hug me. What was unusual was the way his nearness affected me.

"You know I will, Travis. You've always been here for me and my family."

His eyes searched mine for a couple seconds, then he kissed me on the forehead and let me go. "I'll go talk to Jose. Let me know if you find out anything about Rose or George."

"I will." I watched him head down the hall to the door and then slid back into the chair I'd been sitting on like a jelly fish. I put my face in my hands. Sometime in the last couple of years, I'd noticed I had a strong physical pull towards Travis. I'd ignored it, of course, but occasionally it hit me between the eyes like a sledge-hammer. By the look on his face, I was afraid it had hit Travis too.

Jumping up, I took our cups to the sink and rinsed them out. I had to keep busy. I couldn't let these crazy feelings get hold of me. What in the world was the matter with me? I loved my husband. I would never do anything to hurt him even if he was being a poop lately. And what was the matter with Travis? He wasn't the type to go after a married woman. He had plenty of women after him, he didn't need to.

Back in Dad's office I decided to forget about any attraction to Travis and start going through Dad's file cabinet looking for anything pertaining to Rose. In the bottom drawer, the last file I pulled out had a letter in it addressed to me in my father's handwriting. Why hadn't seen it when I'd looked earlier? Had Mitch gone through this drawer and decided I wasn't ready to read a letter from my dad? I wasn't sure I was ready, but I knew I would.

With my hands shaking, I took the letter out and sat down in Dad's chair. I ran my finger over his writing, then I took a letter opener out of his drawer and sliced the envelope open. I pulled the letter out and began to read.

My darling girl,

If you're reading this either you've been snooping, which I know isn't like you, or I've gone on to be with Jesus. Don't cry, sweetheart. As they say, I'm in a much better place. I just hate the thought of leaving you and Bella and your sister.

My hands shook and tears formed in my eyes, sliding down my face. I wiped them away and continued reading.

I know I've told you over and over through the years to take care of Rose. It should've been the other way around. Rose should've taken care of you. But Rose isn't strong like you are, she's easily led and this thing with the cult scares the liver out of me.

I've been trying my best to get her to leave. I hadn't said anything to you because I didn't want to get your hopes up, but Rose has grown disenchanted with Swanson and the Bread of Life. She called me a few days ago and asked me to help her get away. She said they wouldn't let her just walk out because she knew too much.

I put some money and a cell phone in a bag and left it for her in Parkdale. She was supposed to sneak away and get a ride into town and pick it up. She told me if they follow her, she doesn't want them to know I'm involved. As if they wouldn't know! That's been four days ago, and she still hasn't made it to the drop off place. I left the bag with Murray at the gas station in town. He said he'd keep it for Rose and call me when she retrieved it.

Rose planned to take the money and get as far away from Oregon as she could. She said she had to go somewhere they wouldn't follow her. Please take my phone, you know the password, and keep it in case she calls. If she doesn't call, I guess assume she never made it to Parkdale. I know you'll find out what happened to her, one way or another. I must believe she'll make it.

Always remember how much I love you, my baby girl. You are the best part of your mom and me. Never forget that.

Dad

By the time I finished reading the letter I was sobbing. I wanted my dad back. His letter sounded just like him. I missed him so much. Anger burned inside me. Had the Bread of Life cult found out Dad was trying to help Rose escape and killed him because of it?

I had to find Rose. She had the answers. If she was still alive.

I put the letter into the file cabinet and closed and locked the drawer. Then I went in search of my dad's phone. I knew I'd seen it somewhere and thought it was in by his bed.

The drapes were closed in his room, and I flipped on the light switch. I looked for the phone but didn't see it. Dad had been in the living room when he'd been shot. I knew the Crime Scene people had been through the house, but they hadn't found his phone. What had he done with it?

The killer had snuck in after dark and put a bullet through the windows, hitting my dad in the head. Travis had been the one to find him.

I closed my eyes, remembering the phone call and the race out here to Dad's house. Mitch had tried to keep me from coming inside, but I had to see my dad. I don't think I would have believed it if I hadn't seen it for myself.

I don't remember much about the rest of that night. Mitch had held me, then handed me off to Travis while he called for an ambulance and called in the crime scene investigators. I have black holes in my memory of what happened after that.

Now I picked up Dad's flannel shirt from off the bed and held it in my arms, tears streaming from my eyes.

I stood there for a while, holding his shirt against me, inhaling his scent. I wiped my eyes on it and laid it back on the bed. Then I searched dad's room for the phone. Where would he have put it? I opened drawers and cupboards, looked through the bookcase against the wall on the opposite of his bed. I got down on my hands and knees and looked under the bed. Then, I remembered Dad's friend, Murray, telling me Dad had called him the night he was killed.

I walked into the kitchen and looked around every surface, in every drawer. Nothing. Then I went into the living room. I stuck my hand down the sides of my dad's chair and pulled the cushions off the sofa. I didn't find anything.

After a cursory look around, I was about to go back into the kitchen when I noticed something on the floor under the sofa. I bent over and picked it up and sure enough, it was Dad's phone.

Chapter 6

There were no calls from Rose on Dad's phone. I put it in my bag and grabbed the charger to take with me. I looked around the house and thought of everything I needed to do. I'd have to clean out the refrigerator and go through his clothes and donate them. My heart hurt. I didn't want to do this alone, but I didn't have anyone to help me.

Maybe I could hire a service to clean the house and clean out the fridge. That would save me time and then later, when I felt more able, I'd go through his things. I'd have to clean out the refrigerator and go through his clothes and donate them.

I left his house and closed and locked the door. Getting back into my car I headed to Parkdale to talk to Murray.

The rain had slowed to a drizzle, and I barely needed the windshield wipers as I drove up Hwy 35 to the tiny farming community. The town of less than three hundred inhabitants was only a ten-minute drive from my dad's place in Odell.

My phone rang as I pulled into Parkdale, and I hit the button on my steering wheel to answer. My best friend's name had come up on the screen. "Hello, Jenn."

"Liz, how are you doing today? I've been thinking about you." Jenn's voice was soft and soothing.

"I'm okay. Still in shock, I think."

"It was a shock. Listen, I wondered if you and Mitch would like to come over for dinner. Ray is home for once, and I made a big pot of beef stew and I have dinner rolls rising. Why don't you come over and we'll have dinner and visit? We never seem to do that anymore."

A warm feeling spread through me. Jenn always seemed to know when I needed her. "That sounds wonderful. I need to relax. Thank you."

"Of course. What are friends for? Come about six."

"Can I bring anything?" I thought about what I had on hand that I could throw together. The only thing I could think of was a salad. "Maybe a salad?"

"No, that's fine. Just bring that hunk you're married to." Jenn laughed.

"Okay. See you in a few."

I hung up thinking about her remark. She'd told me a few days before my dad died, she thought Mitch was sexy. I'd written it off at the time as Jenn being Jenn, then I'd been so upset about losing my dad, I didn't think about it again. Until now.

Did I need to worry? Should I ask Mitch if he'd noticed Jenn acting different around him? He'd probably shrug it off as nothing. But come to think of it, Mitch had been acting weird lately too. Before my dad was killed, Mitch had been grumpy, moody and he often didn't come home until late and then he'd go to bed instead of sitting with me watching television like he used to.

I shook my head. I knew better than to worry about my husband and my best friend. I was being ridiculous. Jenn loved to flirt with every man she encountered. I knew that. And Mitch was probably going through a mid-life crisis. He was turning fifty soon, and even though he wouldn't admit it, I knew it was bothering him.

The thought of sitting around eating dinner and visiting with friends sounded great after the past week. I knew Mitch would be happy to go. Neither one of us were on duty. I'd taken a couple weeks off work when Dad was killed, and Mitch had taken a few days off.

Now, I parked in front of the gas station and got out. Murray looked up when I walked in. I'd known him most of my life because he and my dad had been friends since high school.

"Liz! How ya doin' hun?" He came around the counter with his arms stretched out for a hug.

I hugged him. He smelled of diesel oil and his wood burning stove. "I'm okay, Murray." My eyes watered. I don't think I'd ever spent time with Murray without my dad there.

"Nah, you're not telling the truth, honey, you're not okay. None of us are."

Murray had tears in his eyes too. I nodded. "You're right. I miss him so much." I let go of my old friend and stepped back. "Dad left me a letter saying he left a package here for Rose?"

Murray nodded.

"Did she come for it?"

He shook his head, taking off his railroad cap, the one he'd worn every day since I could remember, and scratched his head. "No, not yet." He put his hand on my arm and nudged me over to a couple of chairs he kept next to an old wood burning stove.

Murray's gas station had been in his family for generations, and I was sure the stove was original to the building. Maybe the chairs too. They'd always been there as far as I could remember, two old wooden chairs with cracked leather seats. The air smelled of old oil, gas, and wood smoke.

We sat and Murray said, "What do you want me to do with the package, Liz? Give it to you?"

I thought for a minute. "I wish Rose had picked it up. I went to the cult's compound today and they said she left a few days ago. I thought maybe she'd gone to Dad's place, but there wasn't any sign of her there."

Murray shook his bald head. "Rose was never easy to figure out. George worried about her all the time."

"I know." I reached over and patted his hand. "Would you keep the package for a few more days, Murray? Just in case Rose does shows up and ask for it? And if she does, will you call me?"

"Of course, I will. You know I'd do anything for you and Rose."

We talked a while longer, then I said goodbye and went back to my car. I got in and sat for a few minutes thinking about Rose. What happened to her? Was she afraid if she came out of hiding Jeremiah and his goons would find her and hurt her? I wished she'd call me. I could protect her.

The drive back to Hood River didn't take long and soon I pulled into my garage. Mitch wasn't home, and I knew I needed to call him and tell him we'd been invited to Jenn's for dinner in case he decided to stop by the sheriff's office on his way home.

As soon as I stepped into the house, I took my phone out and called him. He answered right away, but when I told him I'd made plans with Jenn he was quiet for a couple minutes.

"Isn't that okay? I figured you wouldn't care. You always say how much you love her cooking."

"No, it's fine. I just thought we could have a quiet evening at home tonight."

That was so unlike him. He was Mr. Social, always wanting to go places and do things after work. "Is everything okay? Are you not feeling well?"

"Yeah, everything's fine." He was quiet for a couple seconds. "I'm just tired. It's been a crazy day. I'll be home in a few minutes. I'm just pulling onto the on-ramp."

We said goodbye and I stood in the kitchen staring at my phone. Mitch had sounded exhausted. Should I call Jenn back and tell her we couldn't go after all? She'd understand. I called Mitch again and asked if he wanted me to cancel. He sighed and said, "No, that's fine. If you want to go, we'll go."

A feeling of guilt swept over me for the way I reacted to Travis. Was I going through a mid-life crisis too? I was only two years younger than Mitch. I shook my head and put it out of my mind. I didn't have time to think about Travis or Mitch. I needed to find my dad's killer.

I glanced at the clock on the microwave and saw it was almost four-thirty. I hadn't eaten all day, but I didn't want to spoil my appetite for dinner, so I poured left over coffee into a mug and reheated it.

My cell phone rang, and I took it out of my pocket to see who was calling me. When the name of my bank came up, I frowned and took the call.

"Liz? This is Sheila at the bank."

I'd banked at the same bank all my adult life and knew everyone. "Hi Sheila, what's up?" In my mind I conjured up the bubbly redhead who always had a joke or a funny story to share.

Her voice wasn't bubbly like normal. "We just had a woman come in and try to take money out of your dad's account."

"What? Who was it? Was it Rose?"

"I haven't seen Rose in years. That's who she said she was, but she didn't look anything like I remember her. I told her your dad's accounts were frozen because of his death, which as you know isn't true, but I wanted to call you before I did anything else."

"Did she have ID?"

"Yeah, she had Rose's ID, and she looked like the picture on the ID card, but there was something off, Liz. I had this bad vibe. I told her to call you because you're in charge of George's account. I hope that's okay."

"You did the right thing. Did she say she'd call me?"

"No, she didn't say anything. She stood up and walked out the door."

Chapter 7

Mitch walked in as I finished my call with Sheila. I told him what had happened. Mitch plugged in his phone and poured himself a cup of coffee.

"Are you thinking it's her?" he asked, taking a sip of coffee, and looking at me over the top of his cup.

"I don't know. Sheila didn't think so, but she said it's been years since she saw Rose. But why would Rose go to the bank and try and get money when Dad left money for her with Murray? None of this makes sense."

Mitch looked thoughtful. "I think we need to go back to the Bread of Life and talk to Swanson again. I'd bet my last dollar he knows more than he's letting on."

Suddenly, I remembered the piece of paper with the phone number on it that Dorcas gave me. I pulled it out of my pocket. "One of the women at the compound slipped this number to me. I tried calling it earlier, but no one answered. I'll try it again."

Mitch nodded and looked at the number. "Do you recognize it?" I asked.

He shook his head, and I called the number. After listening to it ring for ten times I hung up. "Still no answer."

He took the paper from me and stared at it. Then he handed it back. "Did she say anything when she gave it to you?"

"No, but she's the one who told me Jeremiah's wife had left the cult, and Rose had discovered something bad going on at the compound." I looked at the number on the paper. "I wish she would've told me who it belongs to. I'll go back tomorrow and try and talk to her."

Mitch nodded and we got ready to leave for dinner at Jenn and Ray's house.

Jenn and I had been friends since high school. We'd both wanted to go into law enforcement, so we majored in Criminal Justice in college. But Jenn decided to be a parole officer and I wanted to be a police officer. Jenn worked for about five years, but that was enough for her. She quit and stayed home once she married Ray.

Ray's family was wealthy. His grandfather had owned a chain of grocery stores all over the northwest. Ray had been brought up working the family business, then he decided to get into politics and had become an Oregon senator. I had a feeling he wanted to end up as governor or maybe even in Washington, DC.

They'd built a beautiful home on the west side of the valley, up on a hill. Their view was amazing. I had house-envy, but I was happy for Jenn.

When we got there, Ray greeted us with a drink and took our rain jackets. "Glad you guys could come over. We don't see enough of you these days." Ray was older than Jenn by seven years. He was a slender man with even features and a big grin. He always reminded me of a used car salesman, and I thought that was why he had made it in politics. He was a busy man, and we didn't see a lot of him, even though the four of us had done a few things together over the years.

Their living room had windows across the entire front of it with a view of the valley and the Columbia River. Tonight, the lights from town sparkled and I stepped over to look out at them just as I did every time I came to Jenn's house.

The smell of fresh baked bread filled the house and made my stomach growl. I glanced at Mitch, but he was talking to Ray. Was his face flushed? Maybe he was sick. I started to ask him, but Jenn interrupted me.

"We're all too busy," she said, coming into the living room from the kitchen. She was dressed in ankle length skinny jeans and a pink tank that showed the soft curves of her breasts. I noticed my husband's gaze lingering there and I narrowed my eyes at him. He looked away. Jenn gave me a hug and patted Mitch on the arm. "Dinner's ready. Let's eat. We can talk about what you're doing while we eat."

Ray monopolized the conversation during dinner, something he always did. Mitch could hold his own, but I noticed he wasn't saying much. I looked at him and he saw me and gave me a half smile.

"So, tell me what's going on with Rose," Jenn said while we were putting the dishes in the dishwasher after dinner. Ray had taken Mitch into his office to show him something.

I'd told Jenn earlier about the letter Dad left me. Now, I dried the soup pan she'd just washed and put it away. Then I told her about Shelia from the bank calling to tell me Rose or someone had tried to draw money from Dad's account."

"Do you think it was her?" Jenn asked.

I shook my head. "I don't know. Maybe. But if she's okay, why didn't she come to dad's funeral? Something must've kept her from it." I pushed my hair behind my ear.

Jenn rinsed out the sink and dried her hands on a tea towel. Then she picked up hand lotion and rubbed it into her hands. She offered it to me, but I shook my head. "Maybe she was afraid to show up. You know, afraid someone might see her and tell Swanson she was there."

"Or maybe it wasn't her at the bank. Maybe they killed her too," I said, softly.

"No." Jenn shook her head and gave me a hug. I could smell the lemon scented hand lotion. "Don't even go there. Rose is out there somewhere. We need to find her. How can I help?"

I hugged her back. "I don't know. Maybe we could go through Dad's house together. I looked around today but didn't find anything."

"Okay, I'm not doing anything tomorrow. When you get ready give me a call and I'll meet you there."

We took our drinks into the living room and sat down, and the men joined us. Mitch was still quiet. Ray tried to get him to tell him about a burglary in town.

"Did they find the culprit?" Ray asked.

"What?"

"Did they find the culprit?" Ray repeated his question.

"I haven't heard they did, so I'm assuming they didn't." Mitch sighed and sat back on the sofa. "I've been out of the office for a few days. Rodriguez is in charge."

"Of course," Ray said.

After a half hour of stilted conversation from Mitch and questioning looks from Jenn and Ray, I stood up. "I think we should go home. Mitch had to take Bella back to school today and I'm sure he's tired. It's a long drive."

Mitch blinked at me but got up and followed me to the door. Ray handed us our jackets and we said goodnight.

When we got in the car, I turned to my husband. "What's going on? You've been acting funny all evening."

Mitch didn't say anything for a while, then he said, "I guess I'm more tired than I realized."

When we got back to our house my dad's dog, Bailey came to greet us. I bent down to pet her and talk to her, and Mitch went to fill her doggie dish. My phone rang and I stood up and took it out of my pocket. It was the number I'd been calling all day.

"Hello? Who is this?"

A voice I didn't recognize said, "Rose is in trouble. You need to find her before Swanson does."

The phone went black, and I yelled for Mitch.

He hurried in from the pantry. "What's wrong?"

I told him about the phone call.

"Give me the number and I'll have someone find out who it belongs to."

I handed him my phone and he pulled out his own and called the sheriff's office and told Deputy Connolly to check out the number and call him back.

We looked at each other. "Mitch, I'm worried about Rose. This is so weird."

He put his arm around me and pulled me to him. "I know you are, honey. I hate it that you have to deal with this along with losing your dad." He gave me a squeeze and let me go.

The next morning Mitch went into the office. I called Jenn and told her I was leaving for my dad's house. She agreed to meet me there. Bella called to check on me and we chatted for a few minutes before she had to head to class.

I pulled into the farm and parked in my dad's garage next to his pickup. It was a habit, but now as I climbed out of my car, it hit me Dad would never drive his pickup again. A knife-sharp pain filled my chest and I almost fell. Instead, I grabbed hold of the car and forced myself to stand upright and take deep breaths.

I closed the garage door and headed into the house. It was an old farmhouse, but Dad had fixed it up and painted it a dark gray with black trim. He had rose bushes on each side of the front porch. Dad had loved roses. I hadn't thought about what I'd do with the house, but I knew I'd dig up the rose bushes and plant them at my house. I couldn't part with them.

Jenn pulled in a couple minutes behind me. I opened the front door for her. The rain had finally subsided, and the sun was trying to peek out from behind the clouds. I stepped out of the house and waved to her. She got out and joined me on the front porch.

"I'm sure glad the rain has quit for a while. I'm so tired of it," she said.

I nodded and ushered her inside. We'd both dressed in leggings and sweatshirts, and we laughed at each other when we realized they were even the same color.

"Great minds," Jenn said, and I nodded.

Jenn had brought her water bottle, which she never went far without, and I made a pot of coffee. She took a swig of water and asked, "Where do you want me to start?"

"I went through the office yesterday. Do you want to look around in here and the living room? I'll take Dad's bedroom and the guest room, then we can both check out the upstairs."

"Sure." She started towards the living room, then she stopped and watched me make coffee. "How's Mitch this morning? He wasn't himself last night."

"Yeah, he seemed fine. I guess he was tired last night. He's not usually so quiet." I thought about mentioning my worries about Mitch, but for some reason, I didn't.

Jenn nodded. "I hope so." She grimaced. "Men are not easy to live with. I'm so ready for Ray to go back to Salem."

I knew Ray had an apartment in Salem, and he spent a lot of time there when the senate was in session. Sometimes Jenn went with him, but she enjoyed the freedom of him being there and her being in Hood River about one hundred miles away.

"Is there something you want me to look for?" Jenn asked as she walked into the living room.

"Anything that might tell us if Rose was here." I finished making coffee and headed for Dad's bedroom. I'd just stepped through the door when Jenn called out to me.

"You might want to come here." Her voice sounded funny, and I hurried into the living room, but she wasn't there.

"Where are you?"

"In the office."

I ran down the hall to Dad's office. Jenn stood just inside the door. "Someone's been here."

The room was in shambles. Drawers pulled out from the desk, files everywhere, the desk chair turned upside down, and even the pictures were taken down off the wall. It didn't look anything like it had when I'd left the day before. "They sure have."

Chapter 8–Rose

Two weeks earlier

Rose shrank back against the tree. She knew Brother Luke had seen her when he flashed his light on her. Why didn't he say something to Brother Ezekiel? She held her breath. Why had they turned around and come back? Every part of her wanted to turn and run into the forest. The only thing that kept her from following her instinct was she might be lost in the darkness forever.

Rose hated the dark. She always had. As a child, she'd slept with her light on. Especially after her mother left. Nothing was the same when Marta Scott had walked out for the last time.

The car slowed down, and Brother Ezekiel shined a powerful flashlight around the ground. Rose carefully moved to the other side of the tree and peeked around, holding her breath, hoping they wouldn't spot her. She heard the car door open and closed her eyes, praying for a distraction or anything that would get Brother Ezekiel back in the car.

Rose knew Brother Ezekiel was mean and would do something to hurt her if he found her. She'd been the brunt of his jokes when Father wasn't around. And one time he'd caught her arm and twisted it, holding her against him and whispering that he knew what she was about. Whatever that meant.

Brother Luke was different. She hoped if they found her, Brother Luke wouldn't let Brother Ezekiel hurt her. She worried about her dad. She'd overheard Ezekiel telling Father her dad was withholding money from them. He thought they should talk to her dad and shake him up a bit.

Rose had gone in to see Father soon after Ezekiel had left and told him it wasn't true. She assured him she'd given them all the money she'd had when she joined the family.

"I don't know if what you're saying is true, Rose Sari," Father had said in his soft, deep voice. "Ezekiel tells me he knows you held back money. Remember what happened to Ananias and Sapphira in the Bible when they withheld money from the apostles and lied about it?"

She remembered the Bible story. They'd both been struck dead when they lied about their money. It was one of the first Bible stories Father Jeremiah spoke of when someone joined the family. He made it clear no one could lie about their money. Everyone was expected to give everything they had to the family. Rose didn't have any trouble giving her money to the family, but lately, Father had been asking her to ask her dad for large sums of money.

"I know he has lots of money, Rose Sari. We've investigated and found out his worth. Why wouldn't he want to help his own daughter?"

When he put it that way, Rose thought it sounded reasonable. She'd asked her dad if he would like to give money to the Bread of Life family and had been astounded at his answer.

"No, Rose, I'm not giving them a dime. If you want to come home, I'll do everything in my power to help you. I'm saving up money for you, but you won't get it as long as you are a part of that cult."

Rose had tried to convince her dad it wasn't a cult, but Liz had convinced him otherwise. She'd told Father Jeremiah it was her sister who was keeping the money from them.

"You must talk to her, Rose Sari, make her see it is your money, not hers."

Well, it was their father's money, but Father Jeremiah had convinced her it would be part hers someday and her dad and sister should give it to her now. "We need money to get our business going, Rose Sari. You've lived with us for ten years and we've used the money you gave when you joined us. You must come up with more."

Rose had told Mother Priscilla about Father's request. "What should I do?"

Mother Priscilla had shaken her head. "Jeremiah is getting so money hungry. Do not give him more, Rose. He's using it for bad things."

That surprised Rose. "What kind of bad things? I thought he was using it to start the furniture business?"

Priscilla looked around and lowered her voice. "That's not the only business he's gotten into, Rose. I'm not happy with what Brother Ezekiel has brought into this family. He's full of darkness and sin and I'm afraid Jeremiah is listening to him."

Rose was astounded Mother Priscilla would say that about Father. She had questioned her further, but Priscilla had said all she was going to say. A few days later she took Rose aside and told her they needed to leave the cult.

Now Rose listened as Brother Ezekiel and Brother Luke exited the car. "Are you sure you didn't see her?" Ezekiel asked.

"No, I didn't see anything. Maybe you saw a deer. Their eyes shine in the darkness."

Ezekiel flashed his light around. "Maybe you're right. Rose Sarai is such a little pus, afraid of her own shadow, she'd never hide in the forest for this long. Come on, let's go tell Father we couldn't fine her."

To Rose's great relief, they got back in the car and headed towards the compound. Rose stepped out from behind the tree. She had a long walk ahead of her if she wanted to make it into Parkdale before morning.

She'd called her dad and told him she was leaving the cult, but she couldn't show up at his house because they'd look for her there. He'd been overjoyed and told her he'd leave money for her at Murray's gas station in Parkdale.

Rose hoped Mother Priscilla would be in Parkdale waiting for her like they planned. If she wasn't, Rose didn't know what she'd do.

Chapter 9-Liz

Present day

"I wonder what they were looking for?" Jenn said, looking around the torn-up room.

"Money? A way to find Rose. Who knows?" I thought about the cash Dad always kept in a safe in his closet and walked back to his room to look.

Jenn followed me. "What are you looking for?"

"Dad always kept quite a bit of cash in his safe. If Rose came looking for money, or even if she sent someone, she'd know to look there."

I pulled open Dad's closet door and pushed aside his clothes to find the safe which he'd bolted onto the back wall. It was there and still closed, but it looked like someone had tried to pry it off the wall.

"Can you grab Dad's flashlight from beside his bed?"

Jenn got it and handed it to me, and I shined it on the safe. Sure enough, there were marks there where the intruder had worked hard to open the safe, but it was still intact.

I grabbed my cell phone out of my sweatshirt pocket and called the office. The dispatcher answered, and I told her what was going on. "I'll send someone right out," she assured me.

Jenn and I went back into the kitchen. She poured us both a cup of coffee and handed me one. "Rose?"

I nodded and sank onto a kitchen chair. "Why would she do this? Dad left money for her with Murray. Why would she break into his house and try to steal more?"

Jenn had known about the cult, and I'd filled her in on everything I'd found out in the last few days. "Maybe Jeremiah Swanson is pressuring her to give him more money. It must cost a lot to keep his compound going. Where does he get his money? Does anyone there have a paying job?"

"Not that I know of. Rose had to give him all the money she had saved when she joined the cult. I'm sure some of his members have more than others. Good question. He may insist they beg family for money. You should see that place, Jenn, it's gorgeous. It wasn't cheap to build."

Jenn raised her eyebrows. "It's amazing to me intelligent people would buy into that mumbo-jumbo. And give him all their money? I don't think so."

"I know, but Rose was so taken with Priscilla and the idea of living somewhere in an atmosphere of peace and love." I rolled my eyes and Jenn shook her head.

"Not much peace or love if Priscilla felt she had to leave." She opened her water bottle and took a big swig. Then she picked up her coffee and took a sip of it.

I thought for a minute. "You know, maybe I'm going about this the wrong way. Maybe instead of looking for

Rose, I should be looking for Priscilla. She's probably much more visible."

"What do you mean?" Jenn asked.

I was lost in thought and didn't answer for a couple of minutes. "If Priscilla and Rose are missing, which one would you think Swanson would be looking for the hardest?"

"Ah...got ya. Of course, he's looking for his wife. What are you going to do?"

"Go back and ask more questions."

"Will he let you talk to his people?"

"He did yesterday. We can't open an investigation unless there's a witness or a body, and right now we don't have either." I thought for a minute. "But, since I'm Rose's sister, I can start a formal investigation into her disappearance."

My phone buzzed and I took it out of my pocket. It was Mitch. "Hey."

"I heard your dad's place was tossed."

"Yeah, Jenn and I are here now. Are you coming out here?"

"I'll be there in about ten minutes. I went to the bank and picked up a picture off their camera of the woman who claimed she was Rose."

My heart thudded. "Is it her?"

"It sure doesn't look like her to me, but you'd probably be able to tell better than I would. I'll be there in a few."

I hit stop on my phone, picked up my coffee and paced around the kitchen. "Mitch doesn't think the woman at the bank was Rose. He's got a picture."

"Who does he think it is?"

I stopped pacing and took a drink of my coffee. "He doesn't know. Maybe I can recognize her from one of the women I saw yesterday."

Jenn nodded. "Do you need me for anything else? I promised I'd meet Greta for lunch, and I want to go home and change clothes." She looked down at her workout pants.

That was the first I'd heard about her meeting her other best friend. "No, thanks for coming out."

She smiled and gave me a hug. "You'll get this figured out and find Rose. I can feel it." She hit her chest with a fist, and I smiled back at her. Typical Jenn.

I walked her to the door and saw Mitch drive in and park behind her car. She ran out to ask him to move and I watched as they exchanged a few words, then Mitch moved his truck and Jenn jumped into her Mercedes SUV and left.

Mitch looked upset when he came in the house. "Connolly called CSU; they should be here soon. She and Rodriguez are on their way too."

Ah, I thought, my favorite and least favorite co-workers. I liked to work with Enrique Rodriguez, not so much Megan Connolly.

Mitch took the picture out of his shirt pocket and handed it to me, then he went to the coffee maker and poured himself a mug of hot coffee. He held up the pot, silently asking if I wanted a refill.

I held out my mug and looked at the picture while he poured. "This isn't Rose."

"Are you sure?" he asked, looking over my shoulder.

"Of course. Look at her nose, even with the dark glasses and scarf around her neck, I can see this woman has a much bigger nose than my sister. And her chin is pointed. Rose's chin is rounded."

"Do you know her?"

"She looks familiar. I'm wondering if it could be Lydia, Jeremiah's right-hand man."

"You mean woman?" Mitch grinned.

"Yeah." I studied the picture closely, trying to figure out if it was Lydia. It could be, but I wasn't sure.

I put the picture down on the counter and took Mitch in to look at Dad's office. He stood in the doorway. "Rose wouldn't do this."

"I don't think so either."

"If I remember right, she was always neat. She kept a clean house."

"You're right. She even cleaned for dad after she left home."

We walked back to my dad's bedroom, and I showed Mitch where the safe was. He looked it over and pulled on one side. "It's still secure. I'm surprised they gave up so easily."

"Me too. You'd think they'd find a way to get it out if they wanted to." I reached under the dresser and pulled out a box. "Dad left the key to the safe in here."

Mitch raised his eyes. "Not very safe."

I nodded and took the key out and put it in the lock. The safe opened. Inside I found a small handgun and one hundred dollars in twenties. I felt around and didn't find anything else. I took the gun and money out and showed them to Mitch.

"Not enough to break into a house over," he said.

"That's odd." I looked at the money in my hand. "Dad kept several thousand in cash in case he needed it for something. There's only one hundred dollars here."

Mitch rubbed the back of his neck. "Maybe he used it and didn't have time to put it back."

"Maybe." But I wasn't convinced. What would he have needed it for? "I wonder if he gave it to Rose. He left some with Murray for her, but I can't believe he'd leave thousands of dollars for her. And I know he had at least ten thousand in cash because he showed it to me not long before he died."

"Call Murray and ask him to look."

I nodded and made the call. Murray picked up on the first ring. "Okay, hon, I'll check and get back to you."

I put everything back and we went upstairs. "Jenn and I didn't get up here to look around."

The stairs were narrow and steep and at the top was a big room Dad used for storage. When we were girls, Rose and I fought over it. She won because she was the oldest and I had to sleep downstairs.

Rose's bed was still set up with a scrap quilt our grandmother had made lying on top of it. My quilt was at home on our guestroom bed. Rose had an end table and a dresser next to her bed. The room held a faintly sweet smell, and I wondered if her perfume, Chanel #5, still lingered after all these years.

I laid my hand on the quilt, then reached over and opened the drawer of her nightstand. There was the Bible she'd used as a girl. On top of it was a Harlequin romance that had been read many times. There were other odds and ends, a pen and notebook, a few rubber bands, and a church bulletin from twelve years ago.

Mitch's phone rang and he answered it while I walked over to Rose's dresser and opened the top drawer. There were some old sweaters and a pair of jeans, along with a savings account book from our bank.

I flipped it open, expecting to see she'd cleaned it out when she went to the cult, but to my surprise, there was a balance of forty-thousand dollars in her account. "Mitch," I said, softly.

He finished his conversation and came closer.

"Look." I pointed to the bottom line in the book. "Rose has forty thousand dollars in this account."

Mitch took the account book from my hand. "That's a lot of money."

I nodded. "It sure is. I wonder where she got this money. I thought she'd given everything she had to the cult when she joined."

"How much did she have when she left?"

"Remember, she sold her house. I thought she gave all the proceeds to Swanson, but she must've kept some in case she wanted out."

Mitch nodded.

I squinted at the bank book. "That doesn't make sense, though. I remember Dad saying Rose gave Swanson everything she got out of the house. And why would Dad give her ten thousand if she had forty in her account?"

"Maybe she needed cash fast and didn't have time to get to the bank."

I nodded. "I've got to find out what's going on. Do you want to drive out to their compound with me?"

"Yes, but I need to tell you something." He took hold of my shoulders and turned me towards him. My heart skipped a few beats.

"What?"

"That call was from Connolly. She tried to find out who owned the phone that messaged you. It's a burner and she's looking into it, but we probably won't get anything off it."

"Probably not."

"But Liz, she told me something. We knew The Bread of Life cult was being investigated by the FBI, but apparently, they've upped their interest in the last few weeks."

"Do you know why?"

"How does theft, sex trafficking and maybe even murder sound to you?"

Chapter 10

"**Y**ou're kidding me. Murder? Sex trafficking?"

Mitch nodded. "We shouldn't be surprised. I had a feeling Swanson wasn't the upstanding man he claimed to be."

"That must be why Priscilla wanted out. I wonder if Rose knew about it?"

Mitch shrugged. "It sounds like there was someone else killed several years ago. They've been trying to pin the murder on Jeremiah, but the evidence isn't there."

"Who was it?"

He shrugged. "I don't know. Someone from another state. Evans made it sound like it was a man and he was abducted and killed in Oregon."

I grabbed Mitch's arm and squeezed. "We need to find out who he was. Maybe if we figure out why he was killed, we'll know why my dad was."

My husband held me close, and I leaned my head on his shoulder. Fear for my sister and anger for my dad carved a dark, bitter hole in my heart.

My phone rang. It was Murray. "I opened the envelope George left for Rose. There's nine thousand, two hundred dollars."

"Did he say why he wanted to give her so much cash?"

"He said she was trying to leave that gul-durned cult and needed cash to live on."

I thanked him and disconnected. That made sense unless you knew about the forty thousand she had stashed in a bank account.

The two deputies arrived as we were leaving the house and Mitch gave them a rundown of what was going on. They went in to look around and wait for Oregon State's crime scene people. We left my car and drove away from the farm in Mitch's truck. "If Rose found out, she would've left. I'm sure of it."

He nodded but kept his eyes on the road. "I don't know if the FBI will like us getting involved in their investigation."

We both knew the answer. "I'm not giving up the search for my sister. I don't care what the FBI says."

Mitch put his hand on top of mine. I turned my hand over and held his. It felt so warm and strong. We held hands until we reached the drive into the cult. We hadn't done that in a long time.

Mitch drove down the winding road into the compound with its manicured lawns, beautifully cared for buildings and riot of flowers everywhere. Mitch whistled softly. "Nice place."

"Yeah, Jenn asked me where they get their money. Do any of them work?"

"Not that I know of. I think he takes it from the members. When they come here to live, they sign over all their assets."

I thought about Rose and how she hadn't given Swanson all of her money. Had he found out? Did he demand she get the money and give it to him? And when she refused, did he kill her and send Lydia or another one of the "sisters" to clean out her accounts? I had so many more questions than answers.

Mitch pulled up and parked the pickup close to the front door. There were people moving around today unlike the day before when everyone had been inside out of the rain. One man was mowing the lawn, another painting the trimming on the building next to the main house.

"I'm going to look for Dorcas. You keep Jeremiah busy, okay?"

Mitch nodded. We got out of the car, and he headed to the main building while I took off to the right where Dorcas had told me the school was. I hoped she was teaching, and I would find her.

No one paid any attention to me as I walked quickly to the schoolhouse and opened the door. I walked into a hallway that led to two double doors, one on each end of the hall. The door opened and a woman in blue cotton pants and tunic with a paper cap on her head, came out carrying a large trash bag that looked full. I peeked inside the room she'd just exited, and it was a kitchen.

Deciding Dorcas and the children must be somewhere else, I headed down the hall to the other set of doors. I reached out and opened the door on the right and sure enough, there was a classroom. There were pictures on the walls of children's book covers and kids playing soccer, basketball, and baseball. There were kid-sized desks on one end and a large desk for the teacher. The children, ranging in age from about five to ten, were gathered around Dorcas who held a little girl in her arms. They sat on the floor and Dorcas rocked her back and forth on her lap. The other children hovered over her.

When they realized someone else had entered the room, they all looked up at me. Then the little girl on Dorcas's lap cried out, "Please, take me to my mommy."

The children's eyes were big, and Dorcas held the little girl closer. "It's okay, Sweetie."

"I want my Mommy!" she cried again. She had a round face and big blue eyes. Her light brown hair was long and silky and curled around her shoulders. She reminded me so much of Bella at that age, my breath caught in my throat.

The door behind me opened and another woman came in and took the little girl out of Dorcas's arms. The girl screamed and tried to bury her head in Dorcas's shoulder, but the woman picked her up and left with her. I watched them leave, then turned back to Dorcas. The children were silent. Dorcas had tears in her eyes.

"Where is she taking her?" I blinked back tears too.

Dorcas shook her head and got to her feet. She sent the children back to their desks and came over to me. "She's taking her to her mom," she said, but the look on her face said something different.

Again, the door behind me opened, and the man I knew as Ezekiel walked in. "Detective, may I take you to see Jeremiah." His deep voice boomed into the room.

I wondered what he'd say if I said, no. "I'd like to talk to Dorcas first."

"I'm afraid that isn't possible. As you can see, Sister Dorcas has duties here. Please, come with me." He held the door open, and I didn't feel like I had a choice. I had a bad feeling about what was going on with the little girl.

"Is she okay?" I asked Dorcas. She nodded once, but I could see fear on her face.

We left the school and walked up to the front door of the main hall. The room was even more beautiful with sunlight streaming through the windows. I hadn't noticed the day before that the windows on each side of the huge fireplace were made with stained glass. Both had a picture of Jesus holding a lamb, with his hand out to others. The sunlight through the colored glass was breathtaking.

Jeremiah and Mitch stood when I walked over to them. Jeremiah saw me look at the stained glass and smiled. "It is beautiful, isn't it?"

"It is."

"Jesus and I have a lot in common." He beckoned me over to the sofa and we all sat down. "We both love our little lambs."

I glanced at Mitch and saw his eyes widen. This guy is scary, I thought as I followed Jeremiah. "I want to know what is going on with a little girl I just saw in the classroom. She was crying for her mother."

A flash of irritation spread over Jeremiah's face. He frowned. "I don't know what you're talking about." He glanced up at Ezekiel who shook his head.

"None of the children were crying when I was in there," the man said.

"That's because one of the women came and got her. But she didn't want to go with the woman, and I want to know if she's okay." My voice was full of steel. I wasn't backing down.

"Maybe you could have the child brought in so we could see for ourselves that she's okay," Mitch offered.

Jeremiah didn't like it, but he waved Ezekiel towards the doorway. The other man stared at Jeremiah for a few seconds, then headed across the polished floor. His boots made harsh statements the whole way to the door.

"Please sit down." Jeremiah indicated the sofa in front of the fireplace. There wasn't a fire today, but we sat down, and Jeremiah sat across from us. "I was answering a few of the sheriff's questions."

"Have you heard from Rose?" I asked.

Jeremiah sighed. "No, I haven't heard a word from her. We assumed she went to your father's funeral and didn't come back. But you said she didn't show up there, so I don't know where she is."

He looked into my eyes and my skin crawled. I knew he wasn't telling the truth. "When I was here yesterday, someone had already packed up her stuff and cleaned out her room. You didn't expect her back."

"I told you she took her personal things with her. Why would we expect her to come back?"

"Did she have any money? How could she leave?" Mitch asked.

"She must've arranged to have someone pick her up. I don't know how she did it, I just know she's gone." Jeremiah's voice had gone from peaceful to annoyed.

"Did you know my father was murdered? Did Rose know?" I watched Swanson carefully, wondering if he'd flinch. He didn't. Then he bowed his head.

"I'm sorry. I hadn't heard until you mentioned it yesterday. I'm sure it has nothing to do with Rose Sari's disappearance."

I didn't know whether to believe him or not, but Mitch spoke up before I could say anything more.

"Tell me about your wife," Mitch said.

Jeremiah stared at him. "What about my wife?"

"Where is she? I understand she left about the same time as Rose." Mitch continued.

Jeremiah sighed. "She went away for a few days. There's nothing sinister about it. She just needed a break. She'll be back soon."

I wasn't sure if he was trying to convince us or himself.

Ezekiel came back into the room carrying the little girl I'd been worried about. She had a baby doll clasped in her arms and smiled when she saw us. She looked so much like Bella it was everything I could do not to jump up and take her out of his arms.

Mitch stirred on the sofa next to me.

"As you can see, Mary is fine," Ezekiel said, giving me a harsh look.

I stood up and walked towards her. "Hi honey, are you okay?"

She nodded and held out her baby doll. "Mommy." Then she held the doll close and kissed her.

The hair on the back of my neck stood up. I knew in my heart this child didn't belong to anyone in the cult. But I didn't know how to prove that.

"She's beautiful," I said, softly to the little girl.

A young woman came into the room and took Mary from Ezekiel.

"Is there anything else?" Jeremiah asked.

"Just a couple more questions." I reached into my bag and pulled out my phone with the picture of the woman at the bank and handed it to him. "Do you know who this is?"

He took the picture and looked at it. Then he took his glasses out of his pocket and put them on and looked closer. He shook his head. "No, should I?"

"Look closer. Doesn't it look like Lydia?"

He frowned. "It's hard to see her features because of the glasses and scarf, but I don't think so. Why would the bank have a picture of Sister Lydia?" He handed it back to me.

"Is Lydia here?" Mitch asked. "We'd like to talk to her."

Jeremiah took off his glasses and laid them on the coffee table in front of him. Then he rubbed his eyes. "She's not here today. She went out to do a few errands."

"Do you know when she'll be back?" I asked.

He leaned back and sighed as if he'd had all he could take of us and our questions. "Not really. She should be back this afternoon sometime."

"When did she leave?" Mitch asked.

"I'm not sure." He stood up. "Now, if there's nothing else?"

Like a well-orchestrated play, one of his men walked in and beckoned to Jeremiah. He and Ezekiel went to meet him, and they spoke quietly. Then Ezekiel walked out a side door.

I looked at Mitch who raised his eyebrows and whispered, "I don't think he's going to tell us anything more, do you?"

I took a deep breath and let it out. "Can we demand to talk to some of the other people living here? Rose has been missing for three days that we know of."

"Didn't you talk to several of the women yesterday?"

I nodded, but I wanted to talk to them again, without Lydia there. "Yes."

Mitch stood and offered me his hand. "Let's see if we can get a picture of Lydia. Maybe we can do a comparison with the picture from the bank."

I took his hand and stood up next to him. Jeremiah came back with a relieved look on his face. "I have an appointment, but Brother Luke will see you out."

"I'd like to talk with more of the women. I feel like they were on guard yesterday when Lydia was with us."

He looked surprised. "We are getting ready to congregate for prayers. You will have to talk to them another time."

Prayers? Really? I wondered who they were praying to. Jeremiah Swanson most likely.

"We'd like a picture of Lydia." Mitch said.

"I'm sorry, but we don't have pictures of our family. We feel that is a vanity that isn't needed. All my family are beautiful in my eyes." He held out his hand to

Mitch and the two men shook hands. He didn't bother to shake mine.

I ground my teeth as we followed Luke out to Mitch's pickup. Luke opened the door for me. I stood beside the pickup and looked up at him. "I want to speak to some of the women here."

"You talked to them yesterday."

"Not all of them. I have more questions."

He leaned down and said, "You need to stand down. This is an ongoing FBI investigation." He held my arm as I climbed into the truck. "I'll be in touch."

Mitch started the pickup and drove down the rutted driveway. "What did he say to you?"

I told him. "He must be FBI. What are we supposed to do? Sit back and let them handle it? I don't have any confidence that they'll find my sister. I don't think that's a high priority for them."

"You don't know that Liz. If they think someone was murdered here, they will be looking for Rose. We knew they were keeping an eye on Jeremiah. I'm glad they have someone here. Hopefully, he'll call. Maybe he knows where Rose is."

"Maybe. I still don't think that little girl's mom was there. I have bad vibes when it comes to her, Mitch."

He took his eyes off the road for an instant and glanced at me. "Is it because she looks like Bella?"

"You noticed it too?"

He nodded. "You've been through a lot, Liz. Your dad was murdered, and your sister is missing, and Bella went back to school yesterday. Maybe seeing that little girl who looked so much like her made you jump to conclusions."

I sighed. "Maybe you're right." But I didn't think so and I sat looking out the side windows, thinking about little Mary and my sister. How could I help them? I knew the answers to Rose's disappearance were inside that compound and possibly my dad's murder too. I had to find out what was going on.

Chapter 11

I told Mitch about the incident in the schoolroom, and he advised me to let the FBI know. I knew he was right. I made a mental note to call them.

Mitch dropped me off at my dad's house. He had been quiet on the trip back from the compound. I spent the time trying to come up with a way to sneak into the compound and talk to some of the women. I wanted to get a message to Dorcas.

The crime scene unit was gone. They'd left a mess, so I straightened up the office, putting files back and rearranging the furniture that had been turned over. I felt certain that my dad's murder was tied to the cult, but I didn't know why they wanted him dead. Were they looking for money and he came home and found them going through his house? But no, that wasn't right because Travis found him on the floor near his chair. My heart ached. *What happened, Dad? Who did this to you?*

I looked around the office. What were they looking for? I was sure that most of Dad's money was in the bank. What did they want bad enough that they'd kill an innocent man to get it?

I walked back upstairs to Rose's room. Maybe she'd left something there that would help me find her. Although what it would be was a complete mystery since it had been ten years since Rose stored things in her room. Unless she'd been here without me knowing about it. Maybe that was it. Maybe she left something with dad that was damning to the cult and Swanson sent his goons to get it and Dad intervened.

That made more sense to me than anything else. My dad didn't have enemies, he was a good man.

I went through Rose's dresser drawers, looked in the closet and under the bed. Nothing. Then I remembered that when we were little, Rose showed me a hiding spot she had where she kept her treasures. She made me promise to never take any of them.

I scooted the bed away from the wall and eased a piece of paneling out from its spot beside the headboard. Sure enough, inside the hole was a cardboard box decorated with roses that our grandmother had given Rose.

It felt heavy as I lifted it out of its hiding place, and I tried to remember what Rose had put inside it. I remembered a picture of our mother and a pair of earrings she'd left behind. Rose was certain Mother would come back for them. Did it still hold the same things, or had she changed them as she grew older? I'd never thought to ask.

The lid was taped shut and I pried it off and set it aside. Inside the box were mementos of Rose's girlhood. A few pictures of her and her best friend, Ginny. A paperback romance that had been read so many times the cover was falling off, a small key on an angel shaped keyring, a makeup bag, a stack of pictures, and an earring. It was a silver rose and my sister told me that it was one of Mother's favorites because it reminded her of Rose. My sister never got over our mother leaving us. There was only one earing, and I wondered what happened to the other one. Had mother lost it years ago, or had Rose?

I picked the pictures up and saw our mother as she looked before she left. I'd been nine and Rose twelve when she'd disappeared. We'd come home from school, and she wasn't there. When Dad got home, he told us that Mom had left and wasn't coming back.

We'd both cried, but Rose took it harder, maybe because she was older. I rubbed my finger lightly over the pictures. Most were of Mom and Rose, but I was in a couple. I never understood why Mom left. All our dad would say was she wasn't happy. He made sure we knew that it wasn't our fault and that he'd begged her to leave us with him. He said he couldn't live without us. I remember as a little girl wondering how Mom could live without us.

Turning the pictures over, I looked to see if there was anything written on the back. A few had dates written on them, but most were blank. I laid them down and picked up the keyring. The key on it was smaller than a house key or car key. What could it be for? I wondered.

A noise disrupted my thoughts, and I looked up, half expecting Mitch to walk into the room. When I didn't hear anything else, I went back to my study of Rose's treasures.

The makeup case was a hard sided one that opened on the top. I opened it and looked to see what was there. I thought I'd see old tubes of lipstick and mascara. Instead, what I saw made me catch my breath.

Inside I found pictures of young children. They looked like they ranged in age from about four to ten. They all had one word written across their faces. MISSING.

Chapter 12

I went through the pictures one by one to see if I recognized any of the children. I didn't. If any of them had been missing from Hood River I would have. Who were they and why did Rose have these pictures in her secret storage place? She had to have been coming and going in Dad's house for a while. Why hadn't he told me? Had he known she was in his house? He'd never acted like he did.

Was she working with the FBI? Mitch had said the FBI was looking into the Bread of Life for sex trafficking as well as murder. Was Rose involved? I had to find her. If she were, she could be in big trouble.

I started to put the pictures back into the case when I heard a noise downstairs. It sounded like someone walking around in the kitchen. I wondered if it was Mitch. I started to call out, then stopped. Mitch would've come looking for me. He would've called my name.

I texted him. *Where are you? Did you come back to Dad's house?*

He texted right back. *No. I'm at the office. What's going on?*

I'm upstairs. Someone is walking around downstairs. My gun is in my purse on the kitchen counter.

Can you hide somewhere? I'll be right there. Don't go downstairs!

Hurry.

I tip-toed over to the stairway, listening. I could hear footsteps and doors opening and closing. I started down the stairs, trying to be quiet so they wouldn't hear me. I could hear someone rummaging around in Dad's office. Had they been interrupted when they came last time? Had they come back to do a more thorough search?

Was it Rose? My heart sped up. Would I get to see my sister after all this time and finally get some answers?

Dad's bedroom was next to the bottom of the stairs. I moved another step down but stopped when I saw a shadow dart from the office into Dad's bedroom. It had to be Rose, didn't it?

Mitch had told me to wait for him, but there was no way I was going to let whoever was in Dad's house get away. I looked around for a weapon, just in case. I knew that going down those stairs without one was probably the worst thing I could do, but I had to. What if it was Rose? What if this was my only chance to confront her?

What if it isn't? A small voice inside my head asked.

I ignored it and grabbed a large flashlight next to the bed. It wouldn't help in a gun fight, but I might have surprise on my side. I crept down the stairs, holding the flashlight next to my leg. As I stepped on the last stair from the bottom, it creaked. My heart sank. I stood still and listened. The house was quiet.

Suddenly Dad's door slammed shut, and I lunged towards it. It wouldn't open. I jiggled the doorknob, knowing it stuck sometimes. Suddenly it opened and I let it slam against the wall. The slider in his room was open and I could see a figure racing for the orchard. I gave chase.

Where was Bailey when I needed her, I thought as I ran full on through the orchard. She would have loved the chase and would have caught the intruder before they made it onto Travis' property, which was the way they ran.

My lungs started to hurt, and I took short breaths hoping I could keep this up. I could see someone moving in front of me, but I couldn't tell if it was a man or a woman. They were too far away. But I could tell whoever it was wore a dark green hoodie and they had the hood up. As I gained ground on them, I knew it was either a woman or a short man.

"Rose!" I screamed, hoping it was my sister.

The other person didn't stop or even slow down. I yelled Rose's name again as I ran through clumps of grass and felt limbs from the pear trees slap at my face. They were full of water, and it rained down on me. My chest burned and my heart raced. I had a pain in my side and knew I couldn't keep this up much longer.

We were close to Travis's property, and I wanted to stop them before they reached the pond. It was placed in such a way that if you didn't know it was there, you could fall in. The sides were steep, and the pond was deep. With the rain we'd been having, it would be easy to slip. I sped up in a last-ditch effort to catch her. They were slowing down. I got close enough to grab at their hoodie. I caught the fabric in my hand and the figure turned to me, fighting to get away. By then I could tell it was a woman and I tackled her to the ground.

When I finally got hold of her arms and held them away from me, I realized I was right. It was a woman. But it wasn't my sister. It was Dorcas.

"Dorcas! What are you doing in my dad's house?"

Dorcas squirmed and tried to get free, but even though she had youth and strength on her side, I was strong and had police training on mine. "Calm down so we can talk."

Her eyes were wild, and I wondered if she was on something. She twisted, trying to get out of my hold, but I held her tighter. "Dorcas, it's me, Detective Ellisen. Calm down."

She made a guttural sound, thrashing her head back and forth. I could hear her whispering something, but I couldn't tell what. I leaned closer to her, and she said, "he'll kill me," over and over.

"Who?" I asked. "Who will kill you? Are you afraid of Jeremiah?"

Tears blurred her eyes and she suddenly quit thrashing. "No, no, no. Brother Luke."

"Brother Luke? Are you sure?"

She nodded. Her eyes were wide with fright.

"If I let you go, will you stay still?" I asked, easing back from her.

She looked up at me. I could see the desire to run in her eyes, but she nodded again. I moved away from her, but still held her arms. "Easy."

We both scrambled to our feet, breathing hard. Dorcas had tears running down her face. She swiped at them, and the hood of her cape fell back. Today her hair was free. It fell in a long silky wave to her waist.

"What's going on Dorcas?"

"I'm sorry. He sent me here to pick up a package he said belongs to Father Jeremiah. I didn't want to come, but Brother Luke said I had to." She pulled the green sweatshirt, around her trembling body.

"You're sure it was Brother Luke who sent you here?"

She nodded. "I don't understand. He said I had to come and break into that house. He even drove me here. I didn't want to." Tears poured down her face. "I'm going to jail, aren't I?"

I studied her for a few seconds. Luke had almost confessed to me that he was FBI. Why would he send Dorcas to get the package and make her believe he was going to kill her if she didn't?

Unless he knew something was going to happen to Dorcas if he didn't get her out of there. Was Luke on the up and up? Was he trying to get some of the girls out of the compound before they were sent to be sex slaves somewhere?

"I'm not going to arrest you, but you need to talk to me."

She stared at me, and I could tell she wasn't quite understanding what I was saying. She acted like she was on something.

"How many girls have gone missing from the compound lately?" I asked.

She shook her head. "The compound?"

"Where you're living."

"Oh. Just Rose. She left a few nights ago and hasn't come back. I'm worried about her."

I took her arm and headed back towards my dad's house. "No others have left or gone missing since you've been there?"

She looked up at me. "Well, there was one girl when I first came. I'd almost forgotten about her. She was like Rose. She was there and then she was gone. I didn't know her well, so I didn't think much about it."

"How long have you been there?"

Dorcas lagged behind. We were both breathing hard, and I could tell she was worn out from trying to get away from me. "About six months. My mother died and I didn't know what I was going to do. I planned to go to college. Mom had left me some money. But then I met Mother Priscilla, and she told me I could live with them, and they'd see to it that I went to college."

"Did they take your mom's money?"

She nodded. "She said they would invest it for me and pay for my college, but even though I keep asking them when I'm going to start, they keep putting me off."

I took a deep breath and put my arm through hers. "Let's get back to my dad's house and I'll get you something to eat and we can talk."

She nodded and followed me. "Are you going to take me back to the family?"

"Do you want to go back?"

She stopped moving and looked at me. I could see confusion in her eyes. "I worry about the children."

"Where are their parents?"

"Some are there at the homestead. That's what Father Jeremiah wants us to call it."

We started walking again. "And the rest?"

"I don't know."

"The little girl I was yesterday who cried for her mom?"

"I don't know. She showed up a week ago and they told me to take care of her. Then after she had the melt-down yesterday, I haven't seen her." Dorcas brushed tears out of her eyes and swayed. She grabbed hold of me and said, "I'm sorry. I feel weak."

"It's okay, we're almost there." We had reached my dad's yard. "Did you ask anyone where she went?"

She nodded. "I asked Sister Lydia. She said they took her home."

Whose home? I wondered as I let us into the house. I felt sick inside. What was going on at that compound?

Chapter 13

M itch drove into the driveway as I took Dorcas's hoodie and hung it in the hall closet. He came in the front door, a look of relief on his face when he saw me. "I've been trying to call you."

"Sorry, I didn't hear my phone." I started to pull it from my back pocket and realized it wasn't there. "It's not here. I must've left it upstairs."

He nodded and zeroed in on Dorcas. "Your intruder?"

"This is Dorcas." I introduced him as my husband, not as the sheriff of Hood River County even though he was in uniform.

"What's going on?" Mitch asked, leaning against the kitchen counter, his arms crossed in front of his chest. "Why were you in Liz's house?"

Dorcas sat at the table with her head in her hands. Her shoulders were slumped. I could tell she was exhausted or drugged. I told Mitch what she'd told me.

Mitch gave her a piercing stare. "So, you just broke in and began looking for money? You could go to jail, you know."

Dorcas shuddered and burst into tears. "He didn't say anything about money. He told me to look for a package with Rose's name on it." She gave me an accusing look. "She said she wouldn't send me to jail."

Mitch glanced at me and raised his eyebrows.

"I need to get Dorcas something to eat, then I'm going to let her sleep for a while. After she wakes up, we can talk."

Mitch nodded and headed for the coffeepot. He made a pot while I fixed Dorcas a sandwich, thankful that I hadn't cleaned out Dad's kitchen yet.

She barely looked at Mitch as she ate. He and I drank coffee once it was made and talked quietly about Bella. Dorcas was asleep on her feet. As soon as she finished, I led her down the hall to the guest room. She took off her shoes and laid on the bed. "I'm so sleepy."

"It's okay. Get some sleep."

She was out before I got out of the door. I went back into the kitchen and Mitch was still sitting at the table. He poured more coffee for both of us. "Tell me everything," he said.

I told him everything I knew. "Do you think they sent her to get the money Dad promised Rose?"

"Could be." Mitch drank his coffee, then put the mug down on the table. He rubbed the back of his head. "I can't imagine anything else that they'd want that badly."

"Me either. Except..."

"Except?"

I told him about the pictures I'd found. "Do you suppose they were looking for the pictures?"

"Maybe. What did you do with them?"

I had put them in my purse to take to the office. Now I took them out and showed Mitch. "Do you recognize any of them?"

He shook his head. "No, but we need to check them against the missing children data base. If these are pictures of children Swanson has been trafficking, it makes sense he wants to get them back."

I nodded, looking at the pictures again. "Something feels off about these." I tapped my fingernail against the stack. "I can't put my finger on it."

"You need to check them out. I'll talk to the FBI about Brother Luke, see if they've planted someone in the compound."

I took his hand. "Mitch, I'm scared for these girls. It sounds to me like Swanson is selling them into the sex trade. We've got to find a way to stop him."

Mitch nodded. "The only problem is, we don't have any evidence that's what he's doing."

I looked down at our hands. "We need to find the evidence. I know it's there. And I know there's something not right about Rose and Priscilla's disappearance."

"Liz, you know Rose could've left on her own. And Priscilla could be visiting friends or family like Swanson said."

"I have this feeling in my gut," I said, quietly.

"Yeah. I feel it too."

His phone rang and I jumped up to get mine from upstairs. I remembered using it, but I didn't remember leaving it up there. I ran up the stairs into my sister's bedroom and looked around. Sure enough, it was lying on the dresser. When I picked it up, I saw I had two calls, both from the same phone number.

I didn't recognize the number. Whoever it was hadn't left a message, and I shrugged and went back downstairs.

Mitch stood in the middle of the kitchen with his phone up against his ear. His face was red, and his eyes were narrowed.

"What?"

He shook his head and said into the phone. "Okay, I'll be right there." Then he turned it off and looked at me.

"What's going on?"

"That was Connolly. A woman's body was discovered not far from Parkdale. She was in one of Bill Yakamoto's cabins."

My heart fell and I clutched my stomach. "Rose?"

"I don't know. Connolly said the body had been there awhile."

"Oh Mitch! What if it's my sister?"

He put his arms around me and held me. "We don't know that yet, honey. It could be anybody."

I leaned into him, then straightened. "I'm going with you."

"What about Dorcas?"

I put my hand to my forehead, trying to think, wanting to see if the body was my sister. "I don't care. I've got to go."

"I'll call Evans. She's off today, but maybe she can come babysit while we go find out what's going on in Parkdale."

I nodded. He called, but Deputy Evans didn't answer. Mitch left a message.

I grabbed my phone and jacket and ran out the door. I knew Dorcas might be gone when I got back or Deputy Evans got there, but I couldn't care about that right then. I couldn't keep her prisoner anyway. I left a note on the table letting her know I'd be back.

I followed Mitch to Parkdale, taking my car so I'd have it if I needed it. My nerves were strung tight, and I knew I probably shouldn't be driving, but I had to.

We drove beyond the small town and turned onto Clear Creek Road between the community center and the historical museum, heading south.

Bill Yakamoto's orchard was a couple miles from town. When we pulled into his long driveway, there were first responder's vehicles parked everywhere. Deputies Connolly and Rodriguez met us as we pulled into the open loading area where Bill loaded fruit bins during harvest.

I turned off my car and jumped out, running towards the cabins. Mitch was right behind me.

"Liz! Wait up. Don't go in there alone."

I didn't listen, just forged ahead, praying that it wasn't my sister's body in there. Afraid that it was. Oh, dear Lord, please don't let it be her.

An older man stood by the door, blocking it. "You don't want to go in there, Ma'am."

"I'm with the Sheriff's office," I said, trying to push past him.

Mitch caught up to me. "Let me go first, Liz."

"No." I glared at the man. "Get out of my way." The cabin was old and smelled musty. There was a small table and chairs, a sink with a hot plate next to it, and a bunk. The woman lay on the bunk, her back towards the door. At first it looked as though she was asleep. I could tell the minute I laid eyes on her that it wasn't Rose.

"Thank God, thank God," I whispered. Then I felt horrible that I was happy some other woman was dead.

Mitch stood beside me and looked down at her. "I wonder who she is."

Connolly and Rodriguez had followed us into the small cabin. "She was murdered," Connolly said.

Mitch looked up at her. "Are you sure?"

She nodded. "Look at the back of her head. Someone bashed her head in."

Mitch leaned over and gently rolled the woman's head towards him. The back of her head was a bloody mess. Mitch looked around at the bed, on the floor, around the walls. "She wasn't killed here. There's no blood splatter, no blood soaked into the mattress." He looked up at the other deputies. "Who found her?"

"The owner. He's just starting to open the cabins for his crew. He came inside to air it out and found her."

Mitch nodded. "I need to talk to him."

Relief that the dead woman wasn't my sister flowed over me. My legs gave out and I sunk to the floor. Rodriguez reached down and touched my shoulder. "Are you okay?"

I nodded. "I just felt dizzy for a second."

When I looked up, Mitch and Connolly were both staring at me. Mitch with concern and Connolly with surprise. I tried to stand up and realized I was shaking.

"What's with her?" Connolly asked. "It isn't like she's never seen a dead body before."

"Back off, Connolly," Rodriguez said.

Mitch put his arm around me. "It's okay. It's not her."

"I know." I leaned into him for a couple seconds, then walked out of the cabin. I could feel Connolly giving me looks as I walked around outside, trying to get myself to calm down.

After a few minutes, I went looking for Mitch who was talking to Bill Yakamoto. Connolly secured the scene, putting up crime scene tape around the cabin. Rodriguez was talking to the first responders and the paramedics.

Bill Yakamoto was an older man. He wore glasses and wasn't much taller than my five feet, four inches. I didn't know him, but I'd heard about him. His family had been in Japanese internment camps during WW2. Some had neighbors who took care of their farms for them while they were gone. Others had to start over when they came home. Bill was one of the lucky ones. His family farm was given back to them.

Rodriguez came over with one of the men he'd been talking to. "Hey Sheriff, we may have a possible ID on the dead woman. This is Gregg Downs." He indicated the man beside him. "He thinks he knows who she is."

Mitch, Bill, and I looked at Gregg. "Who is she?" Mitch asked.

"Well, I'm not a hundred percent sure, but I think it's Priscilla Swanson. She and her husband started that Bread of Life movement about ten miles south of here. The reason I recognize her is because they tried to recruit my sister a couple years ago. I told them to get the hell away from her and stay away."

My glance collided with Mitch's. I hadn't recognized her, but it had been ten years since I'd seen her. Connolly yelled from the cabin, "Hey Sheriff, you might want to look at this."

I followed him back to the cabin. Connolly stood in the door. The medical examiner had arrived. Elaine King was an older woman with short curly gray hair and rimless glasses. She was a little on the pudgy side and looked like someone's grandma, but she was great at her job.

"Doc here started to bag the Vic's hands. Noticed something on her wedding band." Connolly led us over to the cot where the county medical examiner, Elaine King, leaned over the corpse.

"Hey Sheriff, I thought you'd like to see this." Elaine held out her hand where a thick gold band lay in the middle of her palm.

Mitch picked it up. "Her wedding ring?"

"Yeah, look closely." Elaine pointed to the swirling script on the ring. "That's a J and a S. When you turn the ring, you can see a P."

"JSP for Jeremiah and Priscilla Swanson." He turned to me. "I think Gregg is right. This must be Priscilla Swanson." He shook his head. "I think Swanson lied to us about where his wife went."

I nodded and took the ring away from Elaine, letting it roll around in my hand, feeling the heaviness of the gold. "Do you think he knows she's dead?"

Chapter 14 – Rose

Two weeks earlier

The sun was breaking over the mountains when Rose arrived in Parkdale. It had been a long night of walking and hiding, hoping against hope that no one was following her. Mother Priscilla had told her to find Bill Yakamoto's orchards. She'd drawn Rose a map and said she'd be waiting and that she had a friend who would pick them up.

Rose stumbled onto Bill's property at four o'clock in the morning. She was exhausted from walking all night. Mother Priscilla hadn't told her where to meet her, so Rose found the first empty building she came to and went inside. She had brought a backpack with her clothes and a blanket. She pulled the blanket around her and sat on the bare mattress on the bunk. Exhaustion pulled at her, and she felt her eyes begin to close. She curled up on the bunk and fell asleep.

Rose awoke a few hours later to the sound of a tractor starting up. At first, she wasn't sure where she was, then she remembered walking from the homestead to Bill Yakamoto's orchard.

Her stomach growled and she took a bottle of water and a bag of homemade protein bars out of her backpack and ate one, washing it down with water. What she would've given for a cup of strong coffee. Then she pulled a comb through her long blonde hair and pulled it back into a low ponytail. Soon, she'd have to find a bathroom. She knew that most cabins had separate bathroom and shower facilities.

Rose looked out the windows wondering where Mother was. It had taken longer for Rose to walk from the homestead than she'd thought. Had Mother Priscilla given up and gone on without her?

Rose began to shake from the cold and the thought of being stranded. She could always go to her dad's, but it was another long walk, and she didn't know if she had the strength for that. She knew she could walk to Murray's station and call her sister. She had no doubt that Liz would come get her, but fear of Brother Ezekiel and what he might do if he found out where she was, stopped her. She didn't want him anywhere near Liz or her dad.

Was it true what her dad had found out about Brother Luke? She felt queasy inside just thinking about it.

Rose stood and stretched and opened the door of the cabin. It had stopped raining and the sun was trying to peek out from behind the mountains. She looked around and noticed a barn. Next to the barn, bending over a tractor was an older Japanese gentleman. Rose walked over to him.

"Excuse me," she said, softly, not wanting to startle the older man.

He jumped and squinted up at her. "Oh, you scared me." He held his hand over his heart. "I wasn't expecting company."

Rose smiled. "I'm sorry. I was supposed to meet a friend of mine here. My name is Rose Sari. Has anyone been here looking for me?"

The man shook his head. "No, sorry, sorry. No one has come here." He looked at her over the top of his glasses. "You were meeting someone here?"

Rose nodded. "Yes, a friend of mine. She said she'd be here last night, but I didn't get here when I thought I would. Did someone come looking for me last night?"

"No, no. No one came." He shook his head back and forth. "You sure they were supposed to meet you here?"

Rose nodded. She was beyond tired. She felt herself slump and leaned up against the tractor. She yawned and the man peered at her.

"I wish I could help you. If you leave your phone number, I'll call if your friend shows up." He pointed to her backpack.

"Unfortunately, I don't have a phone." She didn't know what to do, then a thought struck her. "I don't suppose you need help around here?"

"Help? What kind of help?"

"I need somewhere to stay until my friend shows up. I could clean house or work in the orchard, whatever you need." She looked at the cabins. "Maybe I could stay in one of the cabins for a while?" She needed time to think about what to do. Where was Mother Priscilla? She wouldn't have gone off and left Rose there without sending word where she was. Rose felt a skitter down her spine. Was Mother all right? Had Father found out she was leaving and demanded she stay? Would she sneak out that night and come find Rose? Or the next night?

Rose felt she needed to stay on Mr. Yakamoto's place, but she didn't know how to convince him. Surprisingly, he didn't take much convincing.

"Can you cook?"

"Yes, I can cook and clean. Do you need someone to cook for your workers?"

He shook his head. "No, but I would love a good meal. I haven't had a good home cooked meal since my wife died." He looked sad, Rose wanted to put her arm around him to offer comfort, but she made herself stand still.

"I'd be happy to cook for you. Would you like some breakfast?"

His smile spread over his face like the sun over the mountains. "Yes, yes, breakfast, then you nap. You look tired. I will clean up the dishes." He started walking towards the house. "Come. Come. We will eat."

Rose followed him into the little house that looked like it hadn't been cleaned properly in years. What had she gotten herself into? She wondered. She wasn't afraid of Mr. Yakamoto, but as she looked around, she realized she had a lot of work to do. Would she be there long enough to do it? If Mr. Yakamoto was kind enough to let her stay for a while, she'd do everything she could to make his house sparkle while she was there. She just wondered how long she'd have to stay before Mother came.

Chapter 15-Liz

P *resent day*

We left Elaine and Connolly and headed back to The Bread of Life compound. The rain that had been dogging us for days had subsided and the sun had come out. I enjoyed feeling it beating down on me as I rode with Mitch. Rodriguez and Connolly said they'd drive my Jeep back to my dad's house. It would be a while before they could leave the crime scene, but I hoped Dorcas would still be there.

Flowers were springing up on the roadside. The daffodils were long gone, but others had taken their place. With the sun shining on them, they'd raised their heads and opened showing their beauty.

We knew something was up the minute we drove down the hill into the compound. There were cars parked everywhere. People walked towards the main building in groups of two or more. They talked excitedly amongst themselves. News vans were parked along the drive and in the parking area.

A huge white tent had been set up on the lawn behind the barn-like structure, and hundreds of people milled around tables filled with food and drinks. Mitch and I looked at each other and he raised his eyebrows. "Wonder what they're celebrating."

"Yeah, me too. They've got something going on." I pointed to the tent. "Look, there's a stage and microphones. I wonder if they've hired live entertainment."

"Let's mingle, see if we can find out what they're doing," Mitch said.

I agreed and we walked to the backyard alongside a group of people in their twenties and early thirties. They held cans of beer and were laughing and joking. One looked at us and said, "Uh-oh, someone informed the sheriff."

Mitch raised his hands in the air. "Just here to see what's going on."

"What is going on?" I asked one of the young women.

"You didn't hear?" She wore a white dress with a jean jacket and cowgirl boots. Her honey blonde hair hung down her back looking like spun silk.

"No, I didn't. We just stopped by and saw all this." I spread out my arms to the crowd.

"The guy in the white tux over there sent out invitations to all the area churches saying he was hosting a revival. He offered food and drink, so we decided to come see what it was all about."

"He invited area churches?" I couldn't believe I was hearing them right.

"Yeah, we're from Portland, but most I think are from the Columbia Gorge area."

I stopped walking and she stopped alongside me. "Why?" I asked.

"Who knows? We came to see. The flyer we read said, join us for an evening of praise and songs. We'll supply food and drinks." She smiled at me. "I mean, who would turn that down? Especially out here in this beautiful setting."

Who indeed?

"They're supposed to have some big-name Christian bands and famous speakers. It's going to be fun."

She hurried to catch up with her group and I looked around for Mitch. He was talking to some young guys near the tent, and I walked in their direction, taking in snippets of the conversations around me.

When I finally got Mitch away from the people he was talking to, I said, "What do you think's going on?"

Mitch shook his head. "Those guys said Swanson is throwing a big concert with famous bands and guest speakers. What do you think he's up to?"

"My bet is that he's trying to recruit people. Let's blend in and find out what's going on."

He nodded and we found a place to stand behind a group of people who seemed to know each other. They were laughing and talking.

We hadn't been there long when a line of people came out of the main building and walked towards the tent. The men wore white shirts and pants, and the women all wore white dresses. Bringing up the end of the line was Jeremiah Swanson, surrounded by a posse of men. Jeremiah wore a white tuxedo.

The crowds parted for them, and we watched in fascination as they moved single file through the people to the tent where they made a half circle in front of the stage. Jeremiah and his posse split off from the group and went up on stage. He walked to the middle microphone. The crowd cheered. Jeremiah waved and the crowds went wild.

"Thank you for coming." His voice boomed over the giant speakers, and everyone quieted. "As you can see, we are celebrating today. This is the anniversary of the start of our campaign to bring everyone to enlightenment." There was a feverish shine in his eyes. "We want to share with you all." He spread his arms out to the crowd.

Mitch and I looked at each other with raised eyebrows while the crowds around us clapped and whistled.

"I have built this beautiful home for my people. It's an exciting time for us. We are on the edge of great things, and we'd love to invite you all to take this journey with us."

Mitch leaned over and whispered. "I hope they don't pass out Kool aid like Jim Jones did in Jonestown."

"Me too." I knew Mitch was thinking about the mass suicide of cult leader, Jim Jones's people back in the late seventies in Guyana, South Africa. He had given them cyanide-laced Kool-Aid and told them they'd wake up in heaven. I shivered, hoping we wouldn't be looking at something so horrible here.

I glanced around, wondering where Lydia was. I hadn't seen her yet. What was her role in this production? Was she behind the scenes, trying to keep track of people and their money? Or was she going to come out wearing a white robe and riding a white horse?

Jeremiah continued. "We are all about loving each other and being kind to your neighbor. If you as a brother or sister have a problem, I will solve it for you. I take care of my own. Ask any of my people. I have built a happy playground here. We work hard and play harder. We grow our food in an atmosphere of love. We have cut off the stress of the modern world and surround ourselves with joy and peace." He motioned to the people in white in the front row. "If you would like to learn more about us, if you'd like to join our family, please see one of my family members. There's no pressure. You will notice we haven't taken up a collection to help pay for food or drink. You are here as my guests." He spread his arms out. "I just want you to have a great time and feel the love."

"Is this not a good time to tell him his wife is in the morgue?" Mitch asked, leaning close to my ear.

"I don't think it's ever a good time, but this guy is something else. He's quite fond of himself."

"To say the least." Mitch shook his head.

Jeremiah came down off the stage. He was greeted by several people who grabbed at his arm and jumped in front of him, calling his name. I was reminded of the people in Bible days wanting to touch Jesus's cloak. Did Jeremiah think he was the messiah? I was pretty sure he did.

The event felt staged to me. Were these people outsiders or were they members of Swanson's family, making it look like they were dying to join his cult.

"Mitch, there's something off about this crowd."

"You can say that again." Mitch rolled his eyes as women screamed and threw themselves at Jeremiah when he walked by. "They're acting like he's some sort of rock star."

"That's just it, Mitch," I whispered in his ear. "I think they're all acting. I think this is a set up to get people hyped so they'll join his cult. I'll bet all those people throwing themselves at his feet are members of the cult."

Mitch looked around. There were lots of people circling Swanson, but there were also lots of people holding back, looking undecided. "You may be right. Let's go ruin his evening."

Chapter 16

It wasn't easy to make our way through the crowds. While we tried, a band went up on stage and began playing praise songs. Praise for whom? I wondered.

I looked around for a better avenue to get close to Jeremiah and looked right into the startled eyes of Dorcas. She turned and headed off in the opposite direction, and I went after her. "Dorcas!"

She either didn't hear me, or she didn't want to, because she kept moving. "Dorcas!" I shouted her name again. I could hear Mitch calling me, but I knew if I hesitated the other woman would be gone. She dodged people with plates of seafood and vegetables piled high. We weaved around tables of food and drink. I put on speed and finally caught her at the door to the main building.

"What's going on?" I grabbed her arm. "Why did you come back?"

"Come back?" Her eyes were wide with fear and something else. "Why wouldn't I? This is my home."

"I would've helped you get away. There are resources to help women like you."

She pulled away from me. "I don't know what you're talking about." She shook her head. "I have to go help bring out the food. Father will be upset if I don't help."

I grabbed her arm again. "Dorcas, Priscilla was killed. Murdered."

Her eyes grew big and filled with tears. "No! Don't say that." She swayed and would have fallen if I hadn't had a hold of her. One of the other women, carrying a pot of coffee saw us and started our way.

"We found her body today. There's something bad going on in this cult. You need to get out of here."

"No. And don't call it a cult. This is our home. All we want is to feel loved and have peace. Now let me go." She pulled away and ran into the building. The other woman, one of the sister's because she wore a long white dress, looked at me then at Dorcas. She finally put the coffee pot on the nearest table and followed Dorcas inside.

"What was that all about?" Mitch had come up behind me and watched as Dorcas pushed and shoved her way to the back door.

I told him what she'd said. "She acted different than she did at my dad's house earlier."

"She's scared," Mitch said. "She's afraid of Swanson and maybe others here who might hurt her."

"I can't help her if she won't let me." I made fists with both of my hands.

He nodded. "We're going to split this group wide open when we start investigating who killed Swanson's wife. We'll see if he has the control over these people that he thinks he does." He turned back towards the party.

"Let's go tell Swanson the news about his wife. See how he reacts."

I followed him through the throngs of people swaying and clapping their hands to the music on the stage. Jeremiah was still surrounded by people, but we pushed our way through them and made our way over to him.

Jeremiah Swanson looked up in surprise when he saw us. "Sheriff Ellisen, Detective, what are you doing here? Did someone call in to say there's a loud party going on? We don't have close neighbors, so I don't know who would complain."

"We need to talk to you, Mr. Swanson. Can we go somewhere quiet?" Mitch asked.

I watched Swanson and saw him pale. Then he turned to the man next to him and whispered in his ear. The man nodded and Swanson looked back at us. "Could whatever it is wait until tomorrow, Sheriff? As you can see, we are right in the middle of a party."

Mitch eyed the other man. "I'm afraid not. It's urgent."

Swanson conceded with a nod and had us follow him to a side door of the main building. "We can go into my office."

One of his men followed us and I felt the hair on the back of my neck stand up. There was something about the guy that creeped me out. I wasn't sure if it was the way he looked at me, or just his dark brooding eyes.

Swanson led us into the main building, up a staircase and to a huge wooden door. He opened it with a key and motioned us in. His smile had slipped since we were no longer with the crowds below.

His office was magnificent. It had natural wood with a huge mahogany desk, a leather desk chair and two leather club chairs in front of it. There was a sitting area with black leather sofas and chairs surrounding a huge fireplace. The man sure liked his fireplaces, I thought. A picture window looked out over the lawns. It was a beautiful view and most people, including me, would have loved to work there.

Pictures of Swanson hung on the walls, making me want to throw up because there were so many. Some with his arm around his wife, but most with other people I didn't recognize. In all of them, Swanson commanded the scene.

Now, he sat behind his desk and motioned for us to sit in the chairs in front of it. The man who followed us stood by the door; his arms crossed across his chest.

"What's this all about Sheriff?" Swanson asked. He leaned forward and rested his clasped hands on his desk.

Mitch cleared his throat. "We're sorry to inform you, but we think we've found your wife's body. We need you to come with us and identify her."

Swanson turned deathly pale. His eyes bulged and I was afraid he might fall over. He sat back in his chair, and it made a loud squeaking noise. "No, this can't be true. I told you that Priscilla is on a little trip. She'll be back soon."

"Why would she go on a trip when you're having a big celebration today?" I asked.

For a split second, Swanson made fists with his hands and his face turned dark. Then he turned his gaze on me. "She went to visit her mother. She hasn't seen her in several months and her mother isn't well. I told her she needed to go."

"Have you been in touch with her in the past few days?" Mitch asked. He had positioned himself between Swanson and the guy at the door, moving his chair so neither one of them were behind him.

Swanson looked down. "It's been terribly busy here. I meant to call her yesterday."

"How long has she been gone?" I asked. I sat in front of his desk.

He looked up at me. "A few days. I did call her on Wednesday, but she didn't answer. I thought that was odd, but as I said, I've been terribly busy. What makes you think it's my wife's body you found?"

I reached into my pocket and retrieved the wedding ring. I set it on the desk in front of him. "Does this look familiar?"

Jeremiah stared at the ring. He didn't move a muscle, just stared at it for the longest time. Then he stood up and roared with pain.

Mitch and I scrambled to our feet. The other man started in Jeremiah's direction, then stopped, watching the cult leader with such intensity, I wondered what was going through his mind.

Jeremiah turned to me and screamed, pointing his finger in my face. "You! This is all your fault! You and that sister of yours. You did this. You killed my Priscilla." He burst into tears, and I stood up and backed away from his desk.

"Mr. Swanson, I assure you Detective Ellisen had nothing to do with your wife's death." Mitch held out a hand toward the man.

"I've never met her," I said, quietly.

But Swanson was having none of it. "You encouraged Rose to leave. She took my wife and now she'll never come back. GET OUT OF MY SIGHT!" he screamed, and Mitch motioned me towards the door.

"But..."

"Just go, Liz. I'll catch up with you in a few minutes."

Swanson had his head in his hands. Deep sobs wracked his body. I backed towards the door and almost bumped into the man I'd forgotten was there. He reached out and opened the door for me. I looked up and saw the evil glint in his eyes and knew the last thing I should do is leave Mitch alone with the two of them.

"Mitch," I said.

He must've heard something in my voice because he looked at me and came towards the door. He nodded at the man standing there holding it open. "We need someone to identify her body."

The man inclined his head. "I will come myself if Father Jeremiah isn't able to."

Mitch and I both looked at Jeremiah who stood next to his desk holding his wife's wedding ring in his fingers. Tears ran in streams down his face and suddenly he shook himself and roared again. He reminded me of a great lion, roaring for his mate.

Chapter 17

The party was going strong as we let ourselves out of the building. The music was so loud I could barely make Mitch hear me. "I want to find Lydia."

He nodded. "I'll go talk to some of the other family members." He headed towards the people in white who were swaying and clapping their hands and I walked towards the food tables.

Lydia had to be around somewhere. I stopped the first family member I came to and asked if she knew where Lydia was.

She frowned and looked around. "She just walked past a few minutes ago. Maybe she's in the kitchen or her office." She pointed to the building I'd just come out of.

I smiled my thanks and headed to the kitchen door. Maybe she was in the kitchen. If I was lucky, she'd be alone in the office.

The kitchen was a beehive of activity. Several women stood at the industrial sized stove, cooking tempting smelling food. Others dished it onto huge silver trays. They all seemed like they were on autopilot. No one spoke or looked up from their tasks.

I stopped the first woman I came to and asked if Lydia was around. She shook her head. "I haven't seen her in a while." She continued dishing up meatballs onto a platter. Sweat had left droplets on her forehead and ran down the side of her face.

"It's hot in here," I said, and handed her a towel.

She took the towel, looked down at it and put it aside. Then she lifted the tray and headed outside.

I asked several others and got the same reactions. What was going on? I wondered. Then I realized they were exhausted. Jeremiah was using them as slave labor and probably had them up since early morning.

Anger rushed through me, and I headed to the stairway to Lydia's office. I'd paid attention when I was there before and knew which hallway to take.

At the top of the stairs were three doors. One was a double door and opened into a game room. There was a big screen TV, slot machines, a shuffleboard, and a pool table. I felt my eyebrows raise to my hairline. "Bet Jeremiah doesn't let his people in here," I muttered as I tried the door on the right.

That door was locked, and I tried the other and it opened into a beautiful room, decorated to look like it should belong in a high-rise office building in Portland instead of a compound in western Oregon.

Lydia sat at a cherry wood desk in the middle of the room. Around her were matching file cabinets, burgundy leather furniture and a wine bar. She stood up when I walked in the door.

"This room is off limits," she informed me in a voice so cold I looked for icicles. "Please shut the door as you leave."

I didn't comply. Instead, I looked her over. She was dressed to the tee and not in white like the rest of the family. She wore a dove gray suit with a pearly white shell, gray heels and gold jewelry glittered at her wrists and ears. She looked every bit the successful executive.

"I need to talk to you." I shut the door and stepped into the room.

"If you will go back downstairs, we can find an empty room and have our talk. I don't allow visitors in here. I'm sure you understand. This is where I do the books for our business."

"Your business? I thought you grew your own food and lived off the land. What kind of business are you in?"

Lydia picked up the papers on her desk and put them into the file cabinet next to her. Then she locked the cabinet with a key she wore on a bracelet on her wrist. "It's none of your business, Detective. We have the permits we need."

"I think it is my business." I walked closer to her desk.

She narrowed her eyes and looked down at a folder on her desk. On the top of it was the name, Redemption Project. "We build furniture. We have a workshop behind the barn, and we build expensive office furniture and sell it through our internet business." She held her hand out to the furniture in the room. "As you can see, what we build is high end."

I nodded and made my way to the chair in front of her desk where I sat down and looked up at her. She finally decided I wasn't leaving until we talked, so she perched on the edge of her office chair. "What can I do for you?"

"You can tell me what happened to Priscilla."

She frowned. "Mother Priscilla went to visit her mother a few days ago. If something has happened to her, I'm unaware of it. Have you asked Father Jeremiah?"

"Yes." I didn't tell her that Priscilla was dead. I wanted to see if she'd offer any information about why their founding mother had fled. "Why would Priscilla leave on such an important day?"

"Important day? What are you talking about?"

"Isn't this a big anniversary celebration? I'm sure that's what I heard Jeremiah say in his speech a little while ago."

She looked like she was about to swallow her tongue. Her eyes grew wide, and she took a deep breath. "Oh yes, of course." She picked up the file and tapped it against her desk. "I found it a little strange that Mother Priscilla left just before the event. She said her mother wasn't doing well and she felt she had to leave. I'm sure she didn't want to."

"Is it possible that she was forced to leave?"

"Of course not." Her cheeks turned pink and sweat collected around her eyes. "Why would you say such a thing?"

"We found a body on a private property in Parkdale. We think it's Priscilla."

She blinked several times. "She's dead?"

"It looks that way. We need a positive ID, but Jeremiah identified her wedding ring."

Lydia closed her eyes and took a deep breath. "Oh, poor Jeremiah."

It didn't escape my notice that she dropped the title of father. "Lydia, what's going on here? Where is my sister? Who would want to kill Priscilla?" I asked her, quietly.

She shook her head. "I don't know. Rose left a few days ago. No one could tell us where she went. I know you're worried about her, but I don't know where she is."

I'm not sure I believed her. "And Priscilla?"

"Jeremiah said she was going to see her mother. I don't know why anyone would want to kill her. She was an important part of this family. Important to Jeremiah." There was a faraway look in her eyes. Then she blinked again and said, "it must've been a random thing. Maybe she was in the wrong place at the wrong time." She stood up. "I have to go to Jeremiah."

"Can you give me Priscilla's mother's name and phone number?"

She nodded and picked up a cell phone, scrolling down her contacts until she came to what she wanted. She recited it, shut off her phone and walked to the door.

Everything inside me wanted to look through her office. I knew there were answers there to some of the questions I had. I could feel it. But she held open the door until I stood and walked out. Then she closed and locked it.

I went to find Mitch to see if he was having any better luck. When I found him, he was standing with a group of men who weren't wearing white. He saw me coming and headed towards me. "Any luck?"

"I talked to Lydia, but she didn't tell me anything except that they have a business making high end furniture. I think Lydia is the brains behind the business. Oh, I did get Priscilla's mother's contact information from her." I motioned to the men he'd been talking to. "Anything?"

He shook his head. "Not really. Most of them were dragged here by their wives or girlfriends. They're enjoying the food and drinks, but most said they were more than ready to leave."

"Did you talk to any of the family?"

Mitch nodded. "Yeah, but the women just looked scared and scurried away. The men said they didn't know where Mother Priscilla went and to ask Father." He rolled his eyes.

"Have you seen Jeremiah since we talked to him?"

Mitch shook his head. "No, he hasn't shown his face. I'm not sure he will. We can hang around for a while and see if he comes out, but I doubt he will."

We stayed for another hour talking to anyone who'd talk to us, then we headed to Mitch's vehicle. Jeremiah didn't make an appearance, and neither did the man who had been with him in his office.

After we got in the car I said, "Jeremiah must've been too upset to come back to the party."

Mitch put the car in gear and started back up the driveway to the main road. "It wouldn't look good if the grieving husband was seen having a good time after he found out his wife was dead."

"Did you think he was faking it? The grief?"

"No, not the grief, but the wailing was as fake as Jenn's boobs."

"Mitch!" My best friend had a boob job a few months earlier. She'd agonized over whether to go through with it or not.

He grinned at me. "Well, it's not hard to tell that she's gotten a little bigger."

"She didn't think anyone would notice."

"It's a little hard not to." He had his eyes on the road. "As for Swanson, he's a showman. I bet he'll use Priscilla's death to bring in more women to fawn over him."

Did I hear a little bit of jealousy in my husband's voice? "Hmm, thinking it might be fun to be a cult leader and have all those gorgeous young women at your disposal?"

"No thanks. I couldn't keep them all straight and would probably get myself into too much trouble."

I laughed, then sobered. "Do you think Swanson will come in himself to identify the body?"

He shrugged. "You'd think so, but with him it's hard to tell. He doesn't play by the rules."

"That's for sure." Jeremiah was an enigma. On one hand he was this humble man trying to spread love to others. But his other persona was showy and fake. Which was the real Jeremiah Swanson?

It didn't take long, and Mitch pulled into my dad's driveway. Connolly and Rodriguez had left my car in front of his house. Mitch pulled around to the front and stopped his truck behind my car but didn't turn it off. "Are you going back to the office?" I asked.

He nodded. "Just for a little while. I have some paper-work I need to get finished. What's for dinner? Is it your night to cook, or mine?"

I laughed as I opened my door. "I guess mine since Jenn took last night. What sounds good?"

We talked about what to have for dinner, finally settling on spaghetti, one of Mitch's favorite meals. He left and I headed home.

When I got there, I pulled out a pan to brown the hamburger, then remembered I needed to call Priscilla's mother.

I dialed the number and waited, but no one answered. I put my phone down and started making dinner. My phone buzzed with voice mail. I picked it up and touched the screen to get me to my voice mail. There were two. The first was a hang up, but the second was a voice I recognized, Murray, my dad's friend in Parkdale.

"Liz, someone's here looking for Rose. Call me."

I called back right away. Murray answered. I could hear tension in his voice. "Are they still there?"

"Yes."

"Did they tell you who they are?" I asked.

"No. She came in and demanded I tell her where Rose is. I told her that I don't know. She said she didn't believe me. She had a gun, Lizzie. I told her I had some money for Rose and that I'd get it for her. I'm sorry, but I wanted to stall her."

For the first time his voice sounded frail, and I remembered that he was close in age to my dad. "Where are you?"

"In my office. What should I do?"

"Try to keep her there. I'm on my way." I turned off the stove and looked around for my bag. Seeing it on a kitchen chair, I grabbed it and headed for the front door. My heart pounded so hard I was afraid I might faint.

"I will, but she doesn't seem like the patient sort. Hurry, Lizzie."

I hung up and hurried to my car, ignoring the speed limits as I drove towards Dee highway and south to Parkdale. It would take me at least fifteen minutes. I pressed down on the accelerator.

Traffic wasn't bad, and I made it there in less time than I thought. I parked a block down in front of the bistro and walked the rest of the way to Murray's gas station. I was almost there and trying to decide if I should just walk in the front door or sneak in through the big shop door when I heard a gun go off. I pulled my Colt .45 out of my bag and ran towards the station.

Chapter 18

I found Murray hunkered down behind a file cabinet in his office. His eyes were wide with fear. "What's going on?" I whispered. "Who's shooting?"

"I don't know. I was waiting for you and suddenly shots went off inside the garage." He whispered and pointed behind us. "At first, I thought she was shooting at me, but I locked the door to the shop. If she was, the bullet didn't come through. This old building was built back when things were made to last."

I held my gun out in front of me with both hands. "Stay here. I'm going to look."

He nodded. "Be careful."

I went out the office door and snuck around the back of the building. There wasn't anyone around. I crept up to the smaller shop door and peeked in. I could hear voices.

"If that old man doesn't come out here pretty soon with the money, I'm going to shoot you." It was a woman's voice, but I didn't recognize it.

I stepped inside. "Sheriff's office. Drop your weapon."

In what seemed like a split second, she turned and fired at me. Luckily for me, her aim was way off. I ducked back out the door and she ran through the big roll up garage door. I followed, yelling for her to stop. She kept running. I had to run through the shop and out the big door. She had a head start on me and took off like a marathon runner.

People stood across the street, pointing towards the old museum. I could hear them calling to me. I kept running. Had I heard sirens in the distance? I hoped so.

My breathing was labored, and I had a stitch in my side, but I kept running. She headed through the field behind the museum and cut across to an orchard. She was far enough ahead of me, I knew if she found some place to hide, I might not catch her. I ran faster.

There was an old barn ahead of us and I knew she'd either go there and try and hide, or she'd bust into the house and hold the owners at gunpoint. I couldn't let her do that.

Suddenly, I heard a motorcycle zoom down the orchard road. It was coming fast and heading straight for the woman I was chasing. I sped up, but the driver flew towards her, slowed down long enough for her to jump on the back and took off at lightning speed.

I stopped running and bent over trying to catch my breath. Once I felt like I could breathe again, I jogged back to the gas station.

Murray waited for me, along with several other people. Murray grabbed me and pulled me into a hug. "I was worried about you, girlie."

I patted his shoulder. "I'm fine, just a little out of breath." I looked around. "Who was she holding hostage?"

"Charlie." Murray pointed towards his shop. "He's pretty shook up. I figured you'd want to talk to him, so I told him to stay around."

A sheriff's car pulled up and Deputy Enrique Rodriguez stepped out. When he saw me, he headed my way. "What's going on, Liz?"

Several people had gathered around us, and they were all talking at once, trying to tell Enrique what they'd seen.

"If you'll give us a minute," he said, looking around at the excited faces. "I want to hear what you all saw but let me talk to Detective Ellisen first."

"You're a detective?" One man asked. When I nodded, he said, "No wonder you could run like that."

Enrique asked if they'd hang around for a few minutes so he and I could talk and most agreed. We walked into the shop with Murray, who hurried over to his friend. Between Murray and I, we told Enrique what had happened. Then we asked Charlie how he'd become involved.

Murray pulled a cola out of a cooler and handed it to Charlie. Then he sat next to him and put his big hand on the older man's shoulder. "Just tell them what you told me."

Charlie nodded. He was in his eighties. His hair was snow white and he had deep groves in his face. His eyes were still blue, but they were clouded with cataracts. He took a swig of the cola and wiped the back of his mouth with his hand. "I was coming in to talk to Murray. Me and him usually sit and pass the bull in the evening after he closes for the day."

He looked at Murray who gave him an encouraging nod. "So, I came in here and Murray wasn't around. There was this woman standing in front of the old pickup Murray's been working on since the 1970's." He gave a mournful shake of his head. "You're never goin' to get that thing running, you know." He took a deep breath. "Anyways, I asked her if Murray was helping her, and she glared at me. I couldn't believe it. Most folks are nice when you first meet them, but this woman was a ripsnorter, that's for sure."

He stopped and took another sip of his cola. "I headed towards the office, and she yelled at me to stay where I was. I tried to explain that I was a buddy of Murray's, and I'd just go find him. But she pulled a gun on me." His hands shook and he almost dropped the cola. Murray grabbed it.

"For no reason," he continued. "Just pulled out her gun and told me if I moved, she'd blast my stupid head off."

"What happened next?" I asked.

"Nothing. I didn't move. We just stood there for a few minutes staring at each other. Where were you, Murray? I thought maybe she'd already shot you dead."

"I was calling for help."

"Well, she finally got tired of waiting and blew a hole in the ceiling." He pointed up the top of the shop.

We all followed his look. "I ducked and she marched around the room, beat on the office door and yelled for Murray." He looked over at me. "Then you came. I gotta tell you, I was never so happy to see someone in my life."

Enrique looked at me. "I take it she got away?"

I nodded. "I chased her, but she had a head start. We ran through the orchard behind the museum and a dirt bike came screaming through the orchard, slowed down enough for her to jump on and took off."

"Do you have any idea who she was?"

I shook my head. "I didn't get a good look at her. How about you guys?" I asked the older men.

"Didn't know her," they said in unison. Murray took off his cap and rubbed his head. "She kept asking me where Rose was. I told her I didn't know, and she started yelling at me, saying I did know. That I was hiding Rose for her sister."

He looked over at me and raised his eyebrows. "I don't know why she thought I'd know anything."

I thanked the two gentlemen, then motioned for Enrique to follow me outside. We talked to the people who had stayed around, and they told the same story about me chasing the woman.

Enrique and I climbed into his car so we could talk privately. I explained to him about the money my dad had left for Murray to give to Rose. "I'm worried about Murray. Now that she knows that he has money he's holding for Rose, she or one of Jeremiah's henchmen will be back."

Enrique nodded and thumbed his fingers on the steering wheel. "I'm afraid you're right. What do you want to do?"

"I can take the money home with me, but that won't stop them from coming back. And we don't have the manpower to leave someone here to keep watch over Murray."

"No, we don't. I wish there was some way we could let this woman know that Murray no longer has the money. The thing of it is, I don't think she cared about that, I think she was just hoping she could make Murray tell her where Rose is."

"She was a lousy shot," I told him. "She tried shooting at me and hit the wall instead." I wondered if it could've been Lydia, but I didn't think it was. Lydia wouldn't do her own dirty work.

"It's a good thing she couldn't shoot. I don't want to have to tell the boss that his wife has been shot." Enrique grinned, then opened his door and got out. "I'll see if I can find the bullet she put into the wall. Maybe ballistics can get something from it."

I climbed out and we walked back to Murray's together. "I'll get the money and ask Murray to go away for a while. I doubt he will, but I'll try."

"Yeah, these old guys don't like thinking they can't take care of themselves."

Murray and Charlie both stood up as we entered the shop again. "Me and Charlie found something." Murray handed me a crinkled envelope. "It must've fallen out when she took her gun out of her jacket pocket."

I looked down at the envelope. It was addressed to Carolyn Butler.

"I don't suppose that means anything to you?" Enrique asked.

I frowned. I'd seen that name before, but at first, I couldn't remember where. Then it hit me, and I raced outside to my car. I pulled my bag out and dug inside it until I came up with another piece of paper. Enrique had followed me. "What is it?"

"I recognized the name. Jeremiah's right-hand woman gave me the same name when Mitch and I were at the compound earlier today."

"Whose is it?"

"Priscilla's mother."

Chapter 19

The next morning, Mitch got a call that Jeremiah was going to the morgue to identify Priscilla's body. Mitch wanted to be there, so he dressed and left for work early.

I had called the number I had for Priscilla's mother several times the night before with no luck. Her mailbox was full so I couldn't leave a message. I decided I'd find out where she lived and if it was close enough, I'd drive there.

I got dressed and fed Bailey. Bella called to check on me and Bailey. I thought she was more worried about the dog, but it was nice to hear from her.

The address I found for Priscilla's mother, Carolyn Butler, was across the river in White Salmon, Washington. It was only about a twenty-minute drive, and I headed out to see if I could talk to her.

It was another beautiful spring day. I hoped the rain was gone for a while. We'd had enough, but I knew that spring in Oregon brought lots of the wet stuff. Mitch called to tell me that Swanson had identified his wife's body.

"With lots of wailing and carrying on?"

"No, he was subdued today. No audience, I guess," Mitch said. "I invited him to the office for a sit down. He didn't want to come, but I assured him we wanted the same thing. To find out who killed his wife."

"Was he alone?"

"No, same henchman that was with him yesterday. Said his name is Noah. If you get a minute, maybe you can figure out who he really is."

"Probably not. Another Biblical name."

"What?"

"Jeremiah has given all of his people Biblical names. Noah, Luke, Ezekiel, Dorcas, Lydia, Sari; they're all from the Bible."

"That's going to make it harder to identify them."

"Probably why he did it," I said. Then I told Mitch where I was headed and to let me know what he found out. He said he would and hung up.

The river was smooth as I crossed the bridge into Washington. I drove through Bingen and up the hill to White Salmon. Carolyn Butler lived near the high school, and I found her with ease.

Her house was a small two-story with a gravel driveway and nonexistent yard. There may have been grass there at one time, but it was mostly dirt with clumps here and there. The front door stood open, and I could hear country music coming from inside as I walked up to the door.

I knocked, but I was sure she couldn't hear me above the music which was cranked up to painful levels. I called out her name and the music stopped. Seconds later, a small blonde woman came to the door.

"What ya need, hun?" She had frizzy hair, pulled back into a ponytail and her skin was fair and so wrinkled I wondered if she was Priscilla's grandmother instead of her mother. Her voice was deep and gravelly, and I assumed she'd smoked all her life. I could smell it coming off her in waves when she moved.

"I'm looking for Carolyn Butler."

She smiled and popped her gum. "You got her. What can I do for you?"

I showed her my badge. "I'm Detective Elizabeth Ellisen from the Hood River Sheriff's office. I'd like to talk to you about your daughter. May I come in?"

She stepped back and motioned me in. "What's she done now?" She led the way into a bright kitchen that smelled of cigarettes and Pine Sol disinfectant.

Because of her yard, I assumed the house wouldn't be much better, but I was surprised. The kitchen was painted white and sparkled with cleanliness. A bouquet of spring flowers sat on the table. She pulled out a chair. "Sit down, Hun, and tell me why you're looking for Pris."

I stood next to the table, hating to sit down when I had to deliver bad news. "I'm sorry to tell you this, but Priscilla is dead."

She stared at me as though she didn't understand what I'd said, then she buried her head in her hands. When she finally looked up, she had tears in her eyes. "Did he kill her?"

"Who?"

"Swanson. That dirty rotten low life scum. Did he kill my daughter?" She started coughing and couldn't stop. She grabbed a glass from one of her cabinets and poured herself water from a pitcher in the refrigerator. "Want some?" She asked when she could finally speak again.

"No, thanks." I sat down across from her. "We don't know if Swanson killed her. Do you think he would?"

"Yes! If she got in the way of his plans. He's a monster. He thinks he's God here on earth and he's not, I can tell you that. He manipulates people, mostly women, to give him their money. I've been trying to get the FBI to investigate that cult for years." She shook her head. "No one would listen to me and now it's too late." Her voice ended on a wail.

"I'm sorry." I handed her a piece of paper towel from the roll on the counter.

She blew her nose and nodded her thanks. "How did he do it?" Her cigarettes and lighter sat on the table and she pulled them close to her, but she didn't take one out of the package.

"He says he didn't."

"Of course, he'd say that." Tears ran down her cheeks. "I tried to talk Priscilla out of marrying him. He had nothing when they married, wasn't even working. She worked two jobs for a while, then he came up with this cult scheme." She shook her head. "Loser. Dirty rotten loser, that's all he is."

"What did Priscilla think about the cult idea?"

Carolyn looked at me. "She thought it was a crock, just like I did. But she wanted him so bad, she would've done anything." She took a cigarette out of her pack and held it between her fingers, running her thumb back and forth over the smooth surface. "He was charismatic, I'll give him that. And such a handsome devil. My poor little girl didn't have a chance."

"I'm sorry."

She nodded, dried her eyes and coughed into her paper towel. "What am I supposed to do now?"

"What do you mean?"

She looked at me and shook her head repeatedly. I thought she would say what was she supposed to do without her daughter, but she surprised me. "How can I get her things? I'm sure she had belongings, clothes, whatever. And there had to be money. I want her money."

I stared at her, and she stared back. "Weren't she and Swanson married? He'd be her next of kin."

"Not legally. They had some mumbo-jumbo wedding out in the forest someplace, but Pris told me it wasn't legal. She found out he was already married. When she called the other day, she said if anything happened to her, I was entitled to everything that belonged to her."

"He was married? Do you know who he was married to?"

She shook her head. "Some gal in Arkansas. He told Pris he couldn't get a divorce because she'd take everything he had. As if he had anything!"

I made a mental note to find out who Jeremiah's legal wife was. "Did Priscilla think her life was in danger?"

"No." Carolyn fiddled with the cigarette. "No, she just said Jeremiah was doing some things that she didn't want any part of. She said she was thinking about leaving him. She was tired of him cheating on her with the other women. She was real upset when she called. I tried to get her to come home." Her eyes filled with tears again and she put her head in her hands.

I hated to add to her suffering, but I knew I had to ask. "Mrs. Butler, were you in Parkdale yesterday?"

She looked up. "Parkdale?"

I took the envelope out of my pocket and showed it to her. "We found this at a crime scene. Do you recognize it?"

She shook her head and stood. "I don't know what you're talking about, Hun. I wasn't in Parkdale." She took the envelope and looked it over. "This is my name and address, but I was at work. You can ask my boss."

"Where do you work?"

Her eyes narrowed. "I'm a waitress at the brewery just down the hill. Ask for Todd."

"I will. Can I call someone to come stay with you?" I asked.

"My son lives next door." She grabbed more paper towels off the roll on the counter and said, "I want to see my daughter. Can you arrange that?"

"Of course." I took a card out of my pocket and handed it to her. "Call me if you need anything, okay? Or if you think of anything else that Priscilla said that might help find out who killed her."

She nodded. "I will."

"Has your son been in touch with Priscilla lately?"

"No, he wouldn't have anything to do with her after she joined up with Swanson. He said she was just as crazy as Jeremiah for taking up with him." She walked me to the door and held up her hands in the sign of prayer. "Just nail this SOB."

"If he did it, we will."

"I know he did it." She followed me outside.

While she headed to her son's house behind the one she lived in, I went to my car. I was about to step in when I saw movement out of the corner of my eye. I walked around the house, worried about Carolyn, thinking she may have fainted, but she wasn't in sight. I heard the door to her son's house bang against the wall.

I decided I should talk to him while I was there and headed in their direction when I saw a dark blue pickup parked in his driveway. In the back was the dirt bike I'd seen the day before.

Chapter 20—Rose

Two weeks earlier

Rose had never felt as appreciated as she did while fixing Mr. Yakamoto breakfast that morning. He had shown her around the small kitchen and watched while she cooked. He sat at the table and smiled at her. "You know how to cook," he said, nodding at her as she whisked eggs in a bowl.

Rose hadn't cooked in a long time, and it felt good to fry bacon, scramble eggs and make toast and coffee. She poured them both a cup as soon as it was made and thought she'd died and gone to heaven when she took the first sip of the fragrant brew.

As soon as breakfast was ready, she asked Mr. Yakamoto. "Ready to eat?" The kitchen smelled of bacon grease and strong hot coffee.

"Yes, yes. It smells wonderful," he told her, scooting up to the table with a big grin on his face. He looked at the meal and nodded. "It's been a long time." He motioned towards the chair across from him. "Here. Sit. Sit. We don't want it to get cold."

Rose smiled and poured more coffee into her cup and refilled Mr. Yakamoto's. Then she sat down and bowed her head, silently asking a blessing on the food.

When she was finished, she glanced up and Mr. Yakamoto nodded and began eating. "This is so good. Thank-you, thank-you."

"No, thank-you, for letting me cook and eat with you."

He put fluffy yellow scrambled eggs on his buttered toast and took a bite, sighing with pleasure. "You must stay as long as you'd like."

Rose thanked him. She'd opened his freezer and seen all the frozen dinners he'd bought. Poor guy, he probably was thankful for a home cooked meal. "How long have you lived alone?"

That question was enough to keep him talking for some time about his late wife, his children who had moved to Seattle and how lonely he'd been.

After they finished eating, Mr. Yakamoto insisted Rose go lie down while he cleaned up the kitchen. "You sleep. I will do dishes, then go work on my tractor."

Since she hadn't slept the night before, Rose agreed and climbed the stairs to the small bedroom he'd shown her earlier. She laid down on the bed and tried to sleep, but her mind wouldn't shut down. She worried about what had happened to Mother Priscilla. Would she come soon? If she didn't, what was Rose to do?

Rose finally went to sleep and slept most of the afternoon. When she woke up, she took a quick shower in the tiny bathroom at the end of the hall and changed into the extra set of clothes she'd brought with her.

Then she took her dirty clothes downstairs to wash and went outside to look around.

The rain had finally stopped and although it was a cool spring day, the sun had peeked out from behind the clouds. She didn't see any sign of Mr. Yakamoto and figured he was somewhere around. His white Toyota pickup was still in the garage.

She walked down to the cabins, hoping she'd look in one and see Mother Priscilla sitting on a bunk waiting for her. She stuck her head in all six of them, but no one was there. Rose walked around to the barn, a big green metal structure, and looked inside. There was old farm equipment, a new tractor, and stacks of aluminum ladders.

Rose wondered where Mr. Yakamoto was. She didn't run into him anywhere while she checked out his labor camp, barn, and outbuildings.

After she'd gone through all the buildings without any sign of Mother Priscilla, Rose headed back to the house. She thought about how it needed a good cleaning and decided she might as well start in. If Mother didn't show up in the next day or so, she'd have to call her dad to come get her. She hadn't seen a phone in the house, but figured Mr. Yakamoto probably had a cell phone. For the first time in ten years, Rose wished she had one. They hadn't been allowed in the family compound.

She was sweeping the kitchen floor when Mr. Yakamoto came in. He stomped the mud off his boots on the porch and started into the house. when he saw what she was doing, he stooped down and took his boots off.

"I have something from your friend."

"You do? What?"

Mr. Yakamoto held out an envelope. "I went to the mailbox, and this was inside."

Rose took the envelope and looked at it. Her name was written across the front in Mother Priscilla's handwriting. She tore the envelope open and read the short note inside.

Rose Sari,

Something came up. Don't go back to the family. Stay where you are, and I will come for you.

Mother

Rose looked up at Mr. Yakamoto. How did Mother know that he would let Rose stay with him? "Do you know Priscilla Swanson?" she asked.

Mr. Yakamoto shook his head. "No."

"Why would she tell me to stay here?"

He shrugged. "I have room."

Rose smiled but she didn't think it was that simple. Mother Priscilla had wanted her here. Why? She looked around the small kitchen. Was it because Mr. Yakamoto was alone? How did Mother know? It was confusing, but Rose had learned over the last ten years not to ask too many questions.

Chapter 21-Liz

*P*resent day

I banged on the door of Carolyn's son's house. A man not much taller than Carolyn opened it. I had to look down on him. He was probably in his forties with straight brown hair and big ears. He had a kind face, which I realized he'd gotten from his mom.

"Yeah?"

I showed him my badge. "Detective Ellisen of the Hood River Sheriff's office. Is that your truck?"

He looked at my credentials then back at me. "Yeah, what of it?"

Carolyn came to the door and stood behind her son. She blew her nose, and her eyes filled with tears. She put her hand on her son's arm. "This is my son, Brandon Butler. What's going on Detective?"

I nodded at the introduction. "Were you in Parkdale yesterday afternoon?"

He looked at me like I was crazy. "I was at work yesterday," Brandon said. "Why?"

"When was the last time your rode your dirt bike?" I pointed to the truck with the bike in it.

He rubbed his jaw. "Probably last weekend. Some friends and I went up to Gifford Pinchot on Saturday and rode around. Why?"

I knew Gifford Pinchot was the National Forest north of us. "You didn't have your bike in Parkdale yesterday?"

"No, What's this all about?" A deep frown formed between his wide spaced eyes.

I looked at Carolyn. She was wringing the tissue between her fingers. "Did your mom tell you about Priscilla?" I asked.

He nodded. "Yes, but I haven't seen her in years."

"So, you don't have any idea who might want to kill her?"

"Besides the idiot she's married to. No. I told her to stay away from him. I warned her that those cults only last so long and then the leader goes berserk and kills everybody off. But she wouldn't listen to me."

"Do you mind if I take a picture of your bike?"

His eyes narrowed. "Why? What's going on?"

"There was an incident in Parkdale yesterday. The suspect had a friend on a dirt bike pick them up. I just want to make sure this isn't the bike in question. Do you own a gun?"

"Of course, I own a gun. How would my bike get to Parkdale? It was parked in the driveway while I was at work." He shook his head like I was the dumbest woman in the world, then said, "go ahead and take a picture. I don't have anything to hide."

I glanced at Carolyn, who was chewing her gum so fast I thought she'd bite her tongue. She didn't meet my eyes. I walked over and took a quick picture of the bike with my phone. "Where's your gun?"

He gestured to the house behind him. "In the gun safe. I have several."

"May I see them?"

He motioned me into the house, and we walked down a small hallway to a bedroom. "I keep all of my guns in here. I'm careful because I've got two young sons. They're with their mom this week, but I keep the guns locked up all the time in case she's brings them over unexpectedly." He opened the gun safe and showed me his guns. They were in racks, and it looked like they were all there. He had so many it would've been hard to get more inside the safe.

I asked where he worked, and he gave me the name of the same brewery where his mother worked. "Thanks. Please call me if you think of anything else that might help me find out who killed your sister."

They both nodded and I left. Carolyn had seemed worried about the bike. She hadn't said anything, but she'd had a frown between her eyes when I looked at her after taking the picture. Had she borrowed her son's bike the day before? Was she the woman who tried to shoot up Murray's gas station?

I stopped at Everybody's Brewery and the manager confirmed that Brandon and Carolyn had both been at work the day before.

Travis called while I was crossing the bridge back into Oregon. His voice was deep and warm like hot chocolate. "I know you're busy, but can we get together and talk about what needs done in the orchard? It shouldn't take long. I just need to run some things by you."

"Of course. When's a good time?"

We decided to meet at my dad's house in fifteen minutes. I stopped and bought coffee at the Starbucks near the bridge and drove to Odell to meet him.

It had turned out to be a beautiful spring day. A few wispy clouds dotted the sky, but mostly it was a deep blue. The buds on the trees were about to burst into bloom. Soon the whole valley would look like popcorn.

My dad loved spring, even though he said it was one of the busiest times of the year in an orchard. I knew there were things that needed to be taken care of and decisions for me to make.

Travis was already parked next to Dad's house when I drove in. He leaned against his pickup, looking at his phone, frowning.

I jumped out of my Jeep and went to meet him. "Hey Travis, something wrong?"

He looked at me like he wanted to say something and changed his mind. "No, it's all good. Just wanted to talk to you about the water system in the north block. George planned to put in solid sets and not have the aluminum pipes anymore."

"That's right. He did tell me that he was changing his system over. Do you think Jose can get it finished?" I handed him the cup of coffee I'd brought for him.

He smiled his thanks. "I can help him. I just wanted to make sure you were on board. We'll have to order more hoses to cover the acres he wanted changed."

The solid sets were so much easier than changing the huge pipes. All you had to do was turn on a facet and turn it off twelve hours later. With the pipes, you had to drag them from row to row. I'd done a lot of that in the summer when I was a kid. "I'm all for it, but I hate to ask you to put in that much time. I know you have lots to do at your own place."

Travis nodded. "Yeah, I can get the hoses for Jose and he and some of the guys can put them in. I'll just check on them once in a while."

"That would be great." I took a sip of my coffee and looked out over the orchard. I could hear the bees buzzing and smell the pollen they were scattering around. "I'm going to need to make up my mind about what to do with this place soon." The thought that my dad would was no longer around to take care of it gutted me.

"Well, I know you don't want to sell, but if you'd like to lease it out, I could take care of it." He chuckled. "I don't know how you could farm and be a detective too."

I shook my head. "Too many acres. Let me think about it and talk to Mitch."

He agreed but gave me a strange look.

"Is there something else on your mind?" I asked him.

Travis cleared his throat. "If you had a friend and you knew something that would really hurt them, would you tell them?"

I stared up into his brown eyes. "Are you talking about me? Do you know something about Rose? Have you seen her? Oh Travis, if you have, you need tell me. I've been so worried about her."

"No, it isn't about Rose, Liz."

I felt my chest clench. "My dad? Have you found out something about his murder?" I realized I'd told myself the cult was behind my dad's murder, but what if I was wrong?

"No." He shook his head. "I probably should keep my mouth shut. It's not about your dad. I'm sorry, Liz." He headed for his pickup. "I'm going to talk to Jose. I'll call you soon about those hoses."

He drove off and I watched him go, wondering what he'd been talking about? I could tell by the look on his face that he knew something, but he didn't want to tell me. He wasn't acting like himself.

I sighed and walked into Dad's house. I needed to find my sister and find out who killed my dad and Priscilla Swanson. My gut told me the answers were at the cult.

Chapter 22

After Travis left, I locked up and drove back to town to the Sheriff's office. It was quiet and the receptionist at the front desk said Mitch had gone out, but she didn't know where. Shoot, I'd wanted to ask him about his talk with Jeremiah.

Both Brandon and Carolyn's alibis for the previous day checked out. I went to work trying to find out who Jeremiah was married to in Arkansas. I'd had my head in the search for a while when Jenn came in.

"Hey girl, what are you doing? You're supposed to be at home taking time off."

She handed me a cup of coffee from the coffee place down the street. "I saw your car outside and thought you might need a cup."

"Oh, thank you. You're a life savior." I took a big gulp of the coffee and almost spit it out. "Uh, what did you get me?"

Jenn set her cup on my desk and picked up mine. She took a sniff and grimaced. "Sorry, looks like they got it wrong. I told them I wanted two mochas."

"They must not have heard you right. This tastes like what Mitch drinks. I don't know how he can stand it plain black with nothing in it."

Jenn handed me her drink. "Here, drink mine. I've probably had enough today anyway. If I drink more, I'll get the jitters."

I waved her cup away. "No, I just had one with Travis not that long ago."

"Oooh, Travis the hunk. Where did you see him?" She leaned over, her eyes alight with excitement. "Tell your bestie every little detail."

"There's nothing to tell. We talked about him leasing the farm."

"Sure, you did." She leaned closer. "You can tell me. I won't tell Mitch." She lowered her voice. "Travis is so sexy. I wouldn't mind getting to know him better."

I shook my head. "Travis is a friend. He's helping me with Dad's orchard."

She drank out of her cup. "Oh, that's right. Lucky girl." She gave me a knowing look and set the cup on my desk next to the one she'd brought me and sank into the chair across from me. Her lips formed a teasing smile. "I wish I had an orchard he could run. I wonder of Ray would buy me one."

"Jenn! That's a terrible thing to say."

"Why?"

"You want your husband to buy you an orchard so you can spend time with another man, and you don't see anything wrong with that?"

Jenn grinned. "You know that old saying, 'Just because you're on a diet doesn't mean you can't look at the pastry.'"

I shook my head. My office door opened, and Mitch stuck his head in. He looked surprised to see Jenn with me. "What are you two doing?"

"Jenn brought me coffee." I held up the cup. "But it turns out she got you coffee instead." I handed it to him.

Mitch looked at the cup in his hands. "Okay, that doesn't make sense, but I'm not going to turn it down." He took a drink. "I need to talk to you when you have a minute, Liz."

I nodded. Mitch left the room and I glanced at Jenn. She had a knowing smile on her face. "What?"

She blinked. "What do you mean?"

"You had a look."

She stood up and grabbed her coffee off my desk. "I did? I must've still been thinking about the sexy Travis. When can we get together? I'm busy this afternoon, but I could meet you for lunch tomorrow if that works?"

We agreed on a time, and I watched her leave the room. I felt like there was something I was missing, but I decided to ignore it, knowing Jenn loved innuendos and being mysterious. I went back to the search for Jeremiah's wife and a half-hour went by before I headed to Mitch's office.

I tapped on his door and went in. Jenn sat on his desk as close to him as she could get and leaned over, showing him her impressive new breasts. Her hand was on his. My heart sank. "Am I interrupting something?" I could hear frost in my voice.

"No!" Mitch stood and came towards me.

Jenn slid off the desk. "We were talking about taking you and Ray on a cruise this summer. Ray should have a break in June. Wouldn't it be fun for the four of us to do a river cruise in Europe?" She talked fast and avoided my eyes.

"I'm not sure that would be a good idea," I said, glaring at her. What was going on with my best friend? Even though she'd always liked to flirt, she'd gone a little too far this time.

Mitch went to his door and held it open. He gave Jenn a meaningful look. "Maybe we can talk about it when this case is over. I have a feeling Liz and I are going to be busy for a while."

"That sounds great." She glanced at me with that smug look she'd worn earlier. "I'll see you tomorrow," she said and walked out the door.

As soon as it closed behind her, I turned to Mitch. "What was that all about?"

He went back to his desk and sat down. "Who knows. You know how Jenn is, Liz. She has to flirt with any guy who is available."

My eyebrows shot up. "I didn't realize you were available."

"That's not what I meant, and you know it." He sighed. "You know Jenn's a flirt. She doesn't mean anything by it."

I did know that, but her pose when I walked in bothered me. "I'm not sure about that."

Mitch rubbed the back of his head, muttered something about women and picked up a paper that had been on the middle of his desk. "I thought you'd like to know what Swanson had to say."

I nodded, but instead of sitting down like I normally would, I stood with my arms crossed, waiting for him to continue. I didn't like the thoughts running through my mind. What was really going on with Mitch and Jenn? Was there something going on?

Mitch continued like nothing had happened. "As you know, Swanson came in and identified his wife's body. He was subdued today. I took him into the interview room, and we talked for a while. He swears he doesn't know what happened to her, but Liz..." He stopped talking and gave me a worried look. "He says he thinks Rose killed Priscilla."

I shook my head. "He's crazy."

"He said Rose was with Priscilla the day before she left. He swears he didn't know Priscilla was leaving. She told him she was going to stay with her mother for a few days and she was taking Rose with her. But he called Priscilla's mother and they never showed up."

"I'm sure he has people who will say that Rose and Priscilla left together. When we were there yesterday, everyone I talked to said they didn't leave together."

"His stories don't quite add up, but we've got to look into his allegations."

"You look. I'm going to find my sister. I know Rose wouldn't kill anyone. What was her motive?"

"Swanson said she wanted to take over the family. He said she'd been sneaking around, trying to undermine him and Priscilla. He said he's afraid for his life."

I knew Jeremiah Swanson was lying about Rose. Rose was the most easy-going woman you could meet. There was no way she'd try to take over his family. But she might want to shut it down. Especially if she thought Swanson had killed our dad.

Chapter 23

I paced back and forth in front of Mitch's desk. "Did he seem anxious for you to find Rose?" I asked.

"Yeah, he demanded I find her." Mitch sat back in his chair causing it to squeak.

"Hmm."

Mitch played with a pen on his desk. He stopped and looked up at me. "What does that hmm mean? What are you thinking?"

"It means I don't trust Jeremiah Swanson. He's up to something."

Mitch stood up. "I think you're right." He walked around his desk and stood in front of me. "We'll find Rose. She can't have gotten far."

I nodded. "I've got a couple people I need to talk to. I'll see you later." I headed to the door.

Mitch followed me, put his hand on the door and held it shut. "Are you okay?"

"Of course, I'm okay." I didn't look at him. I wasn't okay and he knew it.

He put his finger under my chin and tilted my face up to his. "You aren't acting like yourself. There's nothing going on between Jenn and me."

"Maybe you should tell her that."

"I have," he said. He leaned closer and kissed me.

I kissed him back, then he opened the door and I left. My thoughts were in turmoil. Mitch wouldn't cheat on me, would he? We had a good marriage. We even worked well together. Jenn was my best friend. Why would she go after my husband?

Because she's Jenn and she thinks every guy in the world should be in love with her. A small voice inside my head whispered. Yeah, but we've been friends since we were in school, I thought.

I pushed my misgivings away and decided to concentrate on finding my sister. I would confront Jenn when this nightmare with Rose was over.

Back in my office I put in a call to the FBI field office, giving them my credentials and asking for one of their agents to call me. Then I pulled the pictures out of my bag and spread them over my desk.

Cute little gapped-tooth kids looked back at me. "Who are you?" I whispered, going through each picture. "Why did Rose have your pictures hidden at Dad's house?" I decided to search the missing children data base. I knew it would take me forever, but I had to do it. Who were these kids and what was the meaning of the dates scrawled across their names? Were they dates of abduction or of death?

When my phone rang, and I picked it up and said hello.

"Detective Ellisen, this is Agent John Campbell from the Salem field office. I was told to call you." His voice boomed in my ear, and I held the phone away.

"Thank you for calling me back. I have some questions for you about The Bread of Life cult in Oregon."

"Okay, I don't know a lot about them, but go ahead and shoot."

"I'm wondering if you've had any indication that they are trafficking children?"

There was silence on the other end of the line so long I thought he'd hung up on me, but he finally spoke. "What makes you ask?"

"There's something going on there. They were a quiet little group that suddenly started growing. Yesterday their leader's wife was found murdered and the leader, Jeremiah Swanson threw a big party trying to invite people to join."

"Interesting. I'll be at your office first thing in the morning."

The phone went dead. I looked at it. "I wasn't finished asking you questions, you moron." I shook my head.

What was going on at that cult? I went through the pictures again. There were twenty of them, all the children under ten. I felt my skin crawl. The obvious answer was Rose had discovered a child trafficking ring.

There was a knock on my door and Deputy Connolly stuck her head in. "Sheriff wants us all in the conference room."

She left before I could respond. I picked up the pictures and a notebook and pen and took them with me. It was time to let my colleagues in on what I'd found.

Mitch looked at me as I walked in and sat down next to Enrique Rodriguez. Connolly had taken the seat next to Mitch. Several other deputies filled the room. Mitch stood at the head of the table. "As most of you know, Priscilla Swanson, the wife of Jeremiah Swanson of The Bread of Life cult has been murdered. Liz and I talked to Swanson last night. He was throwing a huge recruiting bash."

"Maybe he was happy to be rid of her," Deputy Todd Wilson said with a smirk. Todd may have been a great deputy, but apparently, he was a lousy husband. He'd been married five times.

Everyone chuckled. "Maybe." Mitch said, then he smiled at me. "As you know, we're looking for Priscilla Swanson's killer. What you may not all know is that Liz's sister was part of that group and she's missing. I want her found and I want this killer found."

Everyone turned to look at me and I nodded. "Rose didn't come home for Dad's funeral. It's not like her."

"And," Mitch said, drawing their attention back to him. "I want to know why this cult is suddenly growing. When Liz and I were there last night, they had Christian rock bands performing, free food and drinks, they treated the attendees like royalty. Swanson was in his element."

"How did he act when you told him his wife was dead?" Connolly asked.

Mitch grimaced. "He roared with grief." He looked at me. "I'm not sure if it was an act, if it was, it was a good one. It's hard to tell with Swanson. Have any of you had dealings with him?"

The deputies all shook their heads except for Connolly. "I met him at one of his recruitment get-togethers last summer," she said.

Mitch looked shocked. "You did? What were you doing at a recruitment?"

Connolly shrugged. She had her head down and her straight blonde hair covered the half of her face that faced me. "Curious."

Todd snickered and she gave him a murderous look. "Not like I wanted to join or anything. I just wanted to know what all the hoopla was."

"Hoopla?" I asked. "I thought they'd been pretty quiet up until the last month or so."

Connolly turned towards me. "Where have you been? There have been parties around the valley. There was a big one in Parkdale. Rose was there."

I stared at her for a minute. The room became incredibly quiet.

"She was handing out brochures." She frowned. "Actually, I thought she acted a little weird that day."

"Weird, how?" Mitch asked.

Connolly turned back towards him. "She was there, doing her job, but she didn't seem happy about it. All the other Bread of Lifers had big smiles on their faces, and they were doing their best to make it seem like they had the best life possible. But Rose was different." She turned back towards me. "My thought at the time was that she wanted out."

"Why didn't you let me know?" I asked, softly.

Connolly shrugged. "I assumed she'd call you. I thought you two were close."

The room grew quiet. I stared at her for a long time. Heard Enrique say, "Geeze, Connolly." Mitch shuffled papers against the table. I'd never liked Meagan Connolly, but in that minute, I hated her. Then she made it worse.

"She was here the other day."

"What? When?" I stood up quickly and Enrique reached out and grabbed my chair.

"The day of your dad's funeral." Connolly acted like it was no big deal.

"Did she say what she wanted?" Mitch asked.

Connolly turned to him. "She was looking for you. Said she'd see you at the funeral." She glanced back at me. "I guess she didn't make it."

Chapter 24

It was everything Enrique could do to keep me from lunging at her. Mitch held his hand up. "Let's talk about this later, Liz."

I stared Connolly down. Then I told them that I'd talked to Priscilla's mother and brother earlier in the day. "Their alibi's for yesterday checked out."

Mitch nodded. "Did you get a chance to look for Swanson's first wife?"

"I looked, but I couldn't find anything. Priscilla's mother said that Priscilla and Swanson weren't legally married. Maybe he didn't marry the first one either. I'll keep looking."

He nodded and looked around the room. "Does anyone have anything to add?"

Everyone else, including Connolly shook their heads. I said, "yes," and put the pictures I'd brought with me out on the table. "I found these at my dad's house in some of Rose's things. Does anyone recognize any of these children?"

Enrique looked them over then passed them around the table. Everyone looked at them carefully, then shook their heads.

I glanced at Mitch who was looking at his phone, a tiny frown between his eyes. "Mitch, I'd like some help going through the data base for the last couple of years. Maybe we can figure out who these kids are and where they came from."

He looked up at me, then over at Enrique. "Rodriguez, you help Liz, okay?" He looked at the others. "I want someone talking to Priscilla's mother and brother again. Then talk to their neighbors."

Connolly had her hand up, but Mitch looked past her. "Molly, you and James head across the river and talk to the Butlers, okay? Liz has their address."

Molly Shepperd and James Watkins both stood. "I'll text you Carolyn Butler's address," I told Molly. She nodded and they left.

Mitch gave out orders, sending Don Spears and Marc Larson back to Parkdale to talk to Bill Yakamoto. "I know you've talked to his crew but question them again. Then go around to the neighbors."

They left and Enrique and I got up to go into my office. Mitch pointed his finger at Connolly. "Stay here. I want to talk to Liz then I'll be right back."

She nodded and Mitch followed Enrique and I out the door. In my office, which I shared with Enrique, Mitch stood just inside the door with his arms crossed.

"Do you know why Rose was looking for you?" I asked him.

He shook his head. "She had to know that I'd be with you and Bella." He ran his hand over his chin, and I could hear the scrape of his whiskers. "I don't want any trouble between you and Connolly, Liz."

"Why don't you tell her that? What's with her with-holding information." I put my hands on my hips and glared at him.

Mitch sighed. "I intend to find out. Maybe she didn't realize that you were worried about Rose."

I rolled my eyes. "You've got to be kidding me. She had to know. She kept that little bit of news to herself so she could bring it out when it suited her best."

"How did it suit her today?"

I threw up my hands. "It's much more fun to have something to share with the group than to tell one person. And you know Connolly doesn't like me, Mitch. You know that." I could feel my face grow red and sweat form under my uniform shirt.

Enrique kept his head down, concentrating on the computer screen in front of him.

"I'll get to the bottom of this, Liz. Just stay away from Connolly for a while, okay?"

"That will not be a problem. It's almost as if she's happy Rose has disappeared. You keep her away from me because one more thing and I'm going to deck her."

Enrique's lips twitched and I knew he was doing his best to keep from laughing. Mitch turned towards the door. "That would not be a good idea." He went out and shut the door quietly.

"I think it's a great idea," I told Enrique, who grinned.

He and I spent the afternoon uploading the pictures into a file that we could share within our department and with other departments in the area. Then we started the difficult task of going through the missing children database.

The room was quiet. We both concentrated hard. After a couple of hours of pouring over the pictures online and comparing the ones we had with them, I scooted my chair back and stood up. "I've got to move, or I'll be stiff as a board. Want something to drink?"

Enrique picked up one of the pictures and compared it to one on the screen. He shook his head at the picture. "Want to walk over to Doppio's Coffee and get a cup? It might do us good to get out of here for a while."

I nodded and grabbed my bag. "Let's do it."

The door to the conference room was closed. I poked my head in Mitch's office and he wasn't there, so I assumed he was still talking to Connolly.

A gentle spring breeze was blowing when we got outside. It felt so good after the days and days of rain we'd had. Enrique and I walked down the sidewalk towards Doppio. Several people said hello as we passed. One redheaded woman driving a Mercedes SUV saw us and ran back to her car to put money in the meter.

Enrique waved so she'd know we saw her. She grinned and waved back. The sidewalks were full of shoppers. It was getting close to tourist season when people flooded our small town.

We got our coffee and headed back. "It sure feels good to get out of that office for a while, doesn't it?" Enrique said, taking the lid off his cup and blowing on the hot liquid inside.

"Yeah, but I want to know where Rose got those pictures."

Enrique nodded and blew on his coffee again. "You know, I wonder how old they are?"

"I don't think any of them are over ten."

"No, that's not what I mean. I wonder how old the pictures are. One of those little boys looks like a kid who went missing from The Dalles years ago."

I stopped, forcing him to stop too. "Really?"

"Yeah. I kept looking at that picture and looking at it. Maybe the reason we aren't finding any of these children is because they're all much older now."

I thought of all the young adults I'd seen at the compound. "Like maybe in their early twenties?"

He shrugged. "Maybe. That kid went missing when I first became a deputy. I remember being horrified because he was the same age as my little brother, Juan."

"What happened? Did they find him?"

Enrique started down the sidewalk again and I followed. "I don't know. Maybe. It seems I just quit hearing about him. You don't remember when it happened?"

I shook my head. "No, you know my memory. But I'd think Mitch would."

"If he's even put the two together. That was a long time ago."

I hurried my steps. "Let's get back and see if we can find out what happened to him. There has to be a report somewhere."

Back at the office I got on the computer and looked up missing children in The Dalles ten years ago. Enrique sorted through the pictures and found the one he wanted-ed. When I found the case he was talking about, he held up the picture of a cute little boy with blond hair that stuck straight up and big blue eyes.

"That's him." Enrique said, pointing to the picture on the screen.

"It sure looks like him." I read the article. "It says his mother reported him missing, but there isn't anything here saying whether they found him or not."

"What's her name? Maybe we can find her."

"Oh my gosh, oh my gosh, oh my gosh!" I grabbed Enrique. "Look at her name."

He leaned over and looked at the screen. "You've got to be kidding me."

"Nope. It's Priscilla's mother, Carolyn Butler."

Chapter 25

I stared at Enrique. "Priscilla had a brother who went missing ten years ago and this is the first we've heard about it?"

He nodded. "Well, I did hear about it at the time, but I didn't know he was her brother. I wonder what his disappearance has to do with the cult. How long has it been in existence?"

"Rose joined ten years ago. It had been around a few years before that." I put my hand on the desk and leaned on it, thinking. "Why didn't Carolyn Butler say anything when I talked to her?"

Enrique shrugged. "Ten years is a long time. And you weren't asking about her son, you were asking about her daughter."

"That family. They have a lot going on. We need to talk to Carolyn again."

Enrique glanced at his watch. "Molly and James were just there. We should call them and see what they learned before we head over there."

I agreed and called Molly on my cell phone and put it on speaker so Enrique could hear too. She picked up right away. "Hey Molly, how did the interview go with Carolyn Butler and her son?"

She laughed. "There wasn't an interview. No one was home at her house or her son's. We talked to a couple neighbors, but they had no idea where they were."

I thanked her and pushed the end button on my phone. I looked down at the picture of Carolyn's son on the computer. The report said his name was Corey Butler. "Wouldn't you think that if a mother had a child go missing, she'd still be talking about it ten years later?"

Enrique shook his head. "Not necessarily. Some people can't cope so they choose to forget."

"Hmm." I looked out the windows at cars going by, thinking.

"What does that hmm mean?"

"This whole thing just keeps getting weirder and weirder. Did Swanson take Priscilla's brother into the cult? Did something happen to him? Why did Carolyn just drop it after a few months? Quit looking into it?"

"Let's go talk to Mitch," Enrique said.

We left the office and walked down the hall to the conference room. It was empty and so was Mitch's office. The office manager, Shelley Larson, was at the front desk. "Do you know where Mitch went?" I asked her.

She looked up from her computer. "No, he and Connolly took off about fifteen minutes ago. He said they'd be out of the office for a while and to call him if we needed him."

"What's up?" Deputy Todd Wilson walked up. I filled him in while Enrique called Mitch. The phone rang and rang, but Mitch didn't pick up. Enrique shut his phone down and shook his head. "He's not answering. Liz and I are going back across the river to question Carolyn Butler and her son."

Todd nodded. "Is there anything I can do? I'm probably stuck here because everyone else has run off."

"I'll send you the file Liz and I set up this afternoon and you can go through it and see if you can figure out anything about the other kids in the pictures. I'm assuming they all disappeared about the same time as the Butler boy."

Todd nodded and Enrique went back to our office and sent the file to him.

We headed back out to my Jeep. Enrique got in and handed me the coffee I'd left on my desk. "Thought you might want this."

"Thanks."

I drove back across the Hood River Bridge into Washington. Enrique worked on the iPad in the car, going over the file we'd made. "I keep hoping we'll find a connection to these kids and The Bread of Life cult. If Swanson abducted all of them, we'll find one," I told him.

His phone buzzed and he said, "Mitch," before answering it. "Hey Boss, Liz and I just figured out something about these pictures of missing children."

"What's that?" Mitch's voice came through the speaker on Enrique's phone.

"One of the boys is a brother to Priscilla Swanson. He disappeared from The Dalles about ten years ago. Do you remember when that happened?"

"No but go on."

Enrique shrugged. "I remembered because he was the same age as my little brother. But I don't remember hearing that he was found. Liz and I've been looking into it and there's no mention of him being found anywhere. We're heading back to White Salmon to talk to Carolyn Butler."

"Sheppard and Watkins were there about an hour ago and no one was home."

"Yeah, but Liz knows where they work. If they aren't there, we'll swing by their homes again."

"Okay. Nice work guys."

"Where are you?" I asked, taking my eyes off the road for a half-second and looking at my husband on screen.

"Connolly and I are following up on a lead we have on Swanson."

"You're going back to the compound?" I didn't like the idea of him taking Connolly instead of me.

"No, we're going to talk to a guy who lives in The Dalles. He was in the cult for a few years and left. I'd like his take on what's going on there now."

"Okay." I said, wishing I was with him and knowing I couldn't be everywhere at once.

"Let me know what you guys find out."

"Ditto," I said, and Enrique stopped the call.

He looked over at me. "This is getting to you, isn't it?"

"Yeah. There's just so much going on and I can't find Rose. Someone has to know where she is."

"You're supposed to be on leave. You could let us take care of Priscilla's murder and concentrate on finding Rose."

"Except I'm pretty sure they're tied together." I gave him a quick glance. "And how does my dad's murder tie into this?"

"You don't think Rose...?"

"Of course not, but I do think the cult is involved. I know we decided his murder was a robbery gone bad, but I keep thinking it was Swanson or someone from his cult."

We rode in silence the rest of the way to Carolyn Butler's house. I knew my sister, didn't I? She could never take someone's life. Rose was a pacifist. Anyone who knew her would know she would never hurt anyone. I was the fighter in the family. The thing that tormented me was did she stand by and let something happen to our dad?

There was no sign of life at either Carolyn's or Brandon's house. Enrique and I got out and knocked on both doors. An older model red Toyota Camry sat in Carolyn's driveway, but Brandon's pickup was gone.

"Either they both went to work, or they went somewhere together," I said. "Let's go check out the brewery where they work."

We headed down the street. White Salmon was built on a hill. It was smaller than Hood River and had one main street. In recent years, people had moved there and opened boutique shops and restaurants. There were a couple breweries in town.

I loved how they'd cleaned up the little town. They'd given old buildings a face lift and the city had put hanging flowerpots on lamp posts and big flowering pots were scattered along the sidewalks. All were lush with red geraniums and purple petunias and lots of greenery.

Everybody's Brewery was reputed to have great food along with its reputation for great beer. I'd eaten there a few times with Mitch and friends, and we'd all enjoyed it. I parked down the block, and we got out and went in.

It was pushing five o'clock, but the dinner/drinking crowd hadn't shown up yet. A young girl with bleached blonde hair stood behind the bar with a big smile on her face. She wore torn jeans, a pink and blue plaid flannel shirt and a name tag that said, Kacee. "Hi, what can I get you?"

"We're looking for Brandon Butler. Is he around?" I gave her a smile.

She looked confused. "You from the Hood River Sheriff's office?"

We nodded.

"He's in the back. Hang on a second." She went through swinging doors into the kitchen, and we heard her yell, "Brandon!"

We didn't have to wait long before Priscilla's brother came through the swinging door followed by the young lady who'd greeted us.

"What's up?" Brandon asked, looking first at me then at Enrique.

"Could we talk to you for a minute?" I moved my head towards the tables and chairs behind us.

"Sure, but I told you this afternoon that I don't know anything about Priscilla, and I wasn't in Parkdale yesterday."

Enrique tugged on his vest. "We're following up on some different information. If we could just have a couple minutes of your time?"

He motioned to a seat by the windows, and we followed him. The blonde busied herself wiping down the bar, but she kept a close eye on us.

After we sat down, I said, "Brandon, what happened to your brother, Corey?"

Brandon's face turned white. He looked down at the table. "I should've known you'd come asking me about him."

"Do you know where he is? Was he ever found?" I asked.

Brandon had his elbow on the table in front of him and he leaned his head on his fist for a second before he looked up at me. "Yeah, he came back. But he was never the same."

Chapter 26

Brandon played with the saltshaker, pushing it back and forth on the wooden table.

"Do you know where he is now?" I asked.

"No. He just bums around. Sometimes he stays with Mom for a few days, then he disappears. We've learned to not get excited if we don't see him for a while because he always comes back. Poor mom."

"Why do you say that?" Enrique asked.

He looked up at us with a sad smile. "Because she's always so hopeful that he'll get himself straightened out. He does okay for a while, then it's like he can't stand it, he has to take off again."

"Where does he go?" I asked.

He pushed the saltshaker away and shook his head. "I have no idea, but wherever it is, he doesn't do well there. When he comes back, he's usually filthy from living off the grid. I think he can only take so much civilization, then he goes back to living in the forest somewhere."

"Even in the winter?" I asked.

Brandon nodded. "Yeah. Me and mom bought him a real good sleeping bag. It's one of them that keep you warm when the temps go below freezing. I think this one's rated at twenty below."

Enrique and I looked at each other and Enrique said, "Is he off the grid right now?"

"Yeah, he's going to be a mess when he finds out about Pris. I'm not sure what he'll do."

"Was she his favorite?"

"She's eight years older than him, so she was more of a mom to him than mom was. Mom worked all the time. Never enough to eat when there's six kids to feed."

"And your dad?" I asked, quietly.

"He left when Corey was about four. Mom raised us by herself. Well, with the older girl's help."

I took a deep breath and sat back in the chair. "Where are the rest of your siblings?"

The blonde who'd greeted us came over to the table. "Would you guys like anything to drink?"

Enrique and I both said, no, thanks, but Brandon smiled at her. "A cup of coffee would be great if you don't mind. Thanks, Kacee." He turned back to us. "They're scattered around. One of my sisters and a brother are in the Seattle area. Got a brother in Portland and another sister in Vancouver."

I took a pen out of my pocket and handed it to him. Then I looked around for a piece of paper. "Can you find some paper and write down your sibling's names and contact information for me, please?"

He nodded and got up and got some paper off the bar. Kacee came back in the room with a big white mug full of coffee. "Here ya go, Brandon."

He smiled his thanks and sat back down. He took a sip of coffee then took his phone out and checked his contact list. Enrique and I kept quiet while he worked on the list. After he'd finished, he pushed it towards me. "Here ya go."

"Thanks."

He took another drink of coffee. "Is there anything else you need? I've got to get back to work."

"Your mom isn't home. Do you know where she is?"

"Probably went over to my aunt's house. She lives up by the high school. Sometimes Mom walks up there."

"What's your aunt's name and address?"

"Judy Marshall. I'm not sure about the address. She lives on Loop Road just before the turn off to the high school. It's a big grey house, you can't miss it." He stood up. We stood too and he picked up his coffee and said, "if you find Corey, will you tell him about Pris? It might be easier coming from someone he doesn't know."

We assured him that we would, and he thanked us, said goodbye, and headed to the kitchen and we went outside. "Curiouser and curiouser," Enrique said as we headed to my Jeep.

"Yeah, a sister who joined or helped form a cult. A brother who was abducted, survived and is now some kind of crazy." I reached the driver's door and got in. Once Enrique was in, I said, "Wonder what all the other siblings are like?"

"Can't wait to find out," Enrique said with a grin.

Chapter 27

Brandon was right. It wasn't hard to find Judy Marshall's house. It sat back from the road and had a mailbox in front with Marshall stenciled across the side.

We drove down her drive and parked in front of a two-story grey house with black shutters on the windows. The porch wrapped around the lower story and Judy had white wicker furniture with dark pink pillows on either side of the front door.

Enrique looked over at me and grinned. "Let's do this."

We got out and walked to the door. A calico cat with a half-black and half-calico face came to greet us, winding herself around Enrique's legs. He bent down to pet her. "Hey, kitty."

I could hear her purring. "She likes you."

Enrique patted her head and stood up. "Isn't she beautiful? Look at that face."

The door opened and a little white furball came out ready to take on the world. The cat ran to the nearest tree and the dog followed, barking its head off. A short, thin woman called to them. She looked enough like

Carolyn Butler I was sure it was Judy Marshall. She had short blonde hair that barely covered the diamonds that sparkled in her earlobes. "Maggie, leave Russia alone." She picked up the dog who squirmed in her arms and continued to bark. "Maggie! Stop that!"

She carried the dog to the house, opened the door and set her inside, then she walked back to us. "Sorry about that. Chasing Russia is her favorite thing in the world." She held out her hand. "I'm Judy Marshall, and you are obviously from the sheriff's office. What's up?"

We both shook her hand, and I said, "We just talked to Brandon Butler. He said his mom is your sister and may be visiting you?"

Judy shook her head. "No, sorry. She just left." A tiny frown marred her forehead.

"Do you know where she went?" I asked.

"My daughter drove her into Vancouver. Carolyn has a daughter down there and she wanted to tell her about Priscilla in person. I'm sure, since you're from Hood River, that you know that my sister's daughter was murdered."

I nodded. "We'd like to ask you some questions if that's all right?"

She shivered. "It's cold out here. Why don't you come in?"

We followed her into the house, where the dog greeted us with wiggles and sharp yips. Judy picked her up. "Hush, Maggie."

She led us into the living room. It was a comfortable home with expensive, but comfy leather furniture. Like her sister, Judy kept a clean house. The mantel over a white brick fireplace held pictures of what I assumed were her children and grandchildren. She motioned to the tan leather sofa, and we sat. Everything in the room was decorated in creams and tans with bright blue accents. Judy sat on the overstuffed chair across from us with Maggie in her lap.

"I presume you're here to talk about Priscilla. I haven't seen her in over ten years. Not since she joined that cult." She patted her dog and looked sad. "The family didn't want her hooking up with that Swanson guy, but she wouldn't listen. She took off with him and hasn't tried to keep in touch with anyone except her mom."

"Actually, we'd like to ask you about Corey." I said, leaning forward and looking her in the eye.

Judy deflated. There was no other word for it, her body sunk into itself. "Corey." She said his name softly. "Our poor, sweet boy."

She looked down at her dog and I glanced over at Enrique who raised his shoulders.

"Why do you say that Mrs. Marshall?" Enrique asked. He sat forward with his hands between his knees.

The house had become still, like it waited for permission from its owner to take a breath. Judy shook her head, and I noticed tears in her eyes. "It's such a sad story."

"Will you tell us?" I asked, feeling like we were about to find out a key ingredient to the lives of the people in this family.

"My sister had six kids and raised them mostly by herself. Her husband was a truck driver, and he was gone a lot, and then he disappeared." She looked up and grimaced. "I think he had another family in another state."

"And Corey?" I prompted.

She was quiet for a couple of minutes. "Corey fell between the cracks if you know what I mean. He was the sweetest boy, always bringing Caro flowers and giving her hugs and telling her he loved her. But she was so busy. My husband, Ron, and I could see that Corey wasn't getting the attention he needed. Some kids just need more attention, you know?"

I nodded. Rose had been like that.

"None of us were surprised that Corey was the one who was abducted. He was always out in the woods by himself or walking along the train tracks. Caro couldn't keep him home." She wiped tears from her eyes. Maggie reached up and licked her chin and she smiled and kissed the top of the dog's head.

"How long was Corey missing?" I asked.

"I don't know, maybe six months?"

"Who found him?" Enrique asked.

Judy shrugged. "He just showed up one day. It was the weirdest thing. He walked in the door one night about supper time. Judy said she was making spaghetti and he walked in and said, 'that looks good, can I have some?'"

"Did he say where he'd been? Or what happened to him?" I scooted forward, anxious to hear what she said.

"He said a guy picked him up and said he was taking him to a swimming hole he knew about. He ended up taking him to a farm or camp for kids who are troubled. Corey said he told the guy he wanted to go home, but the man said he had to stay there for a while."

"Did they hurt him? Did he ever find out why he'd been taken there?"

Maggie had given up and gone to sleep in Judy's lap and she slid her hand back and forth over the dog's back. "That's what's so strange. He said they were nice to him, but he didn't know who they were or why he was taken there. When Ron, my husband, tried to take him back to the camp, Corey couldn't find it. We felt at the time that Priscilla and that bonehead husband of hers had taken him there, but they would never admit it."

"Is Ron around?" I asked. "Can we talk to him?"

Judy shook her head, sadness drawing her face down. "No, Ron died a couple years ago."

"I'm sorry."

The room went quiet. I could hear the clock on the mantel clicking off the seconds. Maggie snored little puffs of breath. Judy gazed at her dog and petted her fluffy fur.

"Is there anything else you can tell us? How was Corey after he came home?"

Judy looked up as if surprised we were still there. "He was fine for a while. He seemed like his old funny self, but then he started having nightmares. Caro said he'd wake up screaming in the night. Poor little kid. He could never remember them the next day."

"Was the Bread of Life cult around back then?" Enrique asked.

I wondered if he thought Jeremiah had abducted Corey then brought him back for some reason?"

Judy shrugged. "Not that I know of." She frowned. "Well, maybe it was. Priscilla hooked up with Swanson a couple years before Corey went missing. We thought they were hippies who liked living off the grid, growing their own food, that sort of thing. I didn't hear anything about a cult until a few years later."

"But it could have been," Enrique said.

Judy nodded. "I suppose so. But why would Swanson take Corey and bring him back?"

"That's a good question. Why would anybody?"

She shrugged again. "Corey calmed down after a while. Caro was relieved and things went back to normal."

"How was he as a teenager?" Enrique asked.

"Like the rest of the boys. Adventuresome, liked to hang out with his friends. Then when he got out of school, something changed. He became depressed, and he'd take off for months at a time never telling any of us where he was going. He still does that."

"Do you think it's because of what happened to him when he was a child?" I asked.

"Well, of course it is. He would never talk about what happened. He still won't."

"Did he have anything to do with Priscilla and Jeremiah?"

"Not that I know of."

"Is there anything else you can think of that we should know about Corey?" I tried to think other questions for her, but I was coming up blank.

"No, I just wish..."

"What, Mrs. Marshall? What do you wish?"

She had tears in her eyes when she looked up at me. "I just wish he could find himself. Ron and I tried to get him in to see a counselor, someone who could help him get over what happened to him, but he wouldn't go. He said no one would understand."

She stood up and laid the still sleeping dog on the chair. "I'm sorry I can't help more."

I dug a card out of my pocket and handed it to her. "If you see Corey will you have him call me? Or if you think of anything else that might help us find out who killed Priscilla?"

She nodded. "If you want to know what I think, I think Swanson was responsible for what happened to Corey and Priscilla. I can't prove it, but I wouldn't put anything past that man."

"Why do you say that?" Enrique asked.

Judy shook her head and wrinkled her nose. "He was always so smarmy. You know what I mean? Kind of like the worst sort of used car salesman. He could charm the socks off you one minute and steal you blind the next."

"Did he steal from you or your family?" I asked.

She looked up at me, her bright blue eyes filled with misery. "He stole Priscilla from us. And then he stole Corey. He's a monster, Detective. If you want to find my niece's murderer, look carefully at Jeremiah Swanson."

Chapter 28

"Sounds like we need to find Corey Butler," Enrique said as we left Judy's house.

I nodded and got in the Jeep. "There's something hinky about this whole clan if you ask me."

Enrique got in and buckled his seatbelt. "You mean Aunt Judy too?"

I started the Jeep and pulled out of her driveway. "Aunt Judy seemed to love Corey. But I felt like she was hiding something."

"Like maybe sister Caro was abusive?"

"Maybe. I'm not sure. But it's weird that Corey disappeared for six months and then showed up again and Carolyn never told the Police that he was back."

He nodded. "Yeah, and if Aunt Judy loved him so much, why didn't she tell the police? Have them look for his abductor instead of sending Uncle Ron out into the woods with a little kid hoping to find their camp. I mean, what was he going to do if he found it?"

I headed down the hill towards the Hood River bridge. "It just doesn't add up. We need to find Corey and talk to him."

It was six-thirty when I dropped Enrique at the office. He was off duty for the day and since I was on leave, I didn't have to check back in. I stopped by his car and let him out.

Enrique waved as I drove away. I called Mitch to see if he would be home in time for dinner and he said he would. When I asked how his interview in The Dalles went, he said he'd tell me at home.

I got home and fixed the spaghetti that we were supposed to have the night before, made a salad and put French bread in the oven. Mitch drove in about the time it was ready. He stopped to play with Bailey in the yard for a few minutes. I watched their tussle and felt tears come to my eyes. Bailey missed my dad. They had been constant companions and now she lived with us, and we were gone so much.

Mitch walked in and threw his hat on the island, then walked over to the sink to wash his hands. "Smells great in here. I'm famished."

I served the spaghetti. "Let's eat. We can talk about our day while we do."

Mitch had let Bailey in, and she flopped down on the floor by our feet. I rubbed her back with my stockinged foot. "So, what did you find out from your interview?"

Mitch took a few bites of food and then wiped his mouth with a napkin. "Mmm, this is so good."

I smiled and dug in.

"So, we talked to a guy named, Rusty Evans. He was a member of the cult for several years." Mitch took another bite of spaghetti. After he swallowed, he said,

"I asked him why he got out and if it was difficult to get out."

"He said he got out because he grew up enough to realize it wasn't the life he wanted. He was eighteen when he joined and twenty-three when he got out. He'd wanted to go to college and Swanson had promised he'd help him go, but time went by, and Swanson kept putting him off, saying his time wasn't there yet."

"Dorcas told me the same thing. Swanson must offer them a way to pay for college to snare these kids into joining."

Between bites Mitch said, "sounds like it."

I dug into my spaghetti, enjoying the taste of tomato sauce and spices. "So, did he have trouble getting out?" I mumbled, opening my mouth, and shoving another bite in.

"He said he told Swanson that he was leaving, and Swanson promised him the moon. By that time, Rusty said he'd heard it all and knew it was empty promises, so he just walked out one day and didn't look back.

"But here's the most interesting thing, Swanson sent one of his goons to rough Rusty up and tell him he'd better not tell anyone what went on in their 'family gatherings'---Mitch made air quotes with his fingers---or he'd be back, and it wouldn't be pretty."

My appetite vanished and I set my fork down. "Did he tell you what went on?"

"He said he imagined I could guess, and I can. Lots of sex with underaged kids. That's what usually goes on in these cults." Mitch shook his head, a disgusted look crossing his face.

My stomach heaved and I put my hand over my mouth. Thinking that Rose had a part of that made me sick inside. But I'd known for a long time that what Mitch said was true.

"He hinted that there were a lot of bad things going on, but I couldn't get him to tell me what. He said the best thing I could do would be to find a way to shut the cult down."

"Oh Mitch, this just makes me sick." I stirred the food around on my plate. "Did you ask him about Rose?"

Mitch nodded. "Yeah, he was surprised that Rose had left the cult. He said she was close with Priscilla and Jeremiah. But he was glad she did."

"Me too. If she's still alive." My stomach churned. Where was my sister? Had Swanson killed her or had her killed too? What had she done? Did she disagree with his practices? Why now? Surely, he hadn't changed that much. None of this made sense.

We were both quiet for a few minutes, thinking our own thoughts. Then Mitch asked, "What did you find out from Priscilla's mother?"

I filled him in on our talks with Brandon and Judy. "This family..." I stopped and shook my head. "There's something weird about them, Mitch. I can feel it."

He nodded. "That's obvious. What's your next step?"

I got up and filled our coffee mugs. Then I sat back down and stirred creamer into mine. "I want to talk to Corey Butler. I have this feeling that Corey is somehow involved in this. I wonder if Priscilla asked him to help her get away from Swanson."

Mitch finished his dinner and set his fork down. "Or maybe he killed her."

"What? He's her brother."

"So? Families kill each other all the time. We need to find him and talk to him."

Did Mitch think Rose killed our dad? Surely not, but I knew he was hiding something. Did he know more about my dad's murder than he was telling me? My chest tightened and I watched him as I got up to clean up our dishes. Mitch helped by stacking them into the dishwasher.

When we finished, I wiped down the counters, and Mitch said, "I'm going to take a shower."

"Okay."

He left the room, and I finished cleaning up. Then I headed into the laundry room to put a load of clothes in the wash. I needed the ones in our bathroom and went in there to get them. When I reached out to open the door, it was locked.

We never locked the doors now that Bella was out of the house. I tried again. Then through the wood I heard Mitch say in a soft caress, "I miss you too, babe. I wish we could be together."

I stood in horrified silence. Who was he talking to? My heart pounded and my nerve ends burned. I leaned against the door, a heavy weight against my heart.

Then I heard him say, "Okay, I'll see you soon, baby. I'll tell your mom. I know she's missing you too."

Bella. Relief flooded through me. It was our daughter. I sagged against the door in relief.

Then I thought, why did he lock the door?

Chapter 29-Rose

Two Weeks ago

Rose found she enjoyed her time with Mr. Yakamoto. He had a great sense of humor, always laughing at himself and inviting Rose to join in. While he worked outside, she cleaned his house from top to bottom and fixed meals.

He never asked where she came from or who she was hiding from, and Rose was thankful. How could she explain her family to someone who'd never experienced people living and working together? She knew it wouldn't make any more sense to him than it had her dad and Liz.

There hadn't been anything else from Mother Priscilla and a couple of days after she arrived, Rose had borrowed Mr. Yakamoto's cell phone and called her dad. Mr. Yakamoto went outside while she talked.

When she'd finally gotten hold of him, she'd told him what had happened. "I should have called you sooner, but I was afraid they'd look for me at your house."

"Where are you?" her dad asked. "I'll come get you."

"No. I need some time to try and find Mother Priscilla. She wouldn't go off and leave me here without letting me know what's going on. I'm worried about her."

"What can I do?"

Rose bit her lip. She hated to ask anything of him, but she knew he'd help her. "I need some money, Dad. Is there any way you can get me some without anyone knowing?"

There was silence on the other end for so long Rose thought he was trying to figure out a way to let her down. Then he said, "how about if I leave it at Murray's station in Parkdale. You know we can trust Murray. Can you get there to get it?"

Rose sighed in relief. "Yes. Thank you, Dad."

"How much do you need?"

Rose named an amount that seemed like it would last for a long time but wasn't too much to ask for.

"I wish you'd come home, Rose. I can protect you."

Tears welled in her eyes. "I know you think so, Dad, but I just...I need to do this my way. I'll come home as soon as I can."

They talked a little longer, then Rose promised she'd call him again soon and hung up.

The next day when Mr. Yakamoto came in for lunch Rose told him she was going to walk into Parkdale.

"Do you have driver's license? You can use my car?"

Rose smiled. "Mr. Yakamoto, you are too trusting. What if I take your car and don't come back?"

He shrugged. "I don't think you will do that."

Rose went upstairs to get her bag. She liked Mr. Yakamoto and would miss him when she left. She grabbed her bag from the closet and started back downstairs. She heard Mr. Yakamoto's phone ring and waited in the kitchen for him to finish his call and give her the car keys.

She knew something bad had happened the minute he walked into the kitchen. His face was white, and he shook all over. Rose took his arm and led him to a chair. "Are you okay? Did you get bad news?"

Mr. Yakamoto nodded. "Bad news." He could barely get the words out. "Old friend killed."

"I'm so sorry." Rose sat on the chair next to him and took his hand.

Mr. Yakamoto shook his head. "He was a good man."

"How was he killed?"

"Murdered."

Chapter 30-Liz

Present day

Travis called bright and early the next morning to talk about the orchard. I was up drinking coffee and trying to decide what I needed to tackle first.

Mitch stumbled out while I was on the phone. He poured himself a cup of coffee, bent down and kissed the top of my head, and headed for the bathroom mumbling about an upcoming meeting.

I'd asked him the night before why he'd locked the bathroom door, telling him I'd wanted in to get the dirty clothes out of the laundry basket. He'd shrugged and said he didn't know. Maybe because Bella had just been home, and he'd gotten used to locking it again.

It was a reasonable explanation and I let it go.

Travis's voice pulled me back into our conversation. "I can start Jose and some of your guys planting trees if you'd like," he said in my ear, bringing me back to the problem of the orchard. "I got a call that your trees came in yesterday. Mine did too. I'll pick them up from the packing house and take them out to Jose."

My dad had told me that the nursery delivered trees to the packing house, and they were stored in the cold storage until farmers could pick them up. "That would be great, Travis. I'm sorry I'm not more involved, but I'm so caught up this case and trying to find my sister, and now we have another murder to deal with. I know the orchard needs me, what with the spring work and everything."

"Hey, don't worry about the orchard, Liz. I've got you covered. I just wanted to check in and let you know what's going on. If you'd rather I take care of things and you call me when you have time, that's great too."

I felt so bad. This was too much to dump on Travis. But how could I farm, look for my sister and find a killer too? "You can call any time, Travis. I'll try and get out to look at what the guys are doing soon. I know this isn't fair to you. We need to talk about you leasing the place. I know that's what Dad would want."

"Don't stress about that right now. Let's just get through the next couple of weeks. I know you're busy dealing with lots of stuff."

I thanked him and hung up. I didn't know what I'd do without him, but Dad had told me that he and Travis had talked about Travis leasing the orchard when Dad got too old to do it himself. Who knew it would be so soon? I knew I couldn't run it and work too.

The washing machine dinged, and I went in to put another load in and pull last night's wash out of the dryer. Just as I walked into the laundry room, my phone pinged. It was a text.

Meet me at Dad's at noon.

I texted back. *Rose?*

Nothing. No answer. I walked back into the kitchen and sat at the table staring at my phone. That's where Mitch found me when he came downstairs.

"What's going on?"

I showed him my phone.

"I'm sure it's another burner phone. I'll go with you."

"Why is she being so obtuse? Why can't she just come here or answer the phone when I try and call or text?"

Mitch put his hand on my shoulder. "I don't know, honey. I think she's trying to get information to you, and she's probably being monitored by Swanson or his goons. Let's just go talk to her and see what she can tell us."

"If it's her." I motioned towards my phone. "There have been so many texts and phone calls and dead ends." I shook my head. "None of this makes sense."

"I know, but we'll figure it out." He looked at his watch. "I need to get to the office. Are you coming in today?"

"First, I'm going to call Carolyn Butler and talk to her, see if she knows where Corey is. I may have to make another trip over there to see her."

He nodded. "Okay, I'll meet you at your dad's house at noon." He started for the door, but I called to him.

"You don't have to go to my dad's. I can do that."

He frowned. "Are you sure?"

"It's okay. I know you're following up on other leads. I'll go talk to Rose. If she shows up." I wasn't convinced the text was from her.

"Okay, call me if you find out anything or if you need me."

After he left, I called Carolyn Butler's number. She didn't answer so I went in to take a shower and get ready for the day.

I tried her number again when I got out. Still no answer, so I called her sister. Judy picked up right away.

"This is Detective Ellisen. I've been trying to call Carolyn and can't get her. Do you know if she's home?"

"She might still be asleep. I gave her one of my sleeping pills last night, and they knock her out for hours. Wish they did that for me, but they don't. But Caro could always sleep ten hours a night."

"I'm looking for Corey. Did you ask her if she knows where he is?"

"Yes, but she doesn't. She said he hasn't been around for a couple of months. I was sure he hadn't, but you never know when he might show up for a few hours, have a shower and something to eat, then head off again."

"Okay, if you talk to her please tell her that I need to talk to her too."

Judy assured me that she would, and we disconnected the call. I sat at the table with a notepad trying to make a list of things I needed to concentrate on. Of course, the main thing was finding Rose.

I was sitting at the table thinking about Rose when I remembered I was supposed to meet with the FBI agent that morning. I hurried and got ready and headed into work.

Agent John Campbell was in Mitch's office when I got there. I walked back and tapped on Mitch's door. He answered it and motioned me in.

"John, this is Detective Ellisen, my wife."

John Campbell looked more like a football player than an FBI agent. He was built like a linebacker and had a baby face. I could tell he smiled a lot from the crinkles around his eyes. "Your wife, huh? Nothing like keeping it in the family." His voice was as loud in person as it was on the phone.

"She's the best detective I've got," Mitch said, grinning.

John looked at me. "I'm sure she is. Hey, tell me what you know about The Bread of Life people. Sheriff was just filling me in."

I took the chair next to him in front of Mitch's desk and told him what we'd found out so far. "I talked briefly to the agent you've got planted there."

"Excuse me?" John sat up and leaned closer. "We don't have an agent there."

I looked over at Mitch then back to John. "He told me he was FBI."

"What did he look like?"

I described him as best as I could. "He wasn't tall, but he had muscles. Broad shoulders, big arms, like he works out a lot. He had dark hair and wore a baseball cap. Oh, and he had a slight overbite."

John frowned. "Doesn't sound like anyone I know, and I'm sure I would've been told if an agent had been assigned to infiltrate that compound."

I'd been lied to. It wasn't the first time since this nightmare began, I was sure of that.

We showed him the pictures of the children that I'd found, but since they were old, he wasn't interested.

"They're grown now. May still be there, but not much we can do if they're adults."

Soon after that he left telling us to keep in touch. Mitch had a meeting with the mayor, so I decided to drive over to my dad's and start going through his stuff. I didn't want to get rid of anything until Rose had a chance to go through it, but I knew I could go through his office and figure out what to do with his financial records. That way I'd be sure and not miss Rose if she came.

Bailey went with me. She barked and danced back and forth in the back of the Jeep as I pulled into the driveway. She probably thought Dad would be there and she could go home. Tears blurred my vision as I drove in and parked in Dad's garage.

I let her out, and she went crazy, tearing around the house, barking, and running like a wild thing. I let her go, knowing the exercise would do her good.

The house smelled musty when I went in. It amazed me how fast a house would smell funny when no one was living there. I opened the windows and doors to let fresh air in. The rain that had plagued us for weeks had finally subsided and we were having a beautiful spring day.

The apple, pear and cherry blossoms had begun to flood the valley with beauty. Every year in April it looked like someone had tossed cotton balls in the air and they'd fallen in neat rows across the valley.

Dad had loved blossom time, even if he had to get up at night and start up the huge orchard fans so the temps would warm up enough not to freeze the buds.

"Oh shoot," I said as I wandered through Dad's house opening windows. "I need to find out if someone filled the tanks on the fans."

I went into Dad's office and found the number for the propane company and made the call. The guy who answered told me that Travis had already called them, and they had filled up the tanks earlier that morning.

"God bless Travis," I whispered as I shut off my phone and looked around the office wondering where to start.

My heart wasn't ready to do this, and I wished that Rose was with me. Although, to be fair, she probably wouldn't have been a lot of help. Rose couldn't handle real life. Going through our dad's house would've been too hard for her. I thought about how she'd acted after our mother left. She couldn't get out of bed for days, just laid there and cried. I was young, but I'll never forget how worried Dad had been. I'd had to pretend that I was okay, because I didn't want to upset my dad more. He had enough to deal with taking care of Rose.

Outside I could hear a tractor running and Bailey barking down by the barn. I thought about walking down to see what had riled her up, but I knew I was procrastinating, and I needed to dig into the job.

I'd been going through drawers, pulling out old files and making stacks until I had Dad's desk covered with them. I went to the kitchen to find trash bags and my phone pinged. I took it out of my pocket and saw I had another text from Rose.

They're spying on me. I'm not safe anywhere. Sorry.

I sank into a kitchen chair and put my head in my hands. I wanted to cry, scream, throw things, but I knew that wouldn't help.

Suddenly, a chill spread across my shoulder blades. I felt someone's eyes on me. I turned towards the kitchen door and saw a man looking in at me. He was wearing blue jeans and a blue and green flannel shirt. His face was screwed into a mask that would cause nightmares. I stood up and fumbled for my gun which was locked up in the Jeep.

"We need to talk," he said, his voice deep and gruff.

"Who are you?" My heart thundered. The hair on the back of my neck stood up and my shoulders tensed.

He stepped into the room, and I wished fervently for some way to protect myself. "We need to talk about Rose."

I blinked. Suddenly, I recognized him from the compound. "You work for Jeremiah Swanson," I said, trying to keep my voice steady.

He nodded. "We're trying to find your sister. We think she'll contact you." He smiled, which eased the lines around his eyes making him seem nicer, less like a bad guy. "Maybe we can help each other."

"How?"

He held his hand out. "May I come in?"

I moved towards the door. "I'll come out." My pulse had calmed a little since I realized who he was.

He backed up and I walked out onto the deck. The sun was strong and warmed me as I stood shading my face, waiting for him to speak.

"Do you know where your sister is?" He leaned against the deck rail and folded his arms over his chest. He reminded me of Jeremiah, same longish dark hair, broad shoulders, and keen brown eyes. But this guy was heavier, more muscular.

"No, I was hoping you did."

He shook his head. "When she left, she took money belonging to Jeremiah. We think that's how she got away."

"How much money?" This didn't sound right to me. Rose wasn't the type to steal. Or at least I didn't think so, but I hadn't been around her for ten years. Who knew what bad habits she'd picked up at the cult. But I knew she had forty thousand in the bank and Dad had left money for her with Murray.

"We usually keep several thousand in petty cash. When Jeremiah looked this morning, it had been wiped out."

"What makes you think Rose took it?"

He pulled a piece of paper from his pocket and handed it to me. I glanced down at it and sucked in a quick breath. It looked like my sister's handwriting.

I'm taking this with me. Sorry if that upsets you, but I need it more than you do.

Rose Sarai

"I can tell by the look on your face that you recognize her handwriting." He said, holding out his hand for the letter.

"Jeremiah found this," I shook the paper at him, "this morning?"

He nodded.

"Rose has been gone several days. Why did he just look this morning?"

Ezekiel took a deep breath. "Jeremiah is too trusting. He would never think one of his own would steal from him."

I chewed on my thumbnail, thinking about the last time I saw Jeremiah. "He accused her of killing his wife."

Ezekiel didn't say anything, but a small tick appeared next to his mouth.

"What do you want from me?" I asked.

"We want to know if you've heard from your sister."

I shook my head. Did he think I'd tell him anything? Was the text I'd gotten that morning even from her? I didn't know and I wasn't about to share anything with Swanson or his goon. "No, I wish I had."

He nodded. Then he looked at the house, studying it like he was thinking of buying it. Or looking for a way in so he could look around.

I heard a vehicle coming down the driveway and saw Travis's pickup. Relief swept through me. Travis pulled up and stopped behind Ezekiel's SUV. He and Bailey jumped out and walked over. Bailey stopped part way and growled. Ezekiel stood still.

Travis put his hand on her head. "It's okay girl. Go to Liz."

She'd been trained by my father to protect. She came and stood between me and Jeremiah's man.

"Hey Liz, I found her down by the pond chasing birds. I wanted to bring you the tree receipts, so I brought her home." He handed me papers, keeping his eyes on the other man. "Thought maybe we could go over the financials while I'm here."

I nodded. "Good idea." Bailey pressed against my leg, and I laid my hand on her head.

The other man moved away from the rail slowly, keeping an eye on the dog. "If you hear anything, let me know." He looked at Bailey who growled low in her throat, then he glanced at Travis. "Could you move your truck so I can leave?"

"Sure." Travis waited for him to walk to his SUV before he went to move his pickup.

After he left, Travis joined me on the deck. "Jose called and said some guy in a big black car was here, so I thought I'd come make sure you were okay."

"I'm glad you did. That was one of Jeremiah Swanson's henchmen." I told him about our conversation.

"Hmm, sounds like Rose gave them the slip. Good for her."

"I'm wondering if he came looking for something and didn't realize I'd be here." I started into the house. "Come on in, I'll make coffee."

Travis nodded and followed me inside.

"They've been extremely interested in Dad's house. This isn't the first-person Swanson has sent over here to look around. Now that I think about it, I wonder what he's looking for. Both Dorcas, the young woman he sent last time, and this guy said they were looking for money Rose had left here. Money that belonged to Swanson."

"But you think she may have left something else? Something incriminating?"

"Either that or they think that." I took coffee out of the freezer where Dad had kept it and filled up the basket on the coffee maker. I checked my phone. Nothing more from Rose, not that I expected her to text again.

Travis and I drank coffee and went through the tree records Dad kept in his office. Dad always had an idea of what he wanted planted next and kept detailed drawings of the orchard and which block the trees went in.

After Travis left, I washed our cups and put papers and things away in the office. My sister still hadn't called or shown up. It was now one o'clock and I knew she wasn't coming. If the text had been from her, which I didn't think it was.

I needed to call Carolyn and ask her about Corey, so I took out my phone and made the call. It went to voice mail. I left a message asking her to call me back. Then I sat at the kitchen table and thought about Rose, the cult and everything I'd learned. A thought struck me that should've a long time before it did: the pictures of the children that Rose had hidden in her room. Was that what Jeremiah was having his people look for? I had to find out where Rose found those pictures and why she'd left them at Dad's house.

Chapter 31

I called Mitch to tell him about my visitor.

"I knew I should've gone with you," he said, sounding mad at himself. "I don't like that guy snooping around. How did you get rid of him?"

"I had Bailey with me. She took off for the pond and Travis brought her home. Bailey didn't like him, so he left. Besides, I don't think he wanted to talk to me with Travis there."

"Good. I'm glad she was with you. May be a good idea not to go to your dad's without your gun and Bailey. Did Rose show?"

"No, I got a text saying they were spying on her. But I don't know if it's even her, Mitch."

He sighed. "Maybe not. Probably someone from the cult."

Bailey whined and I let her outside, then I stood at the kitchen window and watched her chase a squirrel who had snuck up on the deck. "Yeah, I think they're keeping track of me hoping she'll be in contact."

"I wouldn't put it past them. If they think Rose hid something in your dad's house, you know they're going to be trying their best to get in there. I'm surprised they don't break in again."

"I have a feeling they will. I'll make sure the doors and windows are locked when I leave and turn on the alarm. Dad put it in a couple years ago, but he hardly ever used it."

"Probably a good time to start." His voice sounded like it came from a distance.

"You sound busy, what are you working on?" I asked.

"I'm putting out an APB on Rose. She's been gone long enough. I don't suppose you have a current picture?"

"No, I can look around here and see if Dad had one, but I doubt it. Remember, Swanson said he doesn't like his people taking pictures because he thinks it's vain."

"Yeah, I'm surprised he doesn't have a huge one of himself over the fireplace."

"Me too."

"What are you doing this afternoon?"

"I'll look for Corey. I tried to call Carolyn Butler again, but her phone goes to voicemail every time I call. I left her a message to call me."

"Okay, let me know if you find him."

I agreed and we said goodbye. I looked around Dad's house. Maybe I needed to do a more thorough search. If it weren't the pictures of the children I'd found, what would Swanson's goons be looking for? It had to be money.

I heard Bailey barking in the yard and walked over to look out. She was playing with another dog; one I'd never seen before. I went out to shoo it away and found Jose nearby. He was on a tractor and waved as he drove down the orchard road. He whistled and the dogs raced after him. I waved back and went back to my search.

Several hours later I gave up. "It must've been those pictures," I said to Bailey who'd come in from playing with her friend and crashed on the kitchen floor.

She raised her head and thumped her tail against the floor.

"I'm about ready to give it up for the day, Bailey. Are you ready to go home?"

She laid her head down and closed her eyes. I knew that in her mind she was home.

After Bailey and I got home, Mitch called to let me know he wouldn't be there for a while, and he'd get dinner in town. I needed a distraction and called Bella. We hadn't talked for a few days.

"Hi, Mama." Just the sound of her voice made me feel better. "I've been meaning to call. How are you doing?"

"I'm okay. I spent most of the day at Grandpa's going through papers and things."

"I'm sorry, I know that makes you sad."

"Yeah. Tell me about your day."

We talked for over an hour, then she had to go study. I let Bailey out and fixed myself a salad for dinner. Jenn called and I debated whether to take the call or not. I finally did and she sounded just like the old Jenn.

"Ray is in Salem and I'm lonesome. Why don't we go out for a drink?"

I wasn't enjoying my own company and thought, why not? Maybe she'd tell me what was going on with her. "Okay, where?"

We agreed to meet at the Best Western on the waterfront in an hour. I decided to dress up, so I wore a black tee-shirt dress with platform heels. I didn't normally dress for our impromptu get-togethers, but I felt a need to tonight. I hoped it wasn't because my confidence needed bolstered. Jenn always dressed like she was going to a fashion shoot. I'd never tried to keep up with her before.

Taking my gun out of the safe in my bedroom, I locked it into the safe in my Jeep. I wanted to get into the habit of taking it with me.

When I got to the restaurant/bar, I parked my Jeep and made my way up the steps. The hotel had been there for years and had grown with the town. Besides tourists, who we had more than our share of these days, the hotel hosted meetings and conferences. It was usually busy. The bar was just passed the main foyer and to my right. Jenn and I had met there many times and knew the bartender, a gal named Holly.

Holly waved at me from across the room when I poked my head in the door. I waved back and looked around for Jenn. I didn't see her and grabbed a table for two near the bar.

I hadn't been there long when Holly came over. "Waiting for Jenn?"

I nodded.

"Want a glass of Rose' while you wait?"

"That sounds wonderful. Bring two, she should be here soon."

She smiled and went to get it and Jenn walked in. She came around the table and bussed my cheek with an air kiss. "Hey girly, how's it going?"

"Good. I ordered wine." I was glad I'd taken the extra effort to dress up. Jenn had on a tight lilac sweater that showed off her new boobs, a black pencil skirt and black heels. She looked like a million dollars, and she knew it.

"Oh, thank you. I need some." She sat on the chair across from me and picked up a menu. "You know, we should order dinner. I'm famished and I know Mitch won't be home. Are you hungry?"

My ears turned hot, and my chest hurt. "How do you know that Mitch won't be home?"

She looked at me, her smile still in place, but to me it looked a bit forced. "Oh, I stopped to see him a minute on my way down here. I had time to kill."

I narrowed my eyes. My wife-radar was beeping in my brain like an alarm system that had been tripped. "Jenn, what is going on?"

She was reading the menu. She put it down and looked at me. "What do you mean? Nothing's going on."

I took a deep breath. "You've been spending a lot of time with my husband lately."

She stared at me. Then she swallowed. "What are you talking about? I've been friends with Mitch forever, just like I've been friends with you forever."

"I don't remember you stopping by the office to see him all the time until recently." I spoke quietly, trying to keep the censure out of my voice.

She reached across the table and took my hand. "There's nothing going on, Liz, honestly. Mitch and I are like brother and sister. You know that."

Holly came with our drinks and eased the tension. But I wasn't comfortable with Jenn like I'd been since we were in high school. She'd always wanted the guys to make over her. Hence the recent boob job she'd talked about since our school days. And yes, she and Mitch kidded around a lot and hugged each other when they hadn't seen each other for a while.

But this felt different. I knew what Jenn was like when she was on the hunt, and she was on the prowl.

We drank our wine and Jenn ordered a Caesar salad. I sat with her while she ate and we talked, but it was stilted. As soon as she finished eating, I drained my wine glass and stood up. "I should run. I've got a lot to do tomorrow."

She looked up and frowned. "Are you still going through your dad's house? Do you need help?"

I put money on the table for my wine. "Yes, and no. I don't want to get rid of too much until Rose has a chance to look through it."

She nodded. "Okay, well call me if you need me. I'm not doing anything tomorrow." She stood up and picked up her black bag and put it on her shoulder. She looked at me like she wanted to say something, then shook her head. Taking her wine glass with her, she headed to the bar. Several people had come in that she knew, and she was laughing and talking with a couple of guys when I walked out.

I drove to the sheriff's office to see Mitch, feeling unsettled about our relationship and wanting reassurance that we were okay. I'd just pulled up and stopped when several deputies and Mitch came tearing out of the building and ran to their patrol cars.

I got out of my car and raced towards them. "What's going on?" I yelled.

Mitch waved, but he didn't stop, just got in his car, and tore out of the parking lot. I ran inside where people scurried around answering phones and running back and forth between offices. I grabbed Deputy Todd Williams as he started passed me.

"What's going on?"

He stopped long enough to say, "A shooting at Bill Yakamoto's cabins."

Chapter 32

I ran for the door and raced to my Jeep. I climbed in and headed to Parkdale. As I drove up Hwy 35, I thought about Bill Yakimoto. What was going on there? Did this shooting have anything to do with Priscilla's body being dumped in Bill's cabin?

My first thought was for my sister. *Please don't let anything happen to Rose,* I prayed. I didn't think I could take it if my sister were dead.

My Jeep ate up the miles as I flew towards the turn off. I drove south of the tiny berg and soon turned off onto Bill's long driveway. When I pulled into his parking lot, it looked much the same as it had last time I was there when he'd found Priscilla's body, except the EMT's and ambulance, weren't there, just sheriff's cars.

I pulled into a drive row in his orchard and parked. Grabbing my gun and putting it in my bag, I climbed out and went to find Mitch.

Enrique and Conolly stood in the middle of the graveled parking area with a group of men. I raced over to them, but I didn't see my husband. Enrique looked up as I approached.

"What's going on? Was anyone hurt? Where's Mitch?"

He walked over to meet me. "The sheriff is talking to Mr. Yakamoto. We're not sure what happened. Mr. Yakamoto said he came home from dinner out and went in the house. He was in the bathroom and heard a shot. He ran out of the house towards the cabins, but he didn't see anyone. None of the guys living here did either."

"Could he tell which direction the shot came from?"

Enrique shook his head. "That's all I know, Liz. Mitch sent a couple of the guys through the orchard to look around. Connolly and I are going to question the neighbors."

I glanced at the main house thinking I saw movement. "Is there a Mrs. Yakamoto?"

"No, she died a couple of years ago."

Connolly came towards us. "You ready?" she asked Enrique, not bothering to speak to me.

"Yeah." He turned to me. "Do you want to come with us?"

I shook my head. "No, go ahead. I'll see what Mitch wants me to do." I stared at the house.

"Did you see something?"

"Maybe? I thought I saw movement."

Connolly headed in that direction. "Let's go see. It's probably a cat."

Mitch and Bill Yakamoto stepped out of one of the cabins. "Why don't you ask Mr. Yakamoto if there's someone else home instead of us barging into his house and maybe scaring his girlfriend." I told her.

"Or daughter," Enrique agreed.

Connolly walked over to Mitch, and Enrique and I started for the house. We hadn't gotten far when I heard Mitch call my name. I turned around. He, Connolly, and Mr. Yakamoto hurried towards us.

"Bill says there's no one home."

I looked at the older man. His eyes were huge behind his thick glasses. "I live alone," he said, his voice trembling.

"I thought I saw movement." I told Mitch.

He put his hand on Bill's arm. "Stay here, Sir, and let us check it out."

The older man nodded. "I...my housekeeper was here..."

Mitch and I glanced at each other and stopped on the front steps. "Today?" Mitch asked.

Mr. Yakamoto shook his head. "She left yesterday. She said she had some things she had to take care of."

I made a slight movement towards the house with my head and Mitch nodded. Enrique, Connolly and I went on in.

The house was what I'd expect from an older man living alone. It was clean but there were no frills. The front door opened into a living room. We held our guns out in front of us as we checked out the ground floor which consisted of a living room, kitchen, and a small bathroom. The bedrooms were upstairs. There were three small ones and a bathroom on the second level. We each took a bedroom, and I was looking around what must've been Bill's room when I heard Connolly yell, "clear."

Then Enrique's voice saying, "Liz, come here."

I walked down the small hallway to the room he'd gone in and stepped inside. To my surprise, it looked like someone---a woman---had been staying there. There was a plain white nightgown on the end of the bed and a hairbrush and comb on the dresser.

"Maybe his daughter?" I said, hearing the hesitation in my voice.

"He said he lived alone," Connolly put in. "The upstairs is clear. Let's go ask him." She headed down the stairs.

"I think we should take a thorough look at this room," I said, looking around. There wasn't a lot of evidence that someone had been staying there for long. But maybe we'd find something if we looked closer.

Enrique nodded. "You take the dresser and table; I'll look under the bed and in the closet."

The dresser had a couple pairs of small women's plain white underwear and a couple changes of clothes. Nothing fancy, just jeans and tee shirts in the top drawer. The other drawers were empty except for the bottom one and it had a flannel blanket in it.

The bed side table held a Bible and some greeting cards that looked like they'd been there a long time. I picked the cards up and looked at them. They were all addressed to "Mom." Birthday, Mother's Day, and Easter cards. I opened the Bible and found an old bookmark with wildflowers on it and the words, "You are a light in the darkness, a city set upon the hill."

I was sure they all belonged to the late Mrs. Yakamoto and found her name, Mary Yakamoto written in the front of the Bible in beautiful penmanship.

"I don't see anything here except for some clothes. I'm going to check out the bathroom. Maybe she left something in there."

Enrique nodded and I stepped out of the room and into the bathroom. It was big enough for a full-sized tub, toilet, and sink. It was clean and neat like the rest of the house. I didn't find any men's things, shaver, shave cream, men's deodorant, so I assumed there was a bathroom downstairs that Mr. Yakamoto used. There were a few women's things, a purple toothbrush, toothpaste, some moisturizer, and a box of Kleenex setting on the counter.

I opened the cupboard and found towels, wash cloths, and sheets, but nothing personal. It was like looking at a motel bathroom.

Enrique called my name, and I went back into the bedroom. He was looking through an old fabric bag he'd found on the floor. "Look at this," he said.

I looked over his shoulder as he pulled out a wad of money, mostly one-dollar bills, but there were a couple tens there too. Enrique dug a little deeper and pulled out a tube of Chapstick, and a wad of Kleenex.

"There's something stuck at the bottom." He pulled the fabric inside out and a small silver earring blinked at us in the light from the windows.

I took it from him. I recognized it right away because it belonged to my sister. It was a tiny silver rose and matched the one I'd found in her things at my dad's house.

Chapter 33

I carried the earring and Enrique brought the bag with everything else we'd found inside it, down the stairs. I felt shaky and had to hang on to the handrail.

Mitch, Connolly, and Mr. Yakamoto stood in the living room. I took a deep breath and blinked the tears from my eyes, not wanting them to see me cry.

"What did you find?" Mitch asked.

Enrique held out the bag and I showed them my hand with the earring laying in my palm. "Mr. Yakamoto, is there someone staying in your guest room?" I asked.

A dull flush covered his face, and he blinked several times. "Yeah, yeah." He nodded and blinked. Then he shook his head. "I'm a foolish old man."

"Why?" I asked.

"My housekeeper. She came about a week ago and said she needed a job and somewhere to stay." Nod, nod, blink, blink. "I'm a lonely old man. My wife is dead. My son and daughter live in Seattle." Nod, nod, blink, blink. "I let her stay here."

"What's her name?" Mitch asked the same time I said, "is her name Rose?"

Mr. Yakamoto looked at me. "No, no, she said her name is June."

"Did she say a last name?" I asked.

"Yeah, yeah, she said June Smith. Yeah, June Smith." He nodded some more.

"What did she look like?" Mitch asked, watching Mr. Yakamoto carefully.

"She very pretty." He looked up at me and smiled. "She looks like you."

I felt the air go out of the room. My heart stopped beating then began to pound. "Mr. Yakamoto, my sister is missing. I think she may have been your housekeeper. Do you know where she went?"

He shook his head back and forth several times and blinked some more. "No, she said she had to go somewhere, but she's coming back." A big grin spread across his face. "I'll tell her you're looking for her."

"When's she coming back?" Mitch asked.

"I don't know, but very soon, I think. Yes, very soon."

Mitch took a card out of his pocket and wrote on it, handing it to Mr. Yakamoto. "This is my personal cell number. If your housekeeper comes back, please call me on this number."

Mr. Yakamoto said he would, and we all went back outside. Enrique and Connolly headed to the cabins where a couple other deputies were talking to the orchard workers.

I grabbed Mitch's arm to slow him down. "Rose was here."

He nodded. "Rodriguez and Henderson are talking to the neighbors. So far, they haven't found anyone who has been shot, nor have they found blood, and the neighbors are saying they heard the gun go off but didn't see anything."

"Mitch." My heart raced, and I thought I might vomit. I had such a tight hold of his arm, he moved my hand and patted it, letting it go. "They're hunting her."

"What?"

"I thought they were looking for something she'd left at my dad's. Maybe even the pictures of those children, but it didn't make sense because those kids are grownups now. But while we were in Mr. Yakamoto's house, it hit me. They aren't looking for something she took. They're looking for her." Tears cascaded down my face and I wiped them away. "They're hunting her like some animal."

Mitch stared at me. He didn't disagree, which I hoped he would. Instead, he said, "We've got to find her first."

He took my hand, something he never did when we were working, and we ran to his car. "Get in."

"Where are we going?"

"Back to see that freak, and we're going to take that compound apart piece by piece until we get some answers."

Connolly called to us as we climbed into the car. Mitch keyed his mic and told her to search every inch of the Yakamoto place, the barn, the outbuildings, the garage, everything.

"Okay, Sheriff. Where are you heading?"

"Liz's sister was staying here, and that gunshot may have been meant for her."

They signed off and I sat beside Mitch, my body tense with worry. What if we didn't find her in time? My poor sister, what had she been through already? Why had she left the compound? What did she know about Priscilla's murder?

My cell phone rang, and I pulled it out of my pocket. At first, I didn't recognize the number, but something about it looked familiar. Then it hit me. It was Carolyn's sister Judy. I answered, "Detective Ellisen."

"Oh Detective, you've got to get over here. Caro has been missing for a couple days. I was so worried." She shouted into the phone, her words running over each other.

"Did she come home?"

"No, they found her body in the forest behind my house. Someone killed her!"

Chapter 34

I finally got it out of Judy that the police were involved. I told her that I was on a call, but I'd get in touch with her as soon as I could. When I got off the phone, I told Mitch.

"Priscilla's mother?"

"Yes. First Priscilla is killed, and Rose goes missing. Then her mother is killed, and someone is hunting Rose. They have to be tied together."

Mitch nodded. He called Klickitat County Sheriff, Jeanne Walls, to tell her we'd been talking to Carolyn about her daughter's murder. She asked questions and said they'd keep it in mind as they looked for their killer. Mitch asked if they had any clues and she said not yet. He thanked her and said they'd keep in touch. A professional curtesy.

My mind buzzed as we drove towards the Bread of Life compound. I thought about Dorcas and the children, the pictures Rose had left in her room at Dad's house, the murder of Priscilla and now her mother. How did it all tie together?

When we arrived at the road into the compound there was a rope across the road with a sign saying, "Private. Keep out."

Mitch stopped and jumped out and moved the rope. "Private, my ass," he said as he got back in the car and drove down the driveway.

The compound was deserted when we drove in. I wondered where everyone was. Mitch pulled up and parked and we got out. The first thing I heard was a buzzing, like thousands of bees working the blossoms. I looked around for the source of the noise and didn't see anything. "What is that noise?"

Mitch pointed to an area just to the south of us. "Sounds like it's coming from over there."

We walked towards the sound and once we climbed a rise in the lawn, we saw that the cult members were gathered in an arena. This one was different from the one behind the main house that we'd seen the evening of their big revival.

They had made a semi-circle of logs with a platform at one end. The members who sat on the logs all had their eyes closed and hummed and swayed. The platform was empty, but as we watched the humming became louder and one man on the end of a row began to beat softly on a drum he held in his lap.

I mouthed, "What's going on?" to Mitch who shrugged.

A woman who'd been sitting next to the drummer stood and made her way down to the platform where she began to sway to the music. She was dressed in a sarong-style dress, her shoulders and feet bare. She was beautiful, with long dark hair and she was graceful in her movements. Soon a different man joined her. We watched as they swayed, and the audience hummed. The woman began to sing in a hauntingly beautiful voice that sent chills up and down my spine.

Then a deep voice next to my ear said, quietly. "Please come with me."

I almost jumped out of my skin. I glanced at Mitch who nodded, and we followed the man away from the arena.

Back by Mitch's car the man stopped. I didn't remember seeing him before. He was tall and blond and reminded me of Chris Hemsworth. He wore black jeans and a black shirt, and his feet were bare. But his hands weren't. He carried a rifle on a sling over his shoulder, his hands curved around it.

"What can I do for you, Sheriff?" he asked.

"We need to talk to Mr. Swanson," Mitch said, eyeing the man in front of him.

The man shook his head. "I'm afraid that isn't possible right now. We're having a soul session and Father Jeremiah will be speaking to the family. I'm sure you can appreciate that this is private and come back at a more convenient time." He glanced at me. "It would be good if you could call before you come."

"It's important that we talk to Mr. Swanson. We have news of one of his family members," I told him.

Mitch gave a slight start and I hoped he didn't correct me. He recovered himself in time and the other man was looking at me not at Mitch.

A frown formed between the man's eyes. "It can't wait? We're having a funeral for Mother Priscilla. Father Jeremiah is naturally terribly upset. I don't think he'd be happy if I interrupted him to speak to you right now."

Mitch leaned against the car and crossed his arms over his chest. "We'll wait."

"You don't understand. These things can go on for days," Chris Hemsworth's twin said.

Mitch stared at him. "We're not leaving until we see Swanson. I'm sorry if we're interrupting a funeral, but we're investigating a murder."

The other man stared back at him for a few minutes. Then he said, "I'll go talk to him," and walked towards the main house.

We waited in silence for about ten minutes, then Jeremiah Swanson, surrounded by two other men, came out of the building, and walked towards us. His eyes were swollen and red and he acted like he was drugged. He could barely stand and one of the men held his arm.

"Sheriff, could you not let us have this evening to bury our dead?" His voice broke and tears fell down his cheeks.

"I'm sorry to interrupt your funeral, Mr. Swanson, but this can't wait. I need to know what's going on here and I need to know now."

Mitch's voice was filled with steel and Swanson reacted to it by straightening up and holding himself erect.

"The only thing going on here is my wife's funeral service. You've come here and asked questions and upset my people and I've had enough. The answer to Priscilla's murder is not here." He frowned at us. "Have you talked with her family in Washington? That would be the best place to start. They are all a bunch of lying thieves."

"What do you know about them?" Mitch asked.

Jeremiah took a deep breath. "I know they aren't what they seem to be. My wife got away from them as soon as she could. They are murderers and liars and thieves. If you want answers to my wife's death, I'd start there."

Mitch raised his eyebrows. "I would think that we want the same thing, Mr. Swanson. To find out who killed your wife and what happened to Detective Ellisen's sister."

Jeremiah nodded slowly. "Yes, but right now I have to say my goodbyes to my Priscilla."

"Is it true that you were unfaithful in your marriage? Did Priscilla leave because you were enjoying other women?" I asked.

His eyes became slits and he glared at me. "No, it is not true. I loved my wife." He turned to the man beside him and said, "it's time," and they walked away.

The man who had talked to us earlier motioned us back to Mitch's cruiser. "If you would be so kind as to leave now."

Mitch looked at me and started towards the driver's door. I was surprised that he'd give up so easily. I started to say something, but he shook his head at me. I knew him well enough that I figured out he had a plan.

He didn't say anything until we got to the main road. Mitch stopped and put the rope back up, then drove to the next road and turned onto it. He pulled into the first wide spot and shut off the engine. "Let's go to a funeral."

I got out of the car and walked around to his side. Mitch looked down at my feet. "You aren't exactly dressed for a hike. Do you want to stay here while I walk in and see what's going on?"

"No. I'm going too." I wasn't about to hang around and wait for him.

We walked back to the road into the compound. My sandals sank into mud. I finally took them off and went barefooted.

"Every time we go to that place, I come away with more questions than answers," Mitch said.

"I know. They're hiding something, and what's with Swanson trying to make it sound like Priscilla's family is behind her murder?"

"I don't know. He's trying to deflect the attention off his group, I guess."

By the time we made it back to the compound it was getting dark. Yard lights had been installed over their outside gathering area and they were shining through the trees. Mitch and I made our way towards the lighted area, trying our best to stay behind trees and not make a sound.

It was eerily quiet as we walked towards the arena they'd built. They had a huge bonfire going, its flame flicking towards the sky. When we got closer, we saw Swanson standing on a stage with his men surrounding him. The rest of the members sat on logs. They all had the same blank expression on their faces. I grabbed Mitch's arm when I noticed several men carrying a body on a stretcher towards the fire.

"Is that Priscilla? Are they going to burn her body?"

We moved closer and I realized it wasn't Priscilla's body on the stretcher. It was another woman, and the men were hauling her towards the fire. As I stared at her, my heart pounding, trying to see if it was my sister, the woman moved.

"No!" I cried. "They're going to burn her alive."

Chapter 35

Mitch took his gun out of its holster and ran towards the arena with me racing behind him. As we neared the fire, the men swung the woman back and forth, like they were throwing her into the flames as some sort of human sacrifice.

I screamed which started a mass screaming. Chaos erupted. People started getting up and fleeing the area. Mitch pointed his gun at the men holding the stretcher. "Stop!"

He tossed me his radio. "Call for backup."

While I did, Mitch moved closer to the men. Jeremiah Swanson got between him and the body. "What are you doing here, Sheriff? This is private."

"You just made it my business, Swanson. Release that woman at once."

The woman on the cot moaned and I moved closer and looked down at her. "Dorcas!"

She moaned again, moving her head back and forth, but her eyes were shut. I looked up at Mitch. "I think she's drugged." I turned to Swanson. "Did you drug her?"

The men who had carried the cot set it on the stage and I bent over Dorcas, undoing the straps holding her hands in place. Swanson started to object, but Mitch had his gun pointed at the man's head and he backed up, his eyes behind his glasses wide with terror.

"It's not what you think," he cried and moved towards the cot.

"Move another step and I'll blast you into eternity," Mitch said, his voice cold and harsh.

Swanson backed up, staring at Mitch and the gun in his hand.

I took Dorcas's hand and patted it, then her face. "Dorcas? wake up."

She stirred but didn't respond. I stood and turned to Swanson. "What did you do to her?"

He looked down his nose at me and didn't answer. Mitch moved the gun closer to his face. "Answer the detective."

Swanson's eyes widened. "Xanax. A small amount to calm her down."

"She looks more than just calmed down to me. She's practically comatose." I looked down at Dorcas. "Why do you have her on the cot? Were your men going to throw her into the fire?"

"Of course not. It was a test. All of our family must be tested." He mumbled the words while looking at the ground.

I wanted to grab him by the throat and throw him into the fire.

Mitch moved closer to me, but kept his gun trained on Swanson. "What are you testing her for?"

Swanson didn't answer immediately, and Mitch asked again. Swanson looked at Dorcas and mumbled, "her belief in our cause."

"Which is?"

Swanson mumbled again and Mitch reached out and grabbed his arm, twisting it behind him. "Speak up."

Swanson's men started forward, but Mitch waved the gun in their direction. "Stay where you are."

He yanked on Swanson's arm and the other man cried out in pain. "What were you doing to this woman?"

"It's a test of her belief in our way of life," he whispered. "Everyone must face their demons. Sister Dorcas is afraid of fire."

"So, you make a huge bonfire and threaten to throw her in? How does that help her?"

Swanson looked up. "We all have to face our fears."

The fire blazed hotter. Dorcas moaned again. She whispered something that I didn't catch, so I put my ear down closer to her. "It's Detective Ellisen, Dorcas. Are you okay?"

Her head moved back and forth on the cot. "So hot..." she whispered. "Thirsty."

"Hang on. Help's coming," I told her, looking up and willing the ambulance and the other officers to get there faster.

"So hot," she breathed. She squirmed around on the cot, mumbling incoherently, then she cried out, "I believe! I believe!"

I leaned over her. "What do you believe, Dorcas?"

She moved her head back and forth but didn't say anything. I looked up at Mitch. "We need to get her some water."

He nodded. Then he looked at Swanson's men. "Take her to the main building."

They looked at Swanson.

"Now!" Mitch exclaimed.

Swanson nodded at them, and they picked up the cot and carried Dorcas towards the building. I followed, making sure they didn't hurt her. Mitch kept Swanson's hand twisted behind his back and his gun on him as they walked behind us.

We got Dorcas in the building, and I sat with her while one of the women went to get her a drink. Mitch kept Swanson and the other men in place. Ten minutes later we heard sirens and saw a parade of lights coming down the drive.

Enrique was the first one in the door. Mitch told him what had happened, and they handcuffed Swanson and his men. The rest of the family was let go back to their homes.

EMT's came in with a stretcher and checked Dorcas out. The gal in charge looked up at me. "I think she's okay. She'll probably sleep for a long time, but I think she'll come out of it. Do you know what they gave her?"

"He said Xanax, but I'm not sure I believe him."

"We'll get her to the hospital and check her out, but her vitals are good."

I nodded and watched as they loaded Dorcas on the stretcher and headed out with her. She was out cold.

Deputies were cuffing Swanson and his men and leading them out to the cars. I walked over to Mitch. "What are you charging them with? Endangerment?"

He nodded. "They'll spend the night in jail, but Swanson's already called his lawyer. They'll probably be out by morning."

I took a deep breath and let it out. "I thought they were having a funeral."

"They lied. Imagine that."

I shook my head. "I'm going to head back to Mr. Yakamoto's in case Rose shows up tonight."

"Why don't you let one of the deputies do that? You look done in."

He was right. I was exhausted, but I knew I wouldn't be able to rest if there was any hope that Rose would show up at Yakamoto's farm. "It's my sister that's missing Mitch. Who better to stay there in case she comes back?"

"I don't think she will, do you?"

"I don't know, but if she does it will probably be in the middle of the night. She's probably afraid and knows Swanson's goons have been looking for her." I headed towards the door.

"If you're going to stay, I am too," Mitch said.

I looked over at him. "You don't need to do that."

He sighed. "Yes, I do. How can I go home and sleep knowing you're out here by yourself?"

We headed out to his car and drove towards Parkdale in silence. My gut told me that I needed to stay in Parkdale in case Rose came back, but I also felt like someone should be at my dad's house too. "I wonder if we should station one of the deputies at Dad's house?"

"I was thinking the same thing." He got on the radio and talked to Enrique who said he'd do it.

"If you guys are going to stay up all night, I might as well too."

"Thanks man. Tell Connolly she will have to take the morning shift at the office. I don't think I can stay up all night and be there at eight am."

Enrique chuckled. "I'll tell her."

After he finished talking, Mitch turned to me. "Feel better?"

"I'll feel better when we find Rose, and this is over."

"I want to go look around your dad's house before we go home. I assume you want to feed Bailey and change clothes before we go back to Parkdale?"

"Yeah, I don't want to spend the night in a dress. Drop me at my car and I'll follow you there."

He drove into Mr. Yakamoto's ranch, and I got in my car and followed Mitch to Odell. We pulled into Dad's driveway and parked by the house and let ourselves inside. The yard light was on brightening the entryway and the outside deck.

"What exactly are you looking for?" I asked Mitch as he followed me into the kitchen.

"If Rose was staying with Bill Yakamoto and had to leave suddenly, I thought she might come here. I just wanted to look around and see if she'd been here."

I nodded, but I'd been in and out of Dad's place so many times during the last few days, I didn't think Rose would hide there. While we looked, I tried to think about where else she might've gone.

We looked through the house, but there was nothing. No unmade beds, no food taken out of the pantry. I checked the refrigerator and wondered if there were the same items there that had been there the last time I looked.

Mitch checked out the garage and Dad's pickup. He came back in the house shaking his head. "Nothing that I can see."

"I don't think she's been here. If she knows Swanson's goons are looking for her, this would be the first place they'd look."

"Well, let's go home and get ready to head for Parkdale. Enrique should be here in an hour or so."

I looked around Dad's kitchen, thinking. *Rose, where are you?*

Then I remembered her friend, Ginny Miles. Ginny still lived in Hood River. She and Rose had been friends since elementary school and as far as I knew had remained friends until Rose joined up with The Bread of Life cult. I'd talked to Ginny at the time, asking her what she thought about Rose's decision. She'd said she tried to talk Rose out of it, but Rose was determined.

Would Rose go to Ginny if she didn't know where else to go? Maybe.

"Mitch, I just thought of something. Rose had a friend that she was close with, Ginny Miles. I was trying to think of who she might go to if she needed help and maybe she went to Ginny. I'll call her as soon as I get home. Seems like I have a phone number somewhere for her."

"Good idea." Mitch agreed.

We went around switching off lights and I had just turned off the one in Dad's office and walked back into the kitchen when I heard Mitch's phone beep with a new message.

He took it out of his pocket and looked at it, frowned and clicked it off. Something, intuition or my sixth sense, told me it was Jenn. I looked at my husband. He tried to act like nothing was up, but his face was flushed.

"Who was that?"

"It was nothing."

My heart sank. "It was Jenn, wasn't it?"

Chapter 36

I grabbed the phone out of his hand, surprising him into letting go. "Hey!" He exclaimed, trying to get it away from me.

"If it's nothing, why don't you want me to see what she wrote?" I felt sick inside, and so angry. I wanted to scream and throw things at him. I looked down at the phone. The text came up and I read it.

I'm all alone. Why don't you tell Liz you have to go into the office???

Mitch snatched the phone out of my hand. "It's not what you think."

"Oh? What exactly do I think? You tell me because right now I'm thinking some pretty bad things." My voice rose and Mitch's face blanched.

"I haven't given her any reason to think I'm interested. You know, Jenn, Liz. She flirts with every guy she sees. I'm just one of many."

Did he sound upset that he was one of many? I stared at him. "And you haven't encouraged her?" My voice was soft, deadly.

"No! She's been dogging my steps for weeks. Ever since she..." he broke off.

"Got her new boobs?"

Mitch scratched his head. "Well, yeah. I don't know what's gotten into her, but I assure you I didn't start this or encourage her."

"She told me that she went by to see you on her way to meet me tonight."

He looked surprised. "I didn't see her. I was in a meeting."

"How did she know that you weren't going to be home for dinner?"

He threw up his hands. "How should I know? Maybe she has me bugged or something. She seems to know my next step before I do." He shook his head, his eyes pleading with me. "I think she's having a mid-life crisis."

"If she is, she's been having one for years."

Mitch nodded. "I swear..." he held up his right hand, "that I have not initiated any contact with her." He looked around the kitchen as though trying to find something. Then he said, "I swear on Bella's love. I would never hurt you or my daughter."

I stared him down. Was that pleading and a hint of guilt on his face. He wanted me to believe him, but could I? My gut told me there was something there. Something that I wouldn't like.

We were at an impasse. "If I find out that you gave in to her, it's over Mitch. I won't live with a man who doesn't care enough for me or our marriage to stay away from temptations."

He held up his right hand again. "It won't come to that, believe me."

But could I? I wondered. At the very least he was flattered by Jenn's attention. What guy wouldn't be? But where did that leave me and our marriage?

"I don't have time for this right now. I have to find my sister before that cult does."

Relief swept over his face. He put his hand out to me, but I ignored it. "We've immobilized Swanson for a while. Hopefully, Rose will show up tonight."

"You tell Jenn once and for all that she's acting inappropriately." He nodded several times. "I mean it, Mitch. You're the one who has to put a stop to this."

I drove home way too fast, anger pushing my foot down on the accelerator. The minute I pulled into my driveway and parked I was so steamed I took my phone out of my bag and called Jenn. It rang and rang and finally went to voice mail.

"I saw your text on Mitch's phone. Stay away from my husband. I mean it Jenn. I will tell Ray. Just find some other guy to harass."

I hit the off button and slammed my phone back into my bag. Then I marched into the house and up to our bedroom to change clothes. I was so angry I could have taken a chair and thrown it through the window.

Mitch came in and changed also. He watched me from a distance but didn't say anything until he followed me downstairs. I fed Bailey and let her out for a few minutes.

"I called Jenn," he said, quietly while I stood by the door waiting for the dog.

"And?" I kept my back to him.

"She said she hit my name by mistake. That the text was meant for someone else."

I turned to him and rolled my eyes. "Yeah, right. She's covering her butt. She said, tell Liz...how many friends named Liz does she have?"

"She said to tell you that she's sorry. I think she was crying...or drunk."

As if I was supposed to care. Bailey scratched at the door, and I let her in.

"I'm sorry, Liz," Mitch said, quietly.

"So am I."

Whatever happened between Mitch and I, I'd lost my best friend. If I was honest, I knew it had been coming for a while. Maybe Jenn was having a mid-life crisis. I didn't know, but one thing I did know, you don't try to steal your best friend's husband.

We drove in silence to Mr. Yakamoto's place. Mitch had called him and told him we'd be around through the night in case Rose or anyone else showed up.

It was a long night. We didn't talk. I thought about Mitch and what this thing with Jenn would do to our relationship. And I wondered what was going on with her. She hadn't tried to call me back and I was glad. Now that I'd calmed down a bit, I didn't want to talk to her.

We sat in the dark car and waited through the night. We didn't see anything. I was hoping for a shoot-out. It was probably a good thing that no one came around. I could have easily pulled the trigger on my gun even though I knew it wasn't the right thing to do.

I had to get my head back in the game. I couldn't let what happen in my personal life affect the decisions I needed to make as a detective. Finally, around six in the morning, we gave up and went home.

Mitch checked in with Enrique who'd also had a quiet night. I laid down on the sofa and pulled a throw over me, too tired to walk upstairs to bed.

Mitch let the dog out and sat in his chair in the living room until Bailey scratched to be let back in. I was almost asleep when Mitch touched my shoulder. "Let's go stretch out for a while. We're both beat."

We slept in our king-sized bed, me on my side and Mitch on his. Sometime during the sleeping hours, Mitch rolled over and put his arm around me, pulling me close. I snuggled in and slept like the dead.

Chapter 37 – Rose

One week earlier

Rose had been staying with Mr. Yakamoto for a week and still had not heard anything from Mother Priscilla. She knew it was time to do something. She'd been afraid to go to Murray's and get the money her dad left there for her. Afraid that Father Jeremiah had someone watching her. She was afraid something had happened to Mother Priscilla. Maybe she should go back to the homestead and see if Mother gave up and went home.

Rose sighed. She had to get over her fear and do something, but it was so much easier to stay with Mr. Yakamoto and hide. They'd gotten into a comfortable routine. She knew he would miss her if she left, and she would miss being there with him. She felt almost like she had when she first joined Father Jeremiah's family, safe and comfortable.

It was Saturday morning and Mr. Yakamoto was going to his friend's funeral. Rose hadn't asked who his friend was, and Mr. Yakamoto hadn't said. He came out of his bedroom dressed in dark pants and a red and white checked shirt.

"You look nice, Mr. Yakamoto." She'd never gotten passed calling him Mr. Yakamoto, even though he'd told her to call him Bill. She told him her name was June Smith. So original, but it was all she could think of at the time, and he'd accepted it with a smile and nod of his head. He was such a good man. He was a lot like her dad in some ways. Probably because they'd both been farmers for so long.

He smiled. "I don't dress up often. My wife and I used to go into Portland to see shows. She loved to go to plays and to the orchestra."

He sounded so sad. Rose hurt for him. "I know you miss her."

He gave her a sad smile. Then he looked at his watch. "I need to go. You will be all right?"

She nodded. "Of course. I'm so sorry about your friend."

He nodded. "George was a good man."

Rose's heart stopped beating for a few seconds. "George?" No! It couldn't be her dad. "What's George's last name?" She felt paralyzed. She couldn't breathe.

"Scott." He nodded a few times. "Good friend. I hope they find out who killed him."

Rose stared at him in horror. *No!* Her mind screamed. *No! No! No!* Not her dad!

Mr. Yakamoto walked to the door. "I will see you later, June."

After he left, Rose crumpled onto the sofa. All this time she hadn't gone to her dad's because she was afraid for him, and they'd already killed him! Rose sobbed and held her head in her hands.

Later, after she'd cried for her dad for hours, she finally got up and went into the bathroom and washed her face. She knew what she had to do. She couldn't hide any longer. It was time to face Father Jeremiah. She had to ask him the hard questions; what had happened to mother, what was he doing with all the children. Was it like Mother Priscilla had said? Was he selling them? As bad as things had gotten at the homestead the past few years, Rose couldn't believe Father would do something so horrendous. But she could believe it of Brother Ezekiel.

Rose went upstairs and gathered her things and put them in her bag. Then she wrote Mr. Yakamoto a note telling him she had to leave, but she'd be back soon.

It was time to face the family.

Chapter 38-Liz

When I woke up at eleven, Mitch was gone. He'd left a note asking me to call when I got up. Then he texted me that Swanson and his men had made bail and were back home. I couldn't believe they'd been let free after terrorizing Dorcas.

I didn't want to talk to Mitch, so I put the phone down and went upstairs to get ready for the day. The hot shower felt wonderful, and I stayed in longer than usual, washing my hair and feeling the warmth flow over my skin.

When I got out and dressed and blow dried my hair, I went to get my phone which I'd left downstairs on purpose. I had a text from Mitch, one from Jenn and a voice mail from Judy Sherman.

I ignored Jenn's text and called the hospital and asked about Dorcas. They said she'd finally awoke about eight that morning and they were going to release her to her mother. I sighed with relief; glad she was going home. Then I texted Mitch and told him I was up and going to find Ginny Miles. When I listened to Judy's voice mail, she said she wanted to talk to me, so I called her.

"Oh, Detective Ellisen, thanks for calling me back. Could come over here today? We're going through some of my sister's things, and I found something you might want to see."

I agreed and told her I'd be over later that afternoon. Then I found the number for Rose's friend Ginny and called her.

Ginny answered my call, her voice hesitant.

I told her who I was and thought she'd ask about Rose. She surprised me and didn't. After we exchanged pleasantries, I asked if she'd seen Rose.

"Rose? No, I haven't seen her for quite a while."

"She hasn't come by in the past few days?"

There was silence. Then, "no, she doesn't leave home much I don't think. She's still in that cult, isn't she?"

"I don't know where she is. She didn't come home for our dad's funeral. And the cult says she left there a few days before the funeral, and they haven't seen her. I thought maybe she came to see you."

She didn't answer me directly. Instead, she said, "I'm so sorry I couldn't make it to your dad's funeral. He was such a nice guy. But I had a bad cold, and it was so nasty that day."

"Yes, it was. Don't worry about it. Listen Ginny, if you hear from Rose will you please let me know?"

"Oh, of course, not that I expect to hear from her. She's only called me once since she joined tet cult. I think she was upset because I wasn't supportive of her, but I just hated to see her do that, you know?"

"Yes. What did she want the time she called?"

There was silence for several seconds, then she said, "she wanted me to meet her for coffee."

That surprised me. "When was that?"

"Oh, let's see. I think it was last summer. I felt bad, but Sam and I were on a trip. We'd gone up to Leavenworth for a long weekend, so I couldn't meet her."

Leavenworth was a small town in Washington that was modeled on a Bavarian village. Thousands of tourists visited it each year. Mitch, Bella, and I had visited it a couple times.

"If she calls you, will you please ask her to call me? I need to talk to her."

"Of course, but I don't think she will. You take care, Liz. I've got to run. Bye."

She hung up and I stared at my phone. Something seemed off with her. Was she just busy, or was something else going on? It might not hurt to go by her house and see for myself. But first I needed to drive to White Salmon again and talk to Judy Sherman.

I was sure my car could make the trip across the river by itself, I'd driven it so many times in the last few days. It took me twenty minutes to drive across the bridge, through Bingen and climb the hill to White Salmon.

Judy and Maggie greeted me at the door of her house and invited me in. Judy's daughter, Loren was there too. Judy introduced us.

"I'm so sorry for your loss," I told them.

They both had tears in their eyes. "She was so messed up," Judy said.

"What do you mean?" I asked.

We sat at her dining room table, and I could see she had a stack of pictures in front of her. She tapped them with her index finger and said, "I think my sister was blackmailing Jeremiah Swanson."

"What makes you think that?" I leaned closer to see the pictures as she spread them out.

"Look." She pushed a few across the table to me. "I found these in her laptop case under her bed. These are bad, but the rest of these..." she broke off and shook her head. "I don't even want to show them to you."

I studied the pictures she'd pushed towards me. It looked like a party going on in the compound. There were lots of naked young girls, maybe in their teens. It looked like they were dancing for a group of older men who sat in chairs or at picnic tables, watching them.

"How would your sister get these?"

"I don't know. Maybe Priscilla gave them to her." Judy shook her head.

"May I see the rest?" I didn't want to. These were bad enough, but I needed to see what Swanson was up to.

Judy pushed them across to me. "You can have them." She shuddered. "I don't want them in my house."

Her daughter looked green. "How did Priscilla stand to live there? She wasn't like that."

"He brainwashed her," Judy told her.

The young woman got up and went into the kitchen. I could hear her running water.

"I'm sorry you had to find these. Did you show them to your sheriff?"

Judy shook her head. "No, I knew you were looking into the cult, and I wanted you to see them first. If you need to show them to Sheriff Walls, you can."

"She may want to talk to you."

"That's okay. I just can't believe my family is involved with something like this." I knew how she felt. I wanted to look closer at the pictures to see if Rose was in any of them. And do what? I asked myself. *Destroy any with her in it?* A small voice in my head whispered. Could I do that? It would be so tempting.

Loren came back into the room. "You missed one, Mom. I found this one on the counter." She held it up to look at. "This one isn't as bad as the rest." She cocked her head. "Wait a minute. That's Corey."

"What? Carolyn's son?" I stood and walked over to where Loren stood.

"That's where he goes," Loren said.

Judy sat at the table with her head bent.

"Judy, did you know that Corey had joined the cult?" I asked, holding my hand out for the picture.

Judy shook her head. "Not until I found that." Tears formed in her eyes. "It doesn't mean he joined. Just that he was there." She brushed the tears away. "Maybe he went to check on Priscilla."

I took the picture from Loren. Corey Butler looked familiar. Had I seen him at the cult? Or was it that he looked like his brother, Brandon? He stood in front of a fire pit, looking at a crowd of men. The look on his face was one of disgust.

"Whoever those men are, Corey doesn't look happy to be with them."

She nodded. "My poor boy. If she weren't dead, I'd kill Priscilla for this.""Mom!" Loren gasped.

Judy jumped up, tears falling down her face. "He's better than this. Carolyn never gave him any support. She let him slip through the cracks. I begged her to let us raise Corey, but she wouldn't do that. She let him flounder."

I felt their pain and looked down at the picture instead of at the grief on their faces. That's when it hit me. I looked closer. "Judy, are you sure this is Corey?" I held the picture out.

She nodded, miserably.

I looked back at the picture. That wasn't the name I knew him by. He'd told me his name was Luke and that he was with the FBI. He was deeply entrenched in the Bread of Life cult.

Chapter 39

"I talked to him at the compound. He told me he was with the FBI."

"Corey always had an active fantasy life," Loren said, giving her mother a nervous glance. "He loved to play act when we were kids, and he never grew up."

I gathered up the pictures and wondered what an emotionally disturbed man would do when he found out someone had killed his mother. Or was he the killer?

"I'm sure Sheriff Walls asked you all these questions, but do you have any idea who might've wanted to kill Carolyn or Priscilla? Would Corey...?"

Judy jumped up from her chair. "No. He would not. He loved his mother and sister despite the way they treated him."

"So, Priscilla mistreated him too?"

"She got him involved with that cult," Judy said, her eyes on fire.

"But when they were young? How did she treat him when they were young?"

Loren shrugged. "I thought she was okay. She kind of mothered all of the younger kids because Aunt Caro was gone so much."

"Yeah," Judy seemed to deflate, "I didn't notice anything wrong with how she treated him when they were kids. He adored her, followed her around like she was his mother."

"And when he came back from being kidnapped?"

Judy and Loren gave each other uneasy glances. Then Judy said, "he still acted like he was crazy about her when he was her. But his feelings for his mother changed."

"How?"

Judy sighed. "For a long time, he acted like she didn't exist. He'd talk to the other kids, and he'd talk to Ron and me, but he wouldn't speak to Carolyn for the longest time. The counselor said it was his way of getting through the emotional upheaval of what he'd been through. She said to give him time and lots of support."

"We all know how that worked out," Loren said.

I took the pictures and left with a promise that I'd do my best to find Corey. They said they'd let me know if they heard from him. As I drove, I let my mind go back over the things I knew about him. Had he gone crazy and killed his sister and mother? It was a real possibility, but how did Rose fit into the story?

A sharp pain hit my chest. Had he killed her too? And what about our dad? Why was he killed? Was it as simple as a home invasion? Were they looking for money or was it a coincidence and the cult wasn't involved in Dad's murder?

When I got to the office Mitch was in his with the door shut. I tapped on the door and poked my head in. He was on his cell phone, and he looked up and frowned when he saw me.

"I need to talk to you," I mouthed, holding up the stack of pictures. I started to step back and close the door.

"Come in, Liz." He motioned me in, and I walked in and closed the door. "I'll get back to you," he said to the person on the phone.

"Who were you talking to?" I tried to keep my voice light, not asking if it was Jenn, but wanting to know.

Mitch closed his eyes and rubbed the spot between them. "That was Sheriff Walls. Carolyn Butler was murdered somewhere else and dumped where they found her. Just like her daughter."

I put the pictures down on his desk and told him what I'd found out from Judy Sherman and her daughter. Mitch looked them over and shook his head. He rubbed his forehead again.

"Man, this is a nightmare."

"You know if we take these to Swanson, he'll just claim he doesn't know who the people in the pictures are. I didn't see anyone that I recognized from our trips to their compound except Luke, aka Corey Butler, did you?"

"No, and from the picture I can't tell if it was taken at the same time as the other pictures." He took a magnifying glass out of one of his drawers and looked closely at each one.

I went around his desk and leaned over his shoulder to look too. "I mean, it looks like the compound." I pointed to the lawn where the girls were dancing. "If it isn't The Bread of Life compound, where did Carolyn Butler get the pictures?"

"Good question. I think it's time Swanson gave us some answers."

Chapter 40

We headed back to the compound. I told Mitch everything Judy and Loren had told me about Carolyn and Corey. "Judy thinks Carolyn was black-mailing Swanson with the pictures."

Mitch flipped the visor down. The sun was out, and it was a gorgeous day. "That's possible, but where did the pictures come from?"

"Maybe Priscilla took them."

He glanced over. "An insurance of some kind?"

"Could be. I'm sure she didn't like him bringing in young girls to have sex with them. She was his wife."

Mitch's face flushed. "She must've known what his agenda was going into this thing."

"I don't know if she did or not. Rose thought they were going to live together in sweet harmony and grow fruits and vegetables with love. Maybe that's what Priscilla thought too."

"It may start that way, but these cults always morph into orgies."

"And usually with young people who aren't old enough to have a say," I added, my heart sinking.

The compound was quiet just like the day before when we drove in. I looked around. "Do you think they're still humming?" I rolled down my window, but there was dead silence.

"I don't know what they're doing," Mitch said, pulling into the parking area and turning off the engine. He opened his door. "Let's go see."

The silence was eerie as we walked towards the main house. I put my hand on my gun, looking around, hoping to see someone, but there was no one around.

Mitch glanced at me, and I shrugged.

We walked to the front door and Mitch knocked. No one came to the door. He knocked again. Still, no one came.

"Where did they go?" I whispered. "Surely Swanson came back here when he was released this morning."

"I don't know. It's like they vanished." Mitch looked around. "Keep knocking. I'm going to walk around and see if I can find anyone."

I nodded and wrapped on the door again. The door finally opened a crack and a person wearing a hooded jacket held out a piece of paper. I took it and they disappeared back inside.

We are observing a day of mourning for Mother Priscilla. Please allow us this time to grieve.

I knocked again, but no one came to the door. "This is ridiculous," I muttered as I went to find Mitch.

He had taken off across the parking lot to the buildings where Lydia had said they built their furniture. I found him peeking into the first building and showed him the note.

Mitch shook his head. "How long does this go on? They could be in mourning for years."

I stood on my tiptoes and peeked into the windows. "Who knows? Looks like this is where they build their furniture." I tried the door, but it was locked.

We walked around the back of the building and saw several trucks with Redemption Project stenciled on the side. "This isn't a small operation, is it?"

"Nope. Looks like they've got quite the business going. I'll have Garcia look into it." He keyed his mic and told Deputy Garcia to look up everything she could find on the Redemption Project.

"Let's go over to where they were yesterday," I suggested. "Maybe they're still there meditating or something."

We walked around the building, back over the rise to the arena where they mourned for Priscilla the day before. It was empty.

"Okay, this is getting scary. Did he poison them all and leave?"

"This place feels empty."

"Well, there's at least one person because he or she gave me the paper." I held it up.

"Let's go back and demand to see Swanson if he's here. I want to know what's going on."

As we walked through the compound, I noticed most of the windows had black out curtains or were boarded up. "He definitely has moved his people somewhere else," I told Mitch.

"Let's see if he's here." Mitch marched up the stairs of the main building with me right behind him. He pounded on the door.

Nothing.

Mitch pounded again and yelled, "Swanson, this is Hood River County Sheriff, Mitchell Ellisen. You need to come out right now."

The door opened slowly. Mitch and I both pulled our guns and aimed them at the opening. A young woman stepped out with her hands raised. She was shaking and her face was white. "Please, don't shoot."

Mitch lowered his gun. I kept mine trained on the door behind her.

"We need to talk to Jeremiah Swanson. Tell him to get out here now."

The young woman glanced back at the open door. "He can't see you right now. He's in mourning. We are all in mourning. Father Jeremiah asked that you leave. He'll call you when he's ready to receive guests."

Mitch motioned to the door. "We are not guests. Go back in and tell Father Jeremiah that he has about two minutes to show his face."

The girl scampered back inside.

Finally, after what seemed like ten minutes but was probably only two, Swanson appeared in the doorway. He was dressed in white robes with a purple sash across his chest. His congenial manner was gone.

"I am mourning my wife. Why can't you leave us alone?"

"We are conducting a murder investigation. You need to answer our questions." Mitch started towards the door, but Swanson held up his hand.

"I'm sorry, Sheriff, but we have our procedures. Unless you have a warrant, you may not come in."

"I'm worried about the safety of your people. That supersedes a warrant. Where are they?"

"They are safe."

His voice sent chills running up and down my spine. "Safe where?" I asked.

He didn't bother to look at me. "Please leave or I will call the State Police."

"Go ahead," Mitch called his bluff. "They don't have jurisdiction over the sheriff's office."

Swanson stood his ground, but I could tell from the look on his face he wasn't sure what to do. He sighed. "Fine. Come in." He opened the door and walked ahead of us into the building.

Instead of leading us to the sofas by the fireplace, he waved us over to one of the tables. He pulled out a chair and we sat across from him. "How can I be of help?"

"First, I have more news for you. Priscilla's mother was murdered in Klickitat County yesterday. That was one of the reasons we came here to see you."

He nodded, but I got the sense he didn't care one way or another. "Are you certain it was murder?"

"Yes, we're sure. Why would someone be killing your family members, Mr. Swanson?"

"They're not my..." Jeremiah stopped and blinked.

"They're not your what? Family? Had you and your wife divorced?" I asked.

Swanson barely glanced at me. "Of course not. But my family are the people I choose to have as relatives. Priscilla's mother was not one of mine."

Interesting, but not surprising. "Where is your family today?"

A shadow passed over Jeremiah's face. "We are in mourning. We may not mourn like most of society, but we do mourn our loved ones."

"So, you've shut them in a room somewhere?" Mitch asked.

"Of course not." Swanson scooted back in his chair. "Listen Sheriff, we may not do things the way you like, but we haven't committed any crimes." He gave us a smug look. "You put me and my men in jail and we were out before you even left the building. You can't pin anything on us because we haven't done anything wrong."

"Is that right?" Mitch asked. "Drugging and scaring a young woman isn't nothing, Swanson. If she agrees to press charges, I'll..."

"She won't." Swanson said, interrupting him.

"How can you be so sure?" I asked him.

He looked at me with contempt. "I know my people."

Mitch looked at me and I pulled the pictures out of my bag. "Do you recognize any of these people, Mr. Swanson?" I pushed the photographs towards him.

He hesitated for several seconds before picking the pictures up and looking at them. "No, sorry." He shoved them back to me, but I noticed as he did that his hand shook.

I'd held one picture back and I kept my eyes on him as I reached into my bag and drew out the one of Corey Butler. "I'd like to speak to this man. I saw him one of the first times I came here. You called him Brother Luke."

Swanson looked at the picture and shook his head. "I'm sorry. Brother Luke is no longer a part of this family."

Chapter 41

"Why not?" Mitch asked. "Where did he go?"

Swanson raised his hands, palms up. "I don't know where he is. He left a few days ago."

"Why?" I asked.

"It happens. Some people don't fit in here. Brother Luke was one of them. We don't force them to stay if they want to leave."

He'd said the same thing about Rose.

"No, but you warn them to keep their mouths shut, don't you?" Mitch asked.

Swanson looked surprised. "I don't know what you're talking about."

"I think you do." Mitch leaned back in his chair and watched Swanson. I knew his tactic. He'd keep quiet hoping Swanson would offer up something. But Swanson was almost as good at his game as Mitch. He sat with his head bowed.

Finally, Mitch sighed and said, "tell me about Priscilla."

Swanson looked up, surprised. "What about her?"

"You told us that she went to visit her mother. Detective Ellisen talked to Carolyn Butler before she was killed. She said Priscilla had not been in touch with her."

"Well," Swanson looked at his hands which rested on the table, "that's just not true. They had been in touch. I'm afraid my wife had been having some personal problems. Someone had told her untruths and she believed them."

"Had Carolyn Butler ever come here?"

Swanson shook his head. "Not that I'm aware of, but Priscilla may have brought her here to visit while I was away. I'm often away, speaking at engagements across the country."

"What exactly do you talk about? Are you out looking for people to join your...family?"

"Yes, among other things."

"Tell me about the other things," Mitch said.

Swanson drummed his thumbs on the table. "We make furniture. Look around you, Sheriff. My people have made every piece of furniture in this room." He waved his arm around the room. "I go to furniture shows and sell our furniture. It takes a lot of money to keep a group this size fed."

"What else do you do?"

"We grow our food. We have some beautiful gardens in the summer. We bake our bread and we're thinking about raising our own meat too. We are very self-efficient here."

Mitch nodded. "Getting back to Priscilla, what do you think happened to her?"

Swanson glanced at me, and I gritted my teeth. I couldn't let him rile me.

"I think someone wanted her position. Believe it or not, I'm very sought after. Sometimes there are ladies in the family who want to take over and be Mother. Of course, that isn't...wasn't going to happen." A shadow passed over his face. "Sheriff, I loved my wife. She was everything to me."

A tear escaped and rolled down his face. He didn't bother to brush it away. "I don't know who killed her, but I hope with all of my heart that you find out who it was."

"Even if it's one of your family?"

"It won't be."

"So, you don't have any idea who would kill your wife and her mother?"

Swanson shook his head. Then he blinked and gave us a thoughtful look. "There is one possibility."

"Who is that?"

"Her brother. Corey Butler. He has emotional and psychological problems. You may want to talk to him."

"Isn't it true that Corey Butler and Brother Luke are the same person?" I asked.

Swanson looked up at me. "Of course not. Who told you that?"

I pulled Corey's picture out of my pocket and placed it in front of him. "Is this Corey?"

He nodded. "Yes, that's him."

"One time when we were here you called him Brother Luke. He told me that he was with the FBI. Why would you lie to us? Why would Corey lie? What is going on here, Mr. Swanson?" I leaned over the table, getting in his face.

Swanson leaned back and smirked. "Looks like you caught me, Detective."

I stared at him. "Why don't you enlighten me as to your reasons for lying to us."

He pulled on his purple sash and tugged at the collar of his robe. "Corey Butler has been in and out of our lives for years. He was a troubled boy and Pris thought she could help him." He looked me in the eyes. "Carolyn Butler was not a good mother."

"Go on."

He shrugged. "I don't know what you want to know. He'd come, stay a few months, and leave again. I told Priscilla that he needed to decide whether he was going to be part of the family or not and stick to it, but she wouldn't do that. She loved him too much to turn her back on him."

"When he disappeared as a child, was he with you and Priscilla?"

Swanson smiled. "You found out about that, huh? Yes, he came to us and begged us to keep him. He said there was never enough food at home, and Carolyn was gone all the time. We didn't have much either at the time, but we shared. That's what families do."

"Mr. Swanson, if Priscilla and Corey were so close, what makes you think he killed her?"

Swanson squirmed. He looked at his hands, at the large diamond ring on his finger. He sat up and put his hands on the table. "You asked who I thought might have killed Priscilla. I don't know, but I do know that her brother has mental issues. Maybe he went berserk and killed my wife and their mother, maybe it was someone else. I don't know. I just mentioned him as a possibility."

"Mr. Swanson, where is your first wife?"

He looked startled. "Priscilla was my first and only wife."

"That's not what Carolyn Butler told me."

"She was lying." He stood up. "I've answered your questions. You need to look somewhere else for my wife's killer. No one in my family would kill anyone. We are a peaceful people."

Mitch had been quiet during our exchange. He stood up too. "We need to talk to your family members, Swanson. I want to know that they're all right and I want to know what they think about your wife's death."

Swanson said, "My family is sequestered in mourning. Please let us have this time to grieve."

"No. You need to let me see that your family's okay. Let me talk to them. Then you can get back to grieving."

Swanson's face turned dark red. He took a phone out of his cloak and pressed a button. A voice said, "Sir?"

"The sheriff would like to talk to members of the family. Please bring them in a few at a time."

"But Sir, the mourning..."

"Apparently the sheriff doesn't care about our feelings. Please start bringing them in." Swanson's face looked like it had been carved out of stone. His eyes shot lasers at Mitch and me. We ignored him.

Swanson told us there were about a hundred people who lived in the compound. "Do you want to see everyone?"

Mitch nodded. "That would be good. Start bringing them in by those who are in charge. I want to talk to your righthand men and women."

Swanson let his man know what Mitch wanted. Mitch stood at the head of the table, and I chose a place closer to the door where I could observe the room. I wanted to keep a close eye on Swanson and his henchmen.

Several people I'd never seen before filed in. They were all wearing white robes and looking very sober. I didn't know if it was grief written on their faces or if they were coached to keep their eyes downcast and to speak slowly and carefully.

Mitch asked the questions. First, he asked if they were okay. Then he asked if they knew what happened to Priscilla. They all said how sad they were about Mother Priscilla.

It took a long time for all of Swanson's people to file through. Mitch asked about Rose and Corey. No one would admit they knew anything. They were all sad that Rose was gone, all sad that Corey left and several had tears in their eyes when they talked about Priscilla.

By the end of the questioning, I was exhausted. We hadn't found out anything except what Swanson told us, which didn't surprise me, but it was discouraging.

After the last of Swanson's family filed out, he came towards us. I had moved over to stand against the wall beside Mitch. Swanson had been sitting on a chair at the end of the long table. "You've talked to my family. No one knows anything, just as I told you. Now will you please leave?"

Mitch stood up and rubbed the back of his neck. I knew he wasn't satisfied with the interviews, but what else could we do? Then I thought of something. "Mr. Swanson, where is Lydia?"

Chapter 42

S wanson shook his head. "Sister Lydia is away."

I frowned. "Away where?"

He stood up. "She is on a trip to California where she sells the furniture."

"I thought you sold the furniture."

He shook his head. "I'm trying to take our company national. Sister Lydia heads the sales in the Northwest."

I remembered the way Lydia had dressed when Mitch and I were there the night of the revival. She wasn't wearing the white robes like the rest of the family. She was dressed in business clothes. Maybe Swanson was telling the truth this time, but I had a hard time believing anything he said.

"Please let us know when she returns. I'm sure we'll need to speak to her," I told him.

He agreed and we left soon after much to Swanson's relief.

Mitch was quiet as we drove out of the drive. Then he said, "What do you think is going on with them?"

"I think Swanson is doing everything he can to keep us from finding out. I feel like he's putting up roadblocks as fast as he can."

Mitch nodded. "This furniture business, I think it's important that we look into it. Something just doesn't ring true about it."

After we got back to the office, Mitch went in to check with Garcia on her progress looking into the cult's furniture business while I headed over to see Rose's friend, Ginny. I knew she lived on the west side of the valley, near Jenn and Ray, but not as far up the hill.

Ginny's house was off Country Club Road, set on a side hill and tucked back in the trees. It was a small bungalow, painted white with a dark green roof. As I drove in, I thought it was a good place for Rose to hide and my hopes picked up. Maybe she was there. Maybe she could shed some light on where she'd been and what was happening at the compound.

Ginny was divorced and had two children in college. She'd been the secretary at Westside Elementary School for over twenty years. Bella had loved her and spent a lot of time with her when she went to school there.

As I drove up and parked in front of her house, I remembered Rose saying that Ginny had gotten the house in the divorce and her ex had gotten his sports car, a new motor home and a boat.

The lawn was freshly mowed, and someone had been working in the flower beds pulling weeds and putting out fresh bark dust. As I got out of my car, a man came around the back with a wheelbarrow. He stopped when he saw me.

"Hi, I'm looking for Ginny." I didn't know if he was doing yard maintenance or if he and Ginny were together. I guessed I'd find out.

He set the wheelbarrow down and yelled, "Ginny, you've got company."

Rose's friend came out of the house, wiping her hands on a paper towel. Her face froze when she saw me. "Liz."

"Hi Ginny, I hope you don't mind that I dropped by."

Worry lines crossed her forehead and she didn't meet my eyes. "No, of course not. Come in. I was just making Sam and I a cup of coffee. Would you like one?"

I smiled at the man who headed back to his wheelbarrow. "Sure."

Ginny led the way through the living room into her kitchen which was at the back of the house. "Sorry, the house is a mess. We've been working on the lawn and planting a garden, and I've been too tired to clean."

I looked around her bright kitchen. The cupboards, table and chairs were all white. The walls were a soft yellow. There were dishes in a drainer by the sink. A gardening magazine on the table and a few dishes on the counter. "Your house looks fine to me."

She smiled and took three mugs down from the cupboard. "It's so different with Sam here. I've been by myself for so long and the house never got messy. It's amazing how adding one person can change that."

"Yeah, it does make a difference." I thought about Bella's visits from college. She left a mess everywhere she went.

Ginny poured us a mug of coffee and set it down on the table. "Come sit down. Do you want cream or sugar?"

"Cream would be great."

She got a small carton out of the refrigerator and poured a little into each of our cups. Then she sat at the table next to me. "What's going on?" she asked.

I took a sip of the hot coffee and sat the mug back on the table. "Well, like I told you, Rose didn't show up for Dad's funeral, so I went to the cult looking for her. They told me she left a few days before and they haven't heard from her."

Ginny always looked a little worried. I wasn't sure if it was because her brown eyes were set too close together or if she was a little crossed eyed. She had soft brown hair that she wore chin length. She was short and round. "I wish I knew where she was."

"You haven't seen her or heard from her?"

She shook her head, then said, "She did call about a week ago."

"She did? What did she say?" Excitement pounded through me. At least Rose was still alive a week ago.

Ginny drank some coffee. "She said she left the cult and needed somewhere to stay where they couldn't find her. I would have told you, Liz, but she begged me not to. But now..." she broke off her sentence and looked down at her coffee.

"But now?"

She looked up. "She was supposed to come here two nights ago. I told her she could stay with Sam and I, but she didn't come. I kept thinking she would. I can't get her on the phone. I told myself I was going to call you if she didn't show up or call today."

My heart sank. Two days ago, Rose had left Mr. Yakamoto's saying she'd be gone for a while. She must've felt like she needed to move.

"I'm worried about her, Ginny. I think Jeremiah Swanson has sent someone to find her. His wife was murdered a couple days ago and now his mother-in-law. It looks like the wife's brother may have killed them, but why would he go after Rose?" I rubbed my forehead where a headache was forming. "None of it makes any sense."

Ginny didn't say anything. She drank her coffee and looked at me. After a couple minutes she said, "How's Bella?"

I smiled, thinking about my daughter. "She's fine. She had to go back to school the day after Dad's funeral because she had finals. I sure miss her."

Ginny nodded. "It's hard to get used to them being gone, but you do finally."

I couldn't imagine it, but I smiled and nodded. I finished my coffee and stood up. "I should go. If you hear from Rose, please call me."

Ginny stood and picked up both of our mugs, taking them to the sink. "I will." She picked up the cell phone that had been lying on the counter. "What's your number? I'll put it into my contact list so I can call if I hear anything."

I gave it to her, thanked her and headed for the front door. Sam was still shoveling bark dust and he looked up and waved as I passed. Ginny walked towards him.

My cell rang as I got in my Jeep. It was a Parkdale number and I thought it might be Mr. Yakamoto, but when I answered, it was Murray.

"Lizzie, the money your dad left here is gone."

"Gone? Was it stolen?"

"I'm afraid so. I went to get something out of the safe and it wasn't there no longer."

"Was there any sign of a break-in? Were other things missing?"

"No, nothing important. I don't know when it happened, could've been last night or maybe today while I was working. The safe was broken into and it's gone."

Chapter 43

Murray sounded so discouraged. "Did you have money in the safe too, Murray?"

"Just a little bit. Not enough to worry about. I'm just so Gul-durned mad that they got past me and took your dad's money."

I started the Jeep and my phone switched over to Bluetooth. "Maybe it was Rose. She's been in the area."

"She has?"

"Yes. She worked for Bill Yakamoto as his housekeeper for a couple weeks." I signaled and pulled onto Country Club, heading back into town.

"Really? Bill never said a word. He was here this morning."

I thought about the little Japanese man. He'd seemed embarrassed that he'd invited Rose to stay with him. Maybe that's why he didn't say anything. I knew the farmers in Parkdale liked to hang out and drink coffee with Murray in the early mornings before they went to work.

"Don't touch anything, Murray. I'll pick up an evidence kit and be up there soon."

"Okay Lizzie. I'm sure sorry."

"It's not your fault, Murray. I'll see you in a little while."

We said goodbye and I hung up. My phone rang again, and I started to answer, but Jenn's name came up on my screen and I hit decline. She immediately called again.

I so didn't want to deal with her, but I knew she'd keep bugging me until I took her call, so I hit the connect button.

"What's going on Liz? You aren't taking my calls now?"

"I've been busy, Jenn. You know that."

"Are you still maaad at me?" she asked in her whiney little girl voice that always made me gag, but worked with her husband, especially if she batted her fake eyelashes at him.

I sighed. "Listen Jenn, I think you went too far flirting with Mitch. You're supposed to be my friend. What's with giving my husband come-hither looks?"

"You know how I am, Liz. I didn't mean anything by it. Please, please, please, don't be mad."

Ugh. I wanted to throttle her. "Just stay away from Mitch, okay?"

She laughed. "If you'll still be my bestie."

"Look Jenn, I'm busy. I'm in the middle of an investigation and Rose is involved and I don't have time for this crap. I'll call you in a few days."

"Okay. You know I love you, Liz. Byeeee."

Yeah, right, I thought as I hit the off button on the Bluetooth. My teeth clenched so tight my jaw ached.

I drove into town to the sheriff's office to pick up an evidence kit. Garcia came out of the lunchroom and smiled when she saw me. "Hey Liz, are you back to work? I thought you were taking this week off."

I nodded. "I am, but I'm trying to find my sister and her disappearance is tied up with the murder of Priscilla Swanson."

"Be sure you keep track of your hours. I'm sure the sheriff will want to pay you." She winked at me. It was a joke around the office that I got all the best hours, wages, etc., because I was married to the sheriff, even though it wasn't true. Luckily, I got along great with most of my co-workers.

I hadn't even thought of keeping my hours. Since I was doing my own thing and Mitch wasn't telling me what to do each day, I didn't think I was eligible for pay. But you never knew. It might be a good idea to put my hours in.

"Did you have a chance to check on the Redemption Project?" I headed to the back where the evidence kits were kept and picked up a fingerprint kit.

Garcia followed me. "Yeah, I told Mitch that I didn't find out much about them. If they're selling locally, I didn't see any sign of it. So, I broadened my search and found an ad in an obscure magazine back east. It was a picture of some beautiful furniture and a phone number. I called the number, but it said it was no longer in service."

"A front for something else?"

Garcia scrunched her nose. "I wouldn't be surprised. I'll keep looking."

I thanked her, walked back outside to my Jeep, and took off for Parkdale. I wanted to know what the Redemption Project was. Were they laundering money through it? Was it a cover up for a more lucrative business...a less honest business? Just what was Swanson, Lydia, and that cult up to?

Murray gave me a hug when I walked in and showed me the open safe. "See, I didn't touch it."

I had to navigate around old boots, tools, boxes of air filters to get to the safe. The door hung open. Someone had pried it open and took the money, not even bothering to try closing it back up.

I dusted the safe and the wall around it leaving a black dust everywhere. I picked up several prints, but figured they were probably Murray's.

When I finished, I walked back into the main room. Murray wiped his hands on an old rag. He'd never been fingerprinted, so I took his to compare with the others I'd found.

"I've lived a long life and never been finger-printed," Murray said as he watched me put his fingertips into the ink and roll them onto an evidence card.

I smiled, knowing he'd enjoy telling all his cronies about being finger-printed. "You haven't heard anything from Rose?" I put the dust and brush, along with the samples I'd taken back in the kit.

"Nah, nothing." He took his dirty baseball cap off and scratched his head. "I keep thinkin' she might just drop in one day, but she hasn't."

"I doubt it was her who came in and took the money. She would've just asked you for it."

Murray agreed. "Probably someone from that cult. Money grubbing SOB'S." He took a roll of antacids out of his pocket and put one in his mouth. "Did you ever find out who that woman was shooting up the place the other day?"

"No, I'm sure she was a cult member, but we didn't find any evidence and they got away." I still wondered if it was Carolyn Butler, but I didn't know why she would've risked getting caught. I wished again that I'd seen the license plate of the dirt bike. "That was a brazen act."

Murray crunched his antacid. "Shore was." He patted his hip. "Ain't gonna let that happen again." He waved his arm at my concerned look. "Don't worry, Lizzie, I have a carry permit. Had it a long time, just didn't feel like I needed to carry my gun until those cult people started going crazy."

Now I'd have nightmares of Murray shooting at his shadow, but I didn't say that. Just told him to be careful and gave him a hug. "Let me know if you hear anything, okay? I know you've got a good idea what's going on in Parkdale, and Rose is around somewhere."

"'Course I will." He hugged me back and I walked to my Jeep.

Chapter 44 – Rose

One week earlier

Rose felt sick about her dad's murder, but she couldn't bring herself to go to his funeral. She couldn't face Liz and their friends and family. Not now. She had to find out what was going on at the Homestead and she knew her dad would forgive her, even if Liz didn't.

Mr. Yakamoto had shown Rose where he kept his wife's car in a shed behind the barn. "I never drive it," he'd told her, "But I keep it in good condition. If you need to use it and I'm not around, the keys are in the drawer under the left cupboard in the kitchen."

It was a small white Toyota Camry. It was pristine both inside and out. Rose knew he wouldn't mind if she took it to drive back to the homestead. She hadn't driven in ages and hoped she could still do it. It had taken hours to walk to Mr. Yakamoto's, so she found the keys, grabbed her bag, and went out to the shed.

Just as he'd said, the car started easily and Rose drove it out of the shed, stopped and shut the garage door, and headed towards the homestead, hoping for answers.

It didn't take long to get there by car. She wondered what would happen when she pulled in. Maybe she should park on one of the back roads and walk in so she wouldn't be stopped from talking to Mother Priscilla.

Deciding that was a good idea, Rose pulled into a logging road that wasn't used any longer and stopped the car. Grabbing her bag, she got out and locked the car. She didn't want anyone stealing it.

Everything was silent when Rose reached the compound. It was only mid-day, where was the family? she wondered. She kept as quiet as possible, skirting outbuildings and trucks, and crept over to the main hall.

A feeling of dread fell over her. What was going on? She didn't like the silence. Silence meant one of two things. Either someone had died, and the family was in mourning, or a family member was caught doing something against Father Jeremiah's wishes and had to punished.

Punishments, Rose knew, could be quite severe. She'd never understood how a peace-loving family could treat each other so bad. But she'd seen things. She'd turned a blind eye to beatings, family members being isolated in a tomb underground for three days at a time, and shunning's; no one was able to talk to them until they apologized. That was the best punishment. It only lasted a day and was for small transgressions.

Rose knew she'd be given a harsh punishment for running away if Mother Priscilla wasn't around to protect her. She went to the back door of the main building and peeked inside. No one was there. She opened the door as quietly as possible and tip-toed in, hoping to find Mother in her office or sitting room.

The door to Mother's office was locked, so Mother wasn't there. Rose frowned in disappointment, but she knew where the key was. Mother kept it in her sitting room. Maybe if she got into the office, she could find out where Mother was.

The sitting room was next door. When Rose reached out to turn the doorknob, it felt cold to the touch. She eased open the door and went in and took the office key out of the planter on Mother's coffee table. She didn't know who all knew it was there, but Mother had showed Rose that she'd hidden one underneath a succulent plant.

Being as careful as possible, she took the key and put the plant back where she'd found it. Then she went back to the office. She put the key in the lock and went in. She locked the door behind her in case someone came looking for Mother. The office smelled like Mother Priscilla's perfume and Rose felt tears gather in her eyes. Where was Mother? Had she come back only to be punished for leaving? Rose knew she had to find out why the family was in silent mode.

The office was neat and clean. There were plants on the windowsill and a large oak desk sat in the middle of the room. The room had been decorated by Mother Priscilla in creams and browns with rose colored accents. It was a comfy room. One that many of the women family members gravitated to when they had concerns or needed guidance.

The desk chair was pulled out and a rose-colored knitted throw lay across the back. Rose had watched many evenings as Mother knitted the throw. She touched it, running the silky yarn through her fingers. Then she sat in the chair and looked over the desktop.

She didn't know what she was looking for. She guessed some sign of Mother being there in the last few days. But there weren't any notations in the weekly planner she kept in the top drawer. The desk was clear except for a picture of Mother and Father Jeremiah taken at a fund-raising event the previous summer. Rose picked it up and looked closely at them. Did she see strain on Mother's face?

She set the picture back down and continued looking through the drawers, not finding anything. Then she remembered that Mother Priscilla kept an emergency bag in the back of her closet. She'd told Rose that she had it so she could leave quickly if Father wanted her to go somewhere with him on a minute's notice. Now, Rose wondered if she'd packed it in case she had to leave in a hurry.

The closet door was across from the desk and to the right of the outside door. Rose walked towards it, trying not to make any sounds. She didn't want Father walking in and finding her there.

She had reached out to open the closet when she heard someone walking down the hallway outside the office. She opened it wide enough to step in and hunkered down as far back against the wall as she could.

The door to Mother's office opened and two men walked in. Rose couldn't see them, but she could hear them whispering. It was Father and Brother Ezekiel. Rose held her breath.

"We have to find her," Father said. "She found out what we've been hauling in those trucks and threatened to turn us in. Why can't you find her?"

"We've looked everywhere. We checked with her family, but she wasn't there. We leaned on the brother a little, and he didn't cave. Maybe I should go back and lean on him a little harder," Ezekiel kept his voice to a whisper also.

"Yes, I think you should."

Rose could hear Father moving around the room. "I've been through her things several times. There's nothing here indicating where she might have gone. The only thing I can think of is if we find Rose, we may find Pris."

Rose swallowed a gasp, holding her hand over her mouth. Mother was missing. She hadn't come home like Rose thought. A sharp pain hit Rose's chest. She bit down on her tongue so she wouldn't make a noise and alert them to her presence.

She heard their footsteps as they moved towards the door and the sound of it opening.

"We've been keeping an eye on Rose's father's house, thinking she might show up there," Brother Ezekiel said, then the door closed, cutting off Father's answer.

Rose waited for several heartbeats before she opened the closet door. She stepped out, then turned around and searched the floor of the closet to see if Mother had taken her bag. It was gone and so was Mother Priscilla. Where was she?

Chapter 45- Rose

The only other place Rose could think to look for clues to Mother's disappearance was her house. Rose had never been inside the large structure that sat away from the other buildings on the property. The only people allowed in the house were the cleaning crew and maybe Brother Ezekiel since he and Father were so close.

As close as Rose was to Mother Priscilla, she'd never been invited to visit. No one was to talk about the house so there was a lot of curiosity among the family members. There were rumors that it was lavish like the main building, but they were only rumors and Rose didn't know if they were true or not.

The family members lived in nice houses, but they were plain. Not a lot of money was wasted on fixing them up and making them nicer. It was frowned upon to want nicer things than someone else, so most everything was the same. Rose had heard that Sister Lydia's house was furnished with expensive furniture and that it was bigger than the other houses, but she'd never been in there either.

She snuck out of Mother's office and walked down the hall to the door where she'd come in. The building was silent and felt empty. She assumed the family had gathered at the meeting place outside. Father liked to gather there when he talked to everyone if the weather permitted.

Rose wondered if she could get close enough to see what was going on. Once outside, she skirted the gathering area and hid behind an old oak tree that was close enough for her to hear what they were saying, but not so close that they would notice her.

It was so quiet. Rose was afraid she'd step on a stick, and they'd hear her. She peeked around the tree trunk and sucked in her breath. No one stirred, no one said a word. The family gathered on the logs around the staged area. Father Jeremiah and Brother Ezekiel were standing on the stage. Someone was tied to a stretcher. Rose hoped it wasn't Mother Priscilla. She couldn't see very well, but it looked like one of the younger women.

Rose backed away. She didn't want to see what punishment Father dished out. The punishments, even though Father explained they were necessary to keep the family pure, were hard to watch.

Being as quiet as possible, Rose headed for the house where Mother and Father lived. She hoped it wasn't locked. If it were, she didn't know how she would get inside.

Their house was in a grove of trees away from the main compound. Rose and been by it on her walks. It was beautiful, sitting up on the side of the hill with a view of snow-capped Mt. Hood.

Rose felt guilty for invading their private space, but she had to find out where Mother had gone. Even though a part of her wanted to come back to the family, another part knew that she couldn't.

When she finally made it up the hill to the house, she was breathing hard. She stopped to get her breath before she approached the house from where she stood in the trees. It was dark inside, and Rose hoped no one was around.

She went to the garage and tried the door. It opened easily. She walked into the three-car garage where a black Mercedes, a vintage Corvette and what looked like a dark blue Lamborghini were parked.

Rose also noticed a couple of motorcycles parked next to the Corvette. She was beginning to realize that although Father preached simplicity and not needing the finer things in life, he didn't practice what he preached.

She started for the door into the main house, wondering if it had an alarm. If she opened the door would Father and Brother Ezekiel come running? Her heart pounded and she began struggling to breathe. Then she heard a sound behind her and turned. It was a whimpering sound. Did they have puppies?

She walked towards the sound and realized there was a door to another room towards the back of the garage. She walked over and tried the doorknob. It was locked, but the lock was under the knob. With her heart beating so hard, she thought she'd faint; she unlocked the door.

What she saw inside made her burst into tears. The room was large and there were cribs down both sides. In the middle were rocking chairs with two young teenaged girls sitting in them. One of the girls held a baby who cried softly. She looked up when Rose opened the door and said, "Can you help us get out of here?"

Rose knew what was going on and she felt sick to her stomach. Father Jeremiah was kidnapping children and selling them. That was what Mother had tried to tell her. Inside the room were six babies in their cribs. She shook her head, not knowing what to do. How could she get all of them out of there without anyone knowing?

She thought fast. "Gather up what you need, and I'll take you somewhere safe." She glanced around the room. "We won't be able to carry all of the babies, so we'll have to take a couple to my car, then come back for the rest."

The girl nodded. "Thank you. I just want to go home."

"I know. Hurry, we might not have much time."

She and the other girl began to gather bottles and diapers. "There's no time. We'll get them what they need when we get to town," Rose told them. "Just bring the babies."

"We can carry them," the first girl said.

"We have to keep them quiet." Rose told her.

"They won't wake up. He's keeping them drugged."

Rose closed her eyes. When had Father become such a monster? This must've been why Mother left. She couldn't take it anymore. Rose opened her eyes and nodded. "Okay. we'll each carry two, but it's a long walk through the trees. Grab a blanket for each child."

The girls nodded and began picking up babies. Rose took two and herded the girls through the door. Then she turned and tried shutting it with her foot. It wasn't easy, but she managed. She left it unlocked, thinking it wouldn't matter.

They made their way to the door and Rose peeked outside. She didn't see anyone, so she opened it and they hurried out. Rose led them through the forest back to her car. Her arms were breaking by the time they got far enough from the Homestead that she felt she could breathe.

She led them up the road to where she'd parked. The car sat where she'd left it and Rose breathed a prayer of thankfulness. But when they got closer, Brother Ezekiel stepped out from behind the trees. In his hands he held a gun and a rope. "I'm surprised at you, Rose Sari. I didn't think you had it in you to disobey."

Chapter 46-Liz

Present day

I decided to run by and talk to Mr. Yakamoto again before I headed back to the office. Maybe he'd heard from Rose.

There was a tractor off to my right when I pulled into his place. I could tell from the thudding sounds coming from that direction that someone was cutting brush. I remembered my dad pruning the orchard, then going through with a brush cutter and beating up the brush, pulverizing it into mulch that stayed on the ground. My heart caught on the memory. There were so many.

Immediately, I felt guilty. I hadn't checked in with Travis about my dad's orchard in a few days. I needed to call him.

No one was home when I knocked on Mr. Yakamoto's door. I wondered if he was driving the tractor. I walked down to the barn and peeked in the large door. It was empty. Next, I tried the cabins, but I didn't have any luck there either. The place was a ghost town. Where were all of Mr. Yakamoto's workers?

I started through the orchard towards the tractor, wishing I'd worn different shoes. The white canvas tennis shoes I'd put on that morning weren't going to stay white very long walking through the orchard dirt. The brush cutter had left small sticks and dirt clumps and I did my best to avoid them.

When I finally made my way to the row next to the one the tractor came down, I stepped out from behind the trees and waved my arms.

Mr. Yakamoto jumped, but he stopped the tractor, and I walked over to talk to him. He shut the engine off and climbed down, taking off his work gloves.

"Can I help you?" He blinked a few times and nodded. Today he wore tan work pants, a flannel shirt, and a vest. He had an old fishing hat on his head.

"I'm Detective Ellisen," I said, reminding him who I was.

"Oh yes, Detective. What can I do? Have you heard from June?"

"No, I hoped you had."

He shook his head several times. "No, she hasn't come back." He grinned. "But I was out on my tractor today." He pointed behind him to the Kubota tractor and brush cutter, "and I was thinking." He hit his forehead with his forefinger a couple times. "I'm so dumb. So dumb. Why didn't I think of this before?" He looked at me like I might know the answer to his question.

"What did you think of? Was it something to do with my sister?"

"Yes, yes." He nodded and blinked. "June...or Rose...she left something in the kitchen by the telephone."

"What did she leave?"

He bounced back on the balls of his feet. "A notebook. She had phone numbers in it." He nodded. "I looked to see who it belonged to, and it said Rose. I remembered you said June's name is Rose?"

"Yes. What kind of numbers did she have in it?"

He blinked a couple of times. "Phone numbers, I think. And maybe bank numbers or safety deposit numbers. Something like that."

"May I see it?"

"Oh! Yes, yes, of course you can. Come to the house." He started in that direction. "I don't know why I didn't think of it sooner."

I followed him to his house, up the stairs onto the porch and inside to the kitchen. He went to a phone that sat by a microwave. On the counter next to it was a stack of papers and magazines a foot high. Mr. Yakamoto riffled through the stack.

"Now, what did I do with that?" He shook his head, then he smiled. "Oh, yes, yes, I remember. I took it in by my chair. I was going to call you first thing this morning." His face fell. "But I forgot."

"That's okay." I smiled at him and followed him into the living room.

He reached down and picked up a yellow spiral notebook and handed it to me. "I don't know if this will help, but I'm sure June...Rose would want you to have it."

I took it out of his hands and surprised myself by saying, "Thank you for letting Rose stay here. I'm sure it meant a lot to her for you to be so nice. It means a lot to me."

He patted my arm. "You are nice, Detective Ellisen. Just like your sister, and your dad." He nodded and blinked.

"So are you, Mr. Yakamoto. Thank you so much for this." I patted the notebook. "Please call me if you hear from my sister."

"Okay." He walked me to my Jeep, waved and went back to his tractor.

I couldn't wait until I got home, so I paged through the notebook as soon as I got in my Jeep. Mr. Yakamoto was right. There were a lot of phone numbers. There were also names with numbers next to them that could've been bank numbers. I didn't recognize any of the names.

I took out my phone and began calling the phone numbers one by one to see if anyone would answer. No one did. I tapped my thumb on the steering wheel. Think, Liz, I told myself. If Rose had taken the trouble to write the numbers down, they must've been important. It must have something to do with the cult.

I flipped through the notebook for anything else she might have jotted down. Towards the back was a page that had been torn out. But there was one word left at the top. Redemption. And there were three numbers written down after that. I compared them to the numbers on the list and sure enough, the last line which had five numbers, started with the same three numbers. So, I thought, the numbers must have something to do with the Redemption Project. Were these phone numbers for some of their clients?

There were about twenty phone numbers on the list and they each had a line of numbers next to them. Were they extensions? Or were they bank numbers like Mr. Yakamoto thought? I knew I could take them to the bank and ask them if they recognized any of them.

There was nothing to indicate dollar amounts, phone numbers, or anything, just numbers all in a line across the page. I shook my head. I started my Jeep and headed back to the office. Maybe Mitch or one of the deputies could help me figure this out.

My phone rang as I pulled out onto Hwy 35. I didn't recognize the caller, but I answered anyway. For some reason, maybe it was a premonition, I didn't give my name. I said, "yes?" instead.

A voice that sounded familiar said, "This is Judith Moore. May I ask who is calling?"

I thought fast. What could I say? I wanted to throw this person off. Maybe she'd reveal something if I surprised her. "I found this number on my husband's phone. Who are you and why are you calling him?"

There was silence. Then in an ice-cold voice, she said, "You need to talk to your husband. Please don't call this number again." She clicked off.

I stared at my screen. Where had I heard that voice before? Then it hit me. Sister Lydia.

Chapter 47

I dialed Mitch's cell phone, but it went straight to voicemail. I left a message for him to call me, then I called the office. When Deputy Williams picked up, I asked if Mitch was in.

"No," his voice sounded funny.

"Do you know where he is?"

"Um, no, not really."

"What does that mean?"

"Nothing. If I hear from him, I'll tell him you're looking for him."

"Okay." I thanked him and shut off my phone. Then I sat there for a minute with my stomach in turmoil. What was Mitch up to? Was he with Jenn?

I hit Jenn's name on my screen and drummed my fingers on the steering wheel while I waited for her to pick up. When she did, I heard her in the background, giggling. Then I heard her say, "Stop that," in a playful tone.

I hit the off button, turned on the car and headed to her house. I felt sick inside. Was Mitch at Jenn's house? Was I losing my husband to my best friend? My chest ached, my stomach tightened, and my eyes stung.

I ignored speed limits as I tore down Hwy 35 to the Odell Junction, turned and flew through Odell and onto Dee Hwy. I went around a car doing the twenty-five miles an hour speed limit and flew past it and another car.

It was a miracle that I made it to the turn off onto Markham Road. I knew I was driving like a crazy woman, and I took a deep breath and slowed the Jeep back to a reasonable speed. "You idiot," I whispered. "If you have a wreck and kill yourself it will be playing into their hands."

I drove more slowly down Markham and was almost to the turn off to Roirden Hill Road where Jenn lived when my phone rang. It was Mitch. I hit the button. "Where are you? Are you with Jenn?" My voice wavered and I gritted my teeth.

"No. I just walked into the office and Williams said you called. What's going on?"

"I've been trying to get you all day. I called Jenn and she picked up and it sounded like she had someone with her. The way she was giggling, I doubt it was Ray."

"So, you automatically thought it was me." He gave a deep sigh. His voice was full of anger. "I've been in a meeting with the mayor most of the day. You can call him if you want." He hung up.

I drove on to Jenn's house. I don't know what I thought I'd see, but I wasn't prepared for the car I saw sitting in her driveway. It was a black BMW and it belonged to Mayor Cliff Long.

Chapter 48

Relief flowed through me that it wasn't Mitch's car sitting in Jenn's driveway. But he'd said he was with the mayor, and he'd obviously lied to me. Where had he been and with whom?

I turned the Jeep around and headed towards the office to have it out with him. I hadn't gotten far when he called me. "Where are you?" he asked.

Something in his voice warned me that I wasn't going to like what he had to say. "I'm heading to the office. We need to talk."

His voice was quiet, even. "Turn around and go to your dad's house. Knight just called in a possible murder."

"What?" I jerked and the Jeep headed towards the ditch. I wrenched the steering wheel, bringing it back onto the road.

"That's all I know, Liz. Try not to get to upset until we figure out who it is." His voice had softened, and I knew it was a woman.

"It's Rose, isn't it?"

"I don't know, Liz. Please, honey, drive as carefully as you can. I'll meet you there."

"But it's a woman?"

He was quiet for a couple seconds. "Yes, it's a woman."

Travis knew Rose. If he'd found her, he would have called me first, wouldn't he?

I told Mitch that I'd meet him there and headed the Jeep towards Tucker Road and Odell Hwy and my dad's place. My body shook, my head so not in driving. I gripped the steering wheel and made myself pay attention to the road. Maybe it was someone else. Maybe it was one of the cult members. They seemed to be getting rid of themselves one at a time. But in my heart, I knew it was my sister. I knew it was Rose.

Travis came to greet me as I flew into Dad's driveway and slammed on the brakes. I jammed the Jeep in park, shut it off and climbed out, running towards him.

He caught me and held me close for a second. What I feared most was written all over his face. "Where is she? It's Rose, isn't it?"

"I'm so sorry, Liz." He shook his head, crushing me in his arms.

I pulled away and stared at him. "Where did you find her?"

Travis's face looked white and pinched. With one hand he motioned towards the orchard. "In the barn. Jose found her."

Tears spurted from my eyes and Travis held me. Mitch's car pulled in and I backed out of Travis's arms, turning to meet my husband.

He walked slowly towards us. "I'm sorry, Lizzie."

I nodded. I'd prepared myself for this minute for the last ten years. I knew that Rose's decision to join the cult would end badly. Dad did too. "Let's go." I turned and started for the barn. My heart ached. I felt like I'd let my sister and father down. I should have found her sooner.

"Liz," Travis said, reaching out to stop me. "Why don't you let me take Mitch down there. You stay here and wait for the ambulance."

"She's my sister, Travis." I kept walking.

Mitch kept step with me on one side and Travis on the other. "At least let me go in first, Liz."

I didn't answer, just trudged on to the barn.

Dad's barn was a big metal structure. He'd torn down the old wooden barn several years earlier because it was falling in. He put up the metal structure to house equipment. One side was a workshop and the other held small equipment like rakes, hoes, pruning shears, and every other kind of small equipment possible.

Travis pointed to the large opening on the north side of the barn. A tractor was parked next to the door. Several men had gathered. As we walked, pickups and an ambulance came screaming down the drive.

I grabbed Mitch's arm. "Please keep everyone out for a minute. Let me see my sister." I swallowed back tears as I hurried to the barn.

I didn't pay attention to what went on behind me. The barn door beckoned, and I stepped in. The first thing I saw was Jose sitting close to a woman's body. I hurried over and he looked up with sorrow in his eyes.

Jose shook his head. "I'm sorry, Leez."

"I know." I walked around him and leaned over Rose. I squatted down and took her pale hand in mine. Tears ran down my face.

Jose stood up, put his hand on my shoulder for a second and walked away.

Mitch came in and squatted down next to me. "I told Rodriguez to give us a few minutes."

There was no question that my sister was dead. Her eyes were open, staring at the ceiling, unblinking. Her mouth hung open. She had a scarf around her neck which covered the front of her blouse. I moved it and found a hole in her chest from a gun. It wasn't a big hole and the killer had carefully covered it with the scarf. Blood had seeped from the wound, but there wasn't a lot.

I nodded. "She looks so peaceful." I rubbed her hand with my fingers. We sat for several minutes while I held the hand of the sister I hadn't seen in years. Tears filled my eyes and rained down on top of her.

Chapter 49

My mind was numb as I sat on an old four-wheeler and watched the EMT's, Sheriff's deputies and ambulance crew do their job.

I'm so sorry, Dad. I couldn't protect her. Tears burnt the back of my throat.

What good was it for me to be an officer of the law when I couldn't keep my own family safe? I'd promised my dad that I'd find Rose, that I wouldn't let anything happen to her. And I'd let him down. What would he say if he knew? I was glad he didn't have to know what happened to her.

Mitch came over and sat beside me. "It looks like she was killed somewhere else and brought here." His voice was soft, and he sat with his hands between his knees, his eyes on the floor.

I nodded. "Just like the other two."

"Yeah." He put his hand on my shoulder and squeezed. "I'm going to double up efforts to find Corey Butler."

"Corey?" I glanced up at him. "I can see why he'd kill his mother and sister if he felt they didn't protect him when he was a child, but why Rose?"

Mitch rubbed the back of his neck. "I can't figure it out. Rose must've known that he killed the other two. Or maybe she knew he killed Priscilla, so he had to kill her too."

"There's something we're missing." All around me the EMT's and crime scene people were doing their jobs, but I didn't see them. My mind ran through what I knew about the Bread of Life cult.

After a few minutes, I stood up. "I may be wrong, but I don't think Corey's the killer. He loved Priscilla and he had no reason to kill Rose. We've got to keep digging."

Mitch stood and rubbed the back of his neck. "We'll check all possibilities, but I think he did it."

Connolly called his name, and he walked over to talk with her. Enrique came towards me.

"Are you okay?" he asked, putting his arm around me, and giving me a hug.

"I've been so afraid of this. Why would she take off from the cult and not come to me?"

He scuffed the toe of his boot against the floor. "Thinking the cult had her killed?"

"I'm sure of it."

"Have you thought about her past? Maybe someone she ran from when she joined the cult?"

I stared at him. I had been so convinced Rose was running from the cult. Could there have been someone else? "If it were someone from her past, why would they kill Priscilla and Carolyn too? And why wait until now? She's been in the cult for over ten years."

Enrique shrugged. "Who knows? From what I've heard, Rose joined the cult because of Priscilla. Could she have known her before Priscilla married Swanson? Maybe Priscilla talked her into joining because there was someone who was threatening Rose or..." He stopped and shrugged. "I don't know. It just seems like an avenue we should pursue and you're probably the best one to do that."

"Have you told Mitch your theory?"

"Not yet. It just hit me as we were looking around here. It seems like someone has gone to a lot of work to make us think the cult had these women killed. Maybe it's a setup."

We watched as the ambulance crew picked Rose up to move her. There was suddenly a lot of commotion around her body. I hurried over and grabbed Mitch's arm. "What is it? What's going on?"

He held a small notebook in his gloved hand. "This was tucked into her waistband." He opened it, looked down at it, then back at me. "It's her bank book. I think it's the one you found at your dad's house."

I took it from him and nodded. It was the one I'd found in Rose's things.

Mitch handed it to Connolly. "Call this bank and give them the account number. I want to know if the money's gone."

Connolly took the bank book and walked away, taking her phone out of her shirt pocket as she walked.

"It was tucked into her clothing?" I asked.

"Yes, the back of her skirt. Either she put it there or the killer did, trying to make it look like this is all about money."

I told him what Enrique had said. "Do you think it's a possibility that we're looking at this the wrong way? Maybe Enrique's right. Maybe it has nothing to do with the cult."

"I'd swear on my job as Sheriff that Swanson is behind this." He sighed. "But you're both right, we need to check out Rose's past, find out if there was anything going on before she joined the cult to make her want to join." He frowned. "If I remember right, it was a sudden decision, not something she had thought about for months."

I thought back. "Yeah, you're right. She worked at the hospital and the next thing we knew, she'd sold everything, gave it to Swanson and joined his cult." I grimaced and shook my head. "One thing that doesn't make sense, is why did she keep that money in the bank? She gave Swanson everything else, why not that too?"

The ambulance crew were getting ready to load Rose's body to take it to the morgue. They moved her onto a stretcher. A beam of sunshine from a window up high fell on her for just a moment before they moved her. I cried out before I could stop myself.

Mitch had his arms around me before I could put my hand over my mouth. "What, honey? What is it?"

The ambulance crew had stopped still at my cry. They stood holding Rose's body on the stretcher. I shook my head and tried to give them a smile, but my lips wouldn't move. I waved them on.

Mitch held me close to him. I buried my head in his chest. For a few minutes I couldn't breathe. I lifted my head long enough to see Rose carried out of the barn. Tears ran down my cheeks and I brushed them away.

"I'm okay," I said, pulling out of Mitch's arms.

"Are you sure?" He brushed the hair back from my face.

I nodded. "I'm sorry I fell apart like that."

He pulled me close and kissed my forehead. "This has been hard on you and I'm sorry."

I leaned into him for a few seconds. "I had a feeling I'd never see her alive again."

He took a deep breath. "So, did I."

Chapter 50

Mitch and I followed the ambulance to the hospital where the morgue was on the bottom floor. I felt it was the least I could do for my sister. My mind grappled with the fact that she was gone. My heart hurt knowing I'd let her down. Not only her, but my dad too.

Doctor King met us at the door and let us in. "I don't see any need for an autopsy unless you want one?" She waited with one eyebrow raised for our answer.

I shook my head. I knew what had caused Rose's death. "No. Well, maybe a quick look to see if you can find out what kind of bullet was used on her." My voice broke and I swallowed.

The doctor nodded.

I left the room. There was nothing more I could do for Rose there. I had to find her killer.

Mitch came out as I was getting into my Jeep. "Are you going to call Bella?"

"Yes, I guess I should. But I think I'll wait until later. She hasn't been around Rose in years, so I think I'll let her finish her classes today before I call."

He nodded. "Okay. Where are you off to next?" He came over and stood next to my Jeep.

The sun shone on the bonnet causing a glare. I shaded my eyes. "First, I'm going to talk to Ginny again. If Rose was trying to hide from someone when she joined the cult, Ginny would know."

Mitch nodded. "I'll keep looking for Corey Butler. At the least, we need to know if he's alive and if he knows anything."

I glanced up. "You think he's dead too?" I hadn't thought that Corey might've been killed.

"It's possible. If he's not our killer, he's closely tied to two of the victims." He glanced at his phone. "It's after four. I'll meet you at home in a couple hours unless I find Butler. If you get anything out of Ginny, call me."

I agreed and we parted. My Jeep was warm, and I turned on the air as I made my way back to the west side of the valley where Ginny lived. She'd probably think I was nuts coming back to see her the same day, but it couldn't be helped. I needed to let her know about Rose.

Ginny and Sam were sitting on her porch when I drove up. Ginny stood and came to meet me. "What happened?" she asked the minute I stepped out of the Jeep.

My eyes filled with tears and so did hers. "It's Rose, isn't it? She's gone, isn't she?"

I nodded. "I wanted to come tell you before it gets out."

She put her arms around me and held on tight. "Thank you. I'm so sorry." Then she started sobbing and I held her and let her cry for a couple minutes.

"Me, too." I wiped my eyes and stepped back.

"Do you know what happened?" Ginny asked. "Where did you find her?"

I told her everything I knew. "Ginny, I'm trying to follow every lead to figure this out."

She nodded and let go of me. "Of course. Come on over and sit down." She led me to the porch where she had two white wicker chairs with a small table between them.

Sam had gone in the house when I pulled up. He came back out with a tray of glasses and a pitcher of iced tea. He poured the tea and handed me a glass. I smiled and thanked him.

"You girls talk, I'll be inside if you need me."

"You don't have to leave," Ginny said to him, but he shook his head and took the tray into the house.

"He didn't know Rose. I wish they had met."

"Yeah." I took a drink of tea and sat the glass down on the table. "Do you know why Rose joined the cult? Was she trying to escape something?"

Ginny frowned. "Escape something? Like What?"

"I don't know, maybe a bad love affair? Or maybe she hated her job? I'm trying to remember why she joined. The only thing I remember her saying over and over was she wanted to live in peace where she could grow fruits and vegetables, but thinking back, Rose wasn't much of a gardener back then."

Ginny gave a soft chuckle. "No, but she always wanted to learn. She said it was something your mom did when she lived with you guys."

"Ah, that makes sense. Rose never got over our mother leaving us."

"No, she didn't. But I don't think that has anything to do with why she chose to join the cult." Her soft brown hair bounced as she picked up her tea and took a drink. She sat back in her chair and crossed her legs. "You know, it does seem like there was a guy back then, but I don't remember who he was." She set her glass down and put her fingers against her lips.

I let her think, not wanting to say something and make her forget what she was trying to remember.

"Yeah, his name was Dan." She sat forward, her eyes lighting up. "Rose told me she was in love with him. I'd forgotten all about him."

"Dan? Do you remember his last name?"

"Rivers? Yes, I think his name was Dan Rivers. He was a doctor at the hospital." She turned to me, and her brown eyes were wide with excitement. "But Liz, I remember now. She wasn't running away from Dan. She was running to him. Dan had joined the cult."

Chapter 51

I called Mitch to tell him what I'd learned as soon as I got back in my Jeep. "I wonder which of the men at the cult is Dan Rivers. He must still be there."

"I'm tied up this afternoon. Why don't you take Garcia or Connolly and give Swanson another visit? See if you can find Rivers."

"What are you doing?" I didn't mean to sound accusatory. Well, maybe I did.

"I'm working on some things." He sounded distracted. Normally, he would bristle if I accused him of bad conduct. Today he ignored me.

"Okay, I'll see you later."

"Which deputy do you want to go with you?"

"I'll call Enrique."

We disconnected and I fumed. What was Mitch up to? I knew he was busy trying to find Priscilla and Rose's killer. I needed to forget my suspicions about him and concentrate on finding my sister's killer. I knew there was something going on between him and Jenn, but it would have to wait until I found out who killed my father and sister.

I called Enrique and he said Mitch had already asked him to accompany me. I swung by the office to pick him up. He waited in his county issued SUV.

"Let's take this. Makes us seem more official," he said, leaning out the driver's window to talk to me.

I grabbed my gun out of the safe in my Jeep and joined him in his vehicle. "Thanks for going with me."

Enrique grinned. "No problem. I've been dying to visit that cult. You and Mitch have kept all the fun to yourselves."

I laughed. "What have you been working on?"

He drove out of the parking lot and over the Hood River bridge to Hwy 35. Then he headed south. "We've been trying to find Priscilla's killer. I'm confident it's someone in that cult."

"Me too. I've been trying to figure out why they'd kill her. The only thing I can come up with is they're either using that Redemption Project to launder money, or God forbid, traffic children."

"What makes you think they're trafficking children?" Enrique asked.

"Gut feeling. I was there a few days ago and there was a little girl begging for her mom. It about broke my heart. They swore her mom was around and that they took the little girl to her, but she didn't want anything to do with the woman who took her away from Dorcas, her teacher."

Enrique shook his head. "Man, I hope it's not that. I can't take it when children are involved. Tell me what you know about the Redemption Project."

I sat back against the seat and thought about it. "Not a lot. Sister Lydia, who is Swanson's right-hand woman, handles the project. She told me they make high end furniture there and sell it all over the country. But Garcia did a search and couldn't find any mention of their company anywhere except an obscure magazine from one of the eastern states."

"Hmm, curiouser and curiouser. Makes you ask yourself what they're really doing." He turned his blinker on and changed lanes, going around a slow-moving truck.

The day had clouded up and more rain was in the forecast. I hoped it held off for a while. "Wait until you see their main building. It's gorgeous. They do make beautiful furniture, but if they're selling it, they must be hiding it somehow."

He nodded. "Could be doing some under the table business so they don't have to pay taxes."

"That's a possibility."

By the time we drove into the compound, large drops of rain were beginning to fall. The place looked abandoned again and I assumed everyone had gone inside because of the threat of rain.

"Did Mitch tell you what all has been going on here?"

Enrique shook his head. "You know how closed lip Mitch can be. He has a lot on his mind right now with these murders. And the Sheriff of Klickitat is leaning on him hard to help her solve Carolyn Butler's murder. She thinks Carolyn was killed in Oregon and transported to Washington."

"What makes her think that?"

"I think she's so over-whelmed, she doesn't know what to think. She's only been in office for a couple of months and the first thing she gets is a murder in her jurisdiction."

"She signed on for the job." I didn't have a lot of sympathy for her.

"Yeah, I'm sure she'll be fine. She has a lot on her plate right now." He pulled his sheriff's SUV into the paved lot in front of the main building and whistled softly. "Wow. This place is gorgeous."

"Just wait until you get inside."

We got out and climbed the stairs to the main door. Enrique's head was on a swivel, taking in everything.

I knocked and Swanson came to the door. "Deputies." He nodded at us, sighed, and moved back to let us in. "What can I do for you today?"

I didn't correct him by mentioning that I was a detective. "We need to talk. May we come in?"

"Of course." He held the door. Enrique and I entered the large room.

Swanson led us over to the same sofas in front of the fireplace that Mitch and I had sat on. "Please, sit down."

I introduced Enrique and the two men shook hands. We sat down. Enrique and I on a sofa and Swanson in his chair.

"I have come to tell you that we found Rose's body this morning."

Swanson closed his eyes. When he opened them, tears had formed in the corners. "She was killed."

It wasn't a question, more a statement of fact. "Yes."

"I'm sorry for your loss," he said, quietly.

"Thank you." We were silent for a couple of minutes. Then I said, "Mr. Swanson, we need to speak to Dan Rivers."

He stared at me, then nodded. He got up and went to a door just off the main room and opened it, speaking to whomever was in the room. Then he walked back to us. His gait was that of an old man. He sat down again and rested his elbows on his knees.

"Someone is trying to shut us down," he said.

"What makes you say that?" Enrique asked.

Swanson had a fierceness in his eyes that startled me. "They are killing members of my family and making it look like we are killing our own."

"Do you know who would do that to you?" Enrique asked.

"Of course not. If I knew, I'd take care of it." He shook his head.

The door opened and a man came in and stood in front of us. Swanson nodded at him. Then he moved his gaze back at me. "This is Brother Ezekiel. In his past life he was known as Doctor Daniel Rivers."

He was the man who had shown up at my dad's house to warn me off. Enrique shook his hand, and I gave him a hard look.

"Mr. Rivers, my sister, Rose, has been murdered. We found her body this morning."

Brother Ezekiel, or Dan Rivers, whichever you wanted to call him, stared at me. "I'm sorry to hear that." His voice was soft and soothing. I remembered wondering if he and Swanson were brothers because they were both tall, with dark hair and dark eyes. Both good looking men.

"Thank you." I glanced at Enrique. I wasn't sure how to continue but decided to go with the truth. "I've been told that you and Rose were once involved."

"Everyone here is involved, Detective," Dan said, in his deep, soft voice. "We are family."

I stared at him, trying to find emotion, sorrow that my sister was dead. All I saw was the same thing that I'd seen on Swanson's face. Yes, he was sorry, but it wasn't the kind of sorrow a man had for a woman he loved.

"So, you never had a special relationship With Rose?"

"We don't encourage our family to have special relationships, Detective Ellisen," Swanson said. "We are all special here."

My stomach curled, wondering what exactly he meant by that and afraid I knew. I stared him down, then turned back to Dan Rivers. "And before you came here? You and Rose worked together at the hospital, right? Were you the reason Rose joined the cult?"

Rivers wasn't giving an inch. "I believe Rose joined because she and Mother Priscilla became friends and Priscilla encouraged her to come be a part of our family. I had nothing to do with her joining the family, Detective Ellisen."

"Do you know who would want Rose dead?" Enrique asked, jumping into the conversation.

Rivers shook his head. "This is incredulous. Someone is targeting members of our family for no reason. We are peaceful people. We mind our own business. We live simply and beautifully. Look around you, we have a small slice of heaven here."

Enrique and I both nodded, but I couldn't help but think it wasn't heavenly for Priscilla or Rose. "Mr. Rivers, are you saying you and Rose were not involved before you joined the...family?" I almost said the cult and stopped myself just in time.

He inclined his head. "That is what I'm telling you. Rose was like a sister to me, and I'll miss her very much, but we did not have a romance."

I didn't believe him. He was doing his best to pretend it was true, but I didn't buy it. Ginny had said Rose was in love with him. Maybe they were having an affair and he didn't want Swanson to know about it.

Swanson stood and the rest of us followed. "We would like to have Rose buried here on the grounds, Detective. We will have a service for her as soon as you can release her body."

I stared at him. "Rose was my sister, Mr. Swanson. I would like her buried next to our father."

"She may have been your earthly sister, but she was our eternal sister. She would have wanted to be buried here."

Over my dead body, I thought. "We'd like to tour your furniture making buildings while we're here." If he was going to push me, I would push back. "Also, we'd like to talk to Lydia."

Swanson blinked and his eyes widened. "Whatever for?"

"I'd like to know more about your furniture business, and I understand that Lydia is the director of the sales?"

Swanson glanced at Ezekiel.

Ezekiel said, "If you'll excuse me, I have some work to do." He walked towards the back door.

"Brother Ezekiel, please ask Sister Lydia to join us."

Ezekiel or Dan nodded as he went out the door.

All of these, brother this and sister that was giving me a headache. Or maybe it was just being in Swanson's presence and getting the run around that was doing it.

We stood in the main room waiting for Lydia. It wasn't long before she joined us. Enrique took in the room, no expression on his face. I knew him well enough to know what he was thinking. Swanson had quite a racket going on here.

Swanson sat down and put his head in his hands. A delayed reaction to Rose's death? I wondered.

"Yes, Father? Brother Ezekiel asked me to join you." Lydia said after she glided into the room.

Swanson glanced up. He stood and put his hand on her shoulder. "First, it is as we were afraid, Sister Rose Sarai is dead. She was killed just like our beautiful Priscilla."

Lydia stared at him. She didn't show any emotion.

Swanson frowned. "The officers would like to see the production buildings."

"Why?" She kept her eyes on him, avoiding looking at us.

"We're having trouble finding your sales outlets. We'd like to see for ourselves what you build in those buildings." I was tired of playing nice. I wanted answers and I wanted them now.

Chapter 52

Lydia led the way outside, around the main building to the workshop. She didn't speak until we were inside. "As you can see, we are working on several projects at a time. The client likes everything hand made."

"Who is your carpenter?" Enrique asked, running his hand over a chair that was on a table waiting to be sanded. "He does good work."

"She," Lydia said. "Sister Eve is the main carpenter. There are others who help out, but she's a true artist."

There weren't many pieces lying around, but the ones I saw were beautiful. "She sure is. How many people does she have helping her? Why aren't they working today?"

Lydia chewed on her lower lip. It was the first time I'd seen any chink in her armor. "We just finished a big order, so they've taken the day off. I think Sister Eve went to buy supplies. The others are around." She waved her hand like they all were hiding in the woodwork.

Enrique wandered over to a chair that had been built like a throne. "Who is this for?" he asked.

Lydia gave it a brief glance. "Father Jeremiah. His birthday is coming soon, and we wanted to make him something special. That chair is made from mahogany." She walked over and slid her hand down the smooth back of the chair. "One of our sisters is a jeweler. She's going to inlay jewels along the top and the arms."

Enrique whistled. "What kind of jewels?"

"Probably turquoise. Blue is Father's favorite color, and this is an important birthday."

Enrique touched the sliver that had been crafted into the chair. "Fit for a King."

Lydia stared at him. "We can never do enough to repay all that Father Jeremiah has done for us."

As we walked out of the building the rain clouds let loose with a downpour. Lydia ran for the main house and Enrique, and I ran to his SUV. We were soaked by the time we got there and climbed in.

"I didn't think it was supposed to rain this hard," he said, starting the vehicle and turning on the heat.

"Maybe not at home, but this is close to the mountain." I tried to rub the water from my face.

"There are napkins in the glove box. Sorry I don't have a towel."

"That's okay." I opened the glove box and took the napkins out, handing him some. "At least you have a lot of these."

Enrique wiped his face and hands and brushed at his uniform. "So, what did you think of all that?"

I shook my head. "If Rose was in love with Doctor Dan, it was unrequited. The man didn't seem at all upset that she'd been killed."

"Ten years is a long time. Maybe he fell for someone else, or their relationship changed once they moved in with the cult."

I laid the soggy napkins on the floor. "I still don't think all those trucks I saw last time I was here were for hauling furniture. There were too many of them and it sounds like they only make a few pieces of furniture at a time."

"Yup."

Lights came at us from a vehicle coming in the driveway. "Is that one of their trucks?" I craned my neck to see better.

Enrique turned his head towards the drive as a big white panel truck drove past us. "Looks like it."

I pointed to the truck. "Enrique! That's Corey driving."

Enrique put the SUV in gear and followed the truck around the shop buildings. It was going faster than it should and he pushed down on the accelerator. The truck pulled into a large garage through a door which opened and closed as soon as the truck drove in.

"Let's go," I said, opening my door. "We need to talk to him."

We climbed out of the car into the pouring rain and ran to the building. There was a door on the side. I tried to open it, but it was locked. I banged on it instead. Enrique banged on the large garage door and shouted. Rain poured down our backs.

Thunder sounded not far from us, and lightening lit up the sky. I pushed wet hair out of my eyes and pounded the door with my fists, calling Corey's name.

Enrique disappeared into the rain, and I continued to bang on the door.

Soon, he came back, waving for me to follow him. "There's a door on the other side that's unlocked."

We ran around the building and into the dark room. We could just make out the truck in the gloom. "I wish I had my flashlight. Feel around and see if you can find a light switch," Enrique said. He went right and I went left, feeling along the wall.

As far as I could tell, there were no light switches. I started to call out to Enrique, but I heard thumps and grunts coming from in front of the truck. Then a male voice cried out and I took off running towards the sound.

Chapter 53

I hurried through the building towards the sounds of fighting. I couldn't see anything except shadows. Up ahead there were two people scrabbling on the ground. I headed in their direction and tripped on something on the floor, sprawling out on my face.

A scream escaped before I could stop it. I heard a loud "Ummph," and looked up in time to see someone run towards the front of the building and another figure hurry towards me.

"Liz, are you okay?" It was Enrique and he was breathing hard. He bent down and helped me sit up.

"I tripped on something." I pointed to the spot where I'd seen the other guy disappear. "Was that Corey?"

"I don't know. I came around the truck and he tackled me. I almost had him, but when I heard you scream, I let go and he took off."

"Sorry." I rubbed my leg which had hit something causing me to fall.

"Don't worry. We'll catch him." He helped me up and we headed in the direction the other guy went. I limped and Enrique put his arm around me to help.

The building was huge with lots of rooms. The smell of wood and the acid fumes of furniture stain were overwhelming in some of the rooms. I had been so sure that the furniture business was a front for child trafficking. Had I been wrong?

Enrique and I went through the building, but we didn't find Enrique's attacker. We ended up back where we'd started. "What do you want to do? We can go back and talk to Swanson again. Try and find out who was driving that truck."

I nodded. "Yeah, maybe I was wrong. I only caught a glimpse of the driver, but he sure looked like Corey Butler. And he stared straight at me as he went by."

We left the building and ran through the rain towards the main building. My leg was hurting by the time we got to the front door. Enrique banged on the door, and it was opened by a young woman I'd never seen before.

"Hood River County Sheriff's Department. We need to speak to Mr. Swanson." Enrique held up his badge.

She nodded and shut the door in our faces, leaving us standing in the rain.

Soon, the same woman opened the door and ushered us in. Swanson came to greet us.

"Sister Saphira, please get some towels for our guests." He stood in the entryway, not letting us past him. "I thought you left."

"We saw one of your trucks pulling in and the driver looked like Corey Butler."

He shook his head. "I told you that Corey left, and we don't know where he is. Instead of going through my buildings and fighting with my family members, maybe you should look for him."

Wow, I thought, he already knew about the fight. The cult grapevine must be fast.

The young woman came back carrying fluffy white towels like the ones they'd given me the first time I was there. Enrique and I wiped our faces, hands and tried to wipe the worst of the water off our clothes.

"Why did your family member fight with me?" Enrique asked while toweling off his dark hair. The rain caused it to shine, and tiny drops glittered in the light.

"He didn't know you were from the sheriff's office. He thought you were an intruder."

"Word travels fast around here," Enrique said, raising his eyebrows at me.

"We'd like to speak to your driver," I told Swanson.

He sighed and turned to Sister Saphira. "Please bring Brother Mark in to talk to the deputies."

She left again, and we stood in the entry waiting. Soon a young man came in. He wasn't Corey Butler.

"Yes, Father? You wanted to see me?" His voice was hesitant. He looked at Enrique.

So did Swanson. "Is this the man you fought?"

"Yes, sir." He turned to Enrique. "I'm sorry I attacked you. I thought you were an intruder. It was dark in there and I went to turn on the lights and you came out of nowhere."

Enrique nodded. The young man had a bruise forming on his chin. "We're trying to find Corey Butler. Have you seen him recently?"

The young man glanced at Swanson.

"Brother Luke," Swanson and I said at the same time.

"Oh, no, I haven't seen him in days. He comes and goes a lot."

"Just as I have told you," Swanson said to us.

"If you hear from him or if he returns, please let the sheriff's office know," Enrique said.

They agreed and we handed Sister Saphira our towels and let ourselves back out into the rain.

"Was that him?" I asked when we were settled in Enrique's car with the heater and windshield wipers going full blast.

Enrique pulled onto the driveway. "I don't know. It could've been, he had a bruise, but I don't think so. The guy I fought with was bigger, more muscular. Did this guy look like Corey?"

"No, but I only caught a glimpse of the truck driver. Corey is bigger and has light brown hair and Brother Mark's is black. But he had a cap on so I couldn't really see."

Rain splashed against the windshield and Enrique squinted, trying to see. His headlights had come on automatically and the cars coming towards us had theirs on too. We came upon a car driving slow without lights and Enrique flashed his Bright's to let the driver know to turn his on.

We had just reached the Parkdale junction when my phone rang. It was Mitch and I hit the green talk button. "Yeah?"

"Where are you guys?" There was an urgency in his voice, and I glanced up at Enrique.

"We just left the compound. What's up?"

"Get over to White Salmon as fast as you can. Sheriff Walls just picked up Corey Butler. She's charging him with Carolyn's murder."

Chapter 54

"We're on our way. Are you headed there?" I raised my voice because the rain pounded so hard on the car it was hard to hear.

"Yes, I'm about to hit the Hood River bridge. I just got her call as I pulled into the office."

"You want Enrique to come too? Or do you want me to go back to the office to get my rig?"

"He can come. You might want to hurry so you can hear the interview. She wasn't in the mood to wait for us."

"Okay." I said goodbye and shut off my phone.

"So, Corey showed up."

"I guess the guy you fought with wasn't him."

"Apparently not." Enrique flew down Hwy 35 despite the rain. "This should be interesting."

I gripped the door handle. I knew Enrique was a good driver, but he was going too fast for the torrents of rain coming down. "You might want to slow down. I'd like to get there in one piece."

He flashed me a grin. "Don't worry, I can drive in worse weather than this."

I hoped that he was right and held on. The bridge slowed him down, but he picked up speed once we'd crossed.

We got there in fifteen minutes. Mitch was not far ahead of us. He frowned when he saw us walk in. "Did you two fly here?"

"Just about," I said. We'd been shown into an interrogation room. Sheriff Jeanne Walls hadn't made an appearance yet, and neither had Corey Butler.

It wasn't long, though, and Corey was led in by a deputy whose name tag read, John Wright. He nodded to us and helped Corey sit at the table.

Corey's hair was long and greasy, he hadn't shaved in days, and his skin was gray. His clothes were wrinkled and damp in places. From the odor coming off him, I didn't think he'd bathed or changed clothes in days, maybe weeks. I wrinkled my nose.

Corey sat with his head bowed, not making eye contact with any of us. Soon Sheriff Walls came in. She was a small dark-haired woman. She wore her hair short and had a no-nonsense attitude.

"Thank you for coming," she said to Mitch. She gave Enrique and I a quick glance then told Corey she was going to record the interview.

Corey shrugged and she asked him to speak into the recorder, which he did.

She asked him his name and where he lived. He stumbled over his address and finally told her he lived part time with his sister, Priscilla Swanson and part time with his mom, Carolyn Butler.

"Mr. Butler, do you understand that both your mother and your sister are deceased?" Sheriff Walls asked him.

Corey shook his head. "No. That can't be right." He looked confused. "What do you mean? My mom and sister?"

"Yes, sir. We need to know where you were on April 13th."

He seemed confused by her question. "Where I was?"

"Yes, sir."

He frowned.

"When did you last see your mom?"

"I don't remember."

Sheriff Walls glanced at Mitch. He said, "Mr. Butler, do you remember when you last saw your sister, Priscilla?"

He frowned at Mitch. "Pris? I don't know about a week ago maybe."

"At the compound?"

He nodded. Then he shook his head. "They killed her," he said, so quietly I had to lean forward.

"Who?" Mitch asked.

Tears ran down Corey's face and dropped onto his hands. "Swanson. Or Brother Ezekial. He does most of the dirty work."

"And your mother?" Sheriff Walls asked.

Corey didn't respond. His lips moved, but nothing came out. He shook all over.

"Mr. Butler, what happened to your mother?"

He shook his head. "She wasn't my mother. Priscilla was."

Sheriff Walls stepped back. "Carolyn Butler wasn't your mother?"

Corey shook his head.

"Did you kill Carolyn Butler?"

Corey sat with his head down, not saying anything. When Sheriff Walls asked him again, he said, "No, Father had it done." He burst into tears. "I tried to save her!"

"Jeremiah Swanson had her killed?"

He nodded.

"Why would he kill Carolyn?"

Corey kept his head down, sobs tearing through his throat, his chest heaving. Sheriff Walls and I looked at each other. Then she asked again. "Mr. Butler, why would Jeremiah Swanson kill his wife?"

He lifted his head and said, "she knew too much." Then he looked me straight in the eye and said, "you'd better be careful, or you'll be next."

Chapter 55

My heart pounded. "Me?"

He nodded. "You're Rose's sister, right?"

"Yes. You heard about Rose?"

He nodded. "Yes, Rose was my friend. She knew too much."

"What did they know, Mr. Butler?" Mitch asked.

Corey kept his gaze on me. "I think Rose knew."

"Knew what?" I asked.

"About the children." He gave a tired sigh and tears ran down his face. "I tried so hard to save them."

This was it. I knew what he was going to say. "They are trafficking children?" I asked, softly.

His eyes were filled with pain. "His own children. Others in the group's children, children he took from their families, just like he took me when I was a child."

"What happened to you, Corey?" I asked, my voice gentle.

He shook his head, and I heard him whisper, "he's a monster."

"Tell me what happened, Corey. Help us understand what's going on at that cult."

He broke eye contact and looked at Sheriff Walls. "I'd like to call my brother."

"Your brother?" she asked.

He gathered his strength around him and sat up. I watched as he closed his eyes for a minute, took a deep breath, and said, "he's an attorney in Portland."

As soon as Corey Butler was taken from the room, Enrique and I left the sheriff's office and hurried to his car.

Mitch came out behind us and called my name. "Where are you going?"

I looked at him over the hood of the cruiser. "We need to arrest Swanson."

Mitch seemed distracted, but he nodded. "You ride with Enrique. I need to make some calls."

Enrique raised his eyebrows and I stared at Mitch. Then I got in Enrique's car. He didn't say anything as we headed for the cult. Neither did I. Mitch was up to something and my stomach hurt. My wife radar was going off, but I didn't want to say anything to Enrique.

Twenty minutes later we turned into the compound. My phone tinged with a text. I took it out of my pocket and glanced down at it. It was Jenn.

We need to talk. Come see me asap.

My heart dove into my stomach. What did she want? I texted back.

Not now. Busy.

You'll want to hear what I have to say.

I gritted my teeth. Everything was always about Jenn. I shook my head and put my phone back in my pocket.

It buzzed again, but I ignored it. I turned around to look for Mitch's cruiser, but it wasn't behind us.

"What happened to Mitch?" I asked Enrique.

He shrugged. "I'll call him."

He started to talk on his mic, but his phone lit up. It was Mitch.

"Hey Boss, what happened to you?"

"I've got something I have to take care of. You guys go ahead and make the arrest. I'll meet you at the station."

Enrique and I stared at each other. What could be more important than arresting Jeremiah Swanson for murder and child trafficking? My stomach hurt, but I didn't have time to worry about it.

I took out my phone. "I'm going to call Garcia and see if she's found out anything about Swanson's project."

Enrique nodded and I called the other deputy.

"I was just going to call you. I couldn't find much about the Redemption Project on the web, so I did a search of the dark web and bingo. They are on every child trafficking site I found. It's disgusting and horrifying, Liz. Pictures of little kids naked and in suggestive poses. Made me want to vomit." She was quiet for a few seconds, then she asked, "What do you want me to do with this?"

I knew the dark web was an important hub of criminal activity where you could find just about anything you wanted to buy, even children.

Enrique turned green. "Keep the information. We'll need it when we arrest this monster."

"You got it. I hate this stuff. Give me a good robbery any day."

I thanked her and clicked off. Then I looked at Enrique. "Let's go get Swanson."

Enrique nodded, his face a mask of disgust, his eyes glittering. "This guy better not give us any trouble, or I don't know what I'll do, Liz. I hate guys like this who use children for money. They are the worst kind of scum."

"Yes, they are. We're going to get him, Enrique. We've got enough to take the monster down."

To our surprise, on the drive into the compound we encountered three large trucks coming out. "They're taking the children out of here," I said.

The driver of the first truck honked his horn and waved his arms when Enrique turned crosswise in the road. He called for backup. "What are we going to do now? If they have guns, we can't take them all on."

"We don't have much choice." I grabbed my gun and opened my door. "Get on the speaker and tell them who we are and that we want to search their trucks."

Enrique did as I said.

The door of the first truck opened and the guy on the passenger side got out. He came towards us with an assault rifle in his hands.

"Hood River County Sheriff. Stand down!" I screamed pointing my gun at him.

He put up his hands. "We don't want any trouble. We just want to pass."

"I said stand down. Put your riffle down and your hands on your head."

The man turned to me, and I could see indecision in his eyes. Then he turned and nodded at the truck driver and stepped out of the way. The driver gunned the engine and came towards us, picking up speed as he came. I jumped out of the way, hoping Enrique had too.

I fired my gun at the truck, but it kept coming, pushing the cruiser out of the way with ease. I watched as the passenger hopped back in and the other trucks followed.

"Enrique!" I screamed his name and headed for the cruiser.

He met me and we could see that the car had been crushed all down the driver's side. I ran around and tried to get in on the passenger side. A blast hit the ground next to me and Enrique yelled, "get down."

I flattened myself against the ground and heard another shot ring out. It hit the car and I rolled away from it towards the trees, covering my head with my hands. Rain pelted me. A couple more shots and the car blew.

Chapter 56

Enrique called it in, then we took off for the compound, running down the rain-slick road. My feet kept slipping, but I kept running. I thought maybe there were other trucks loading up. I had no idea how many they had.

When we got to the end of the road, my breath came in short gasps. I looked around and didn't see anyone. We headed for the main building.

The front door was locked and even though I pounded on it, no one came. "Let's go look around the factory," I told Enrique.

He nodded. "It's sure quiet."

He was right. Where was everyone? We walked down the hill towards the building where they made the furniture. We didn't encounter anyone.

When we got to the huge building, the over-sized garage doors were open, and it was empty.

"Almost as though they knew we were coming," Enrique said.

I nodded. "Let's keep looking. Maybe some of them are hunkered down in their homes."

We went from house to house, barn to barn, but didn't see anyone. We let ourselves into the main building. It was like they had left so fast they didn't have time to prepare. In the kitchen, there was food preparations on the counters.

"Look at this. They left in a hurry."

Enrique nodded. "Something spooked them."

"Let's go see if we can get into Swanson's office. Maybe he's hiding in there."

We climbed the stairs to the offices, leaving a wet trail on the beautiful wood floor. His was in the back of the building. When we tried his door, we found it locked. We backtracked to the other offices and rooms and every door was unlocked.

"Interesting," Enrique said. "They took the time to lock Swanson's office, but no one elses. Makes you wonder what he's hiding in there."

"Let's look in Lydia's office. She seems like the brain around here."

We walked into the office next to Swanson's. There was a cup of cold coffee on her desk, but everything else was put away. We tried opening file drawers, but they were locked.

"We'll have to come back with a search warrant to get into her files," Enrique said, picking up books off her shelves and flipping through them. Most were accounting books from college courses. "Looks like she was an accountant."

I nodded. "She did the books for the cult. She tried to sell their furniture and didn't get involved in the other things going on as far as I could tell. When Mitch and I were here and they were having a big recruiting party, Lydia was in here working."

We searched for a key to her file cabinet but couldn't find one. Then we searched the other offices. One office belonged to security and the other belonged to Priscilla Swanson.

"Maybe we'll find a key to Swanson's office in here," I said, walking into a room set up with a bank of computers against one wall. There were cameras that showed different areas of the compound, but we didn't find a key.

"This is how he kept an eye on what was going on in his compound," Enrique said, fiddling with one of the computers and bringing up different areas.

I shook my head, feeling sick. "Talk about a manipulator."

"Talk about a sleaze ball," Enrique whispered. He'd pushed a button and brought up the inside of the houses. "He watched them when they were in their own homes."

"We shouldn't be surprised. He had to keep a tight rein on them for this to work."

"Makes you want to throw up."

We continued searching and found a cabinet with several keys, but none of them were for the offices. They were labeled house #1 through #10, storage shed, main building, but none of them were labeled offices.

"Do you think we could break in?" I asked.

"We'd better wait for Mitch. Hopefully he went after a search warrant."

I hoped that was what he was doing. I didn't want to wait, I wanted into that office. I thought for a minute. "Let's go see if there's an entry from either Lydia's office into Swanson's or maybe his wife's office.

"Go ahead, I'm going to keep looking at these cameras. Maybe I can find footage of what went on right before they left."

"Good idea." I left him and walked back into Priscilla's office. If he had a door into her office, they might've left it unlocked. I moved around the room searching for a hidden door or a crawl space. Nothing. I gave up and went into Lydia's office. In her closet I found what I was looking for. A small door at the back of her closet led into a bedroom, which led into Swanson's office.

I opened his door into the hallway and called for Enrique. "I found a way in!"

He hurried to me from the security room. "How'd you do that?"

We walked into Swanson's office together. "Seems that instead of having a door between his wife's office and his, he had one leading into Lydia's office."

"Hmm, a little hanky-panky going on?"

I nodded. "I think there was a lot of hanky-panky going on. Isn't that the big reason these guys start cults? They want to have sex with multiple partners."

"So, they say God told them it's all right and somehow convince all these people that they have a direct revelation from God." Enrique walked into Swanson's office and whistled. "Wow! Doesn't look like Father Swanson spared himself the luxuries, does it?"

"Nope. It must've been awful for him to see it unraveling around him."

"Poor guy." Enrique grinned. "Quite a difference from the homes he gives his children."

"Yeah, I really feel sorry for him." I rolled my eyes. "I so want to be the one to arrest him."

We systematically went through the rooms. We'd always worked well together. Swanson had files on plans for expansions that were interesting, but not what we were looking for.

"He must've had a back-up plan," Enrique said after we'd gone through every file. "An idea of what to do if they had to abandon the compound."

"Maybe he kept it in his head."

"Or maybe Brother Ezekiel has it in his office."

Enrique glanced over at me in surprise. "Does he have another office? I figured he was head of security."

"I don't know. Let's look around and if we don't find anything, we'll go through the other offices. This is a huge building. I'm sure there are more offices up here."

We spent the next half hour going through Swanson's office and although we found a lot of things to make us raise our eyebrows, we didn't find anything to tell us where the family had gone.

We went through the rest of the rooms on the upper floor and didn't find anything except lives disrupted. Downstairs, the kitchen was left with dinner preparations on the counters. The large meeting room had chairs in disarray, something I hadn't seen the few times I'd been there.

When we'd finished, I heard sirens and vehicles driving into the compound. "It sounds like the calvary is coming."

Enrique nodded. "I'm afraid they're too late."

Several sheriff's vehicles pulled in. Mitch was the last one. I went to greet him.

He stepped out of the car. "Where's Swanson?" His voice was razor sharp.

I narrowed my eyes and shrugged. "Anybody's guess. Looks like they all left. The trucks we saw must've been the last of them."

Mitch nodded. "We've got people going in all directions trying to find them. We'll get them." He called the other deputies over. "I want this place searched from top to bottom. Start with that main building. Maybe Swanson is holed up in there."

The deputies headed in that direction.

"Enrique and I searched the buildings. No one is here."

Mitch headed towards the main building. "Won't hurt to look again."

Enrique raised his eyebrows and shrugged. "I guess we go help."

We spread out and searched the entire compound. Mitch and a couple other guys searched Swanson's home. I stayed with Enrique, and we went through the main building again. There was no one around. The whole compound felt like a ghost town.

"It looks like they picked up and left in a hurry," I said to Mitch when we reconvened in the parking area. They had left clothes, household furnishings, and food.

Mitch nodded. "I have a bad feeling between my shoulder blades, like we're missing something." Worry lines deepened in the corners of his eyes as he took in the compound. "I keep thinking about Jonesboro and all those people drinking poisoned Kool aid because some nut case told them to."

I followed his gaze. The rain had eased again giving us a respite. "If they had done that, we'd see their bodies strung around the compound."

"Unless they went somewhere else to kill themselves," Connolly added. She'd walked up from the arena where Swanson held his family meetings when the weather allowed. "No one down there." She pointed back towards the arena.

"You searched his house?" I asked Mitch.

Mitch nodded. "He didn't spare the money there. You should see that place. But it's funny. He had a whole library of self-help books. How to be a great leader. How to stand tall against an enemy. We even found books on his shelves about how a man is to control his wife. That he is her superior in every way." He shook his head and looked at me.

"Well, that wouldn't work in today's families."

"Maybe not in most families, but you'd be surprised," Connolly chimed in. "there are sects of people who believe in men lording it over women."

"These cults are built on one man's absolute rule," Enrique said. "How they convince people to follow them is beyond me."

I thought about Rose. What had drawn her to the cult? Was it because she'd become so disenchanted with her life that she wanted something different? Was she drawn because Priscilla had offered a community, a family and Rose didn't have that at home? Or was it like we thought; that she'd followed a guy. I felt like I'd let her down. Now I'd never know why she joined the cult.

My heart was heavy as I studied my co-workers. Would they feel the same about me if they knew I'd let my family down?

Mitch interrupted my thoughts. "Liz, where would Swanson take his people if he wanted to hide them?"

I frowned. "Enrique and I have been talking about that since we got here. I wish I knew." Then I remembered something Carolyn Butler told me. "Wait a minute. Carolyn Butler told me Swanson owned property in Washington. That's where they started out. Maybe he still owns it. Maybe he moved the family there."

"Where in Washington?"

I pulled my cell phone out of my pocket. "Maybe her sister knows." I called Judy's number, but it rang and rang, and no one answered. There was no voicemail. Just the ringing of the phone. "She's not answering. Call Sheriff Walls and have her ask Corey Butler. I'm sure he knows where it is."

Mitch took his phone out and called the sheriff. I was too agitated to wait and paced back and forth in front of the main building. If they weren't there, where would Swanson have taken them? I had no idea but felt certain Corey would know.

I'd been pacing, waiting for Mitch to get hold of Sheriff Walls when something at the base of the main building caught my eye. The rain had eased off again and the sun was trying to come out. A small point of light hit on something in the flowerbed that didn't look right.

I walked towards it and looked down. It was some sort of metal ring attached to a square of heavy metal. I noticed the ground around the metal ring had been disturbed recently.

"Mitch."

He glanced up from his conversation and something in my voice must have alerted him to the fact I'd found something. He walked closer. "What is it?"

I pointed to the ring. It was the size of a small dinner plate. He got down on his knees and pulled on it. He struggled, his face turning red as he strained to pull it up. I got down next to him and helped pull. Enrique and Connolly must've seen our struggle because they came over to help. Eventually it opened.

It was a small doorway with stairs leading down. I was sure Mitch's expression mirrored mine. Horror and revulsion filled my chest. Was this where Swanson had stashed his people? What if he couldn't make it back to get them out? Would they be able to get out themselves?

Mitch started down the stairs with me right behind him. At the bottom were two openings. One to the right and one to the left. Mitch took the one to the left and I went right.

I took the flashlight off my belt and shone it around. The area had been tunneled out and smelled of fresh dirt. After I'd taken a few steps, I noticed a wooden box sitting in front of me. It was long and narrow. Was it a coffin?

Horror filled me. I called for Mitch, pointing to the coffin when he came up behind me. Mitch and I made our way to the coffin. We could hear what sounded like scratching. Something or someone was in there. I noticed a lock that had been latched, but it wasn't locked. We opened it up and stared down at a white-faced woman. She moved and we jumped.

I realized right away who laid there with a gag in her mouth. It was Dorcas. I undid the gag and she cried, "Please help me. They left me here to die!"

Chapter 57

M itch lifted Dorcas from the coffin and carried her up the stairs because she was too weak to walk. When we asked how long she'd been down there, she didn't know.

"Why did you come back here?" I asked. "I thought you went home with your mother."

Dorcas blinked and squinted. "I did, but Brother Ezekiel came to get me. My mom was at work, and I was alone. He brought me back here." Her eyes filled with tears. "I'm not safe anywhere."

"Why did they put you underground?" I asked.

Dorcas grabbed my hand and held on. "I was being punished," she whispered.

"For what?"

She sobbed and put her free hand up to her face. She shook so hard she almost missed. "For trying to hide the children. They were going to send them away. I was taking them to my mom's, but Father found out, he put me on the stretcher and threatened to put me in the fire." She burst into tears. "Then you guys saved me."

"Oh, Dorcas." My heart went out to the younger woman.

"They were selling them. Little children! They were taking them from their families and selling them. I just couldn't stand it anymore. They were so sad. They cried all the time." She closed her eyes and continued to cry. "Rose tried to get them out of here, but Ezekiel caught her. That's why they had to kill her."

My breath caught in my throat. *Rose.* She'd tried to do the right thing in the end.

"Do you know what they did with the children?" Mitch asked.

She shook her head. "Those poor babies. They just wanted to go home."

Mitch called for an ambulance.

Mitch carried Dorcas into the main building and laid her on one of the sofas. When he started to lay her down, she cried out. "No! Father will be angry!"

I put my hand on her arm. "It's okay, Dorcas. There's no one here."

She tried to sit up but was too weak. She sank back onto the sofa. A confused look crossed her face. "Where is everyone?"

I squatted next to her. She still had a death grip on my hand. "We don't know. We think Swanson moved everyone." My voice was gentle. "Do you know where he would have taken them?"

She shook her head. "No. Why did he move everyone?"

"I hoped you could tell us."

She sighed and leaned her head back against a pillow Connolly had found for her. Then she whispered, "Mother's dead. Sister Rose Sarai is dead. Maybe he was trying to save the family from whoever is trying to kill us."

She grabbed my hand. "You've got to help us. Father says there's a group of people who want to see our family destroyed."

"Did he say who they are?" I asked.

"No, but he said we might have to defend ourselves. He wanted us all to learn to shoot a gun. We were taking lessons." She tried to sit up but groaned and laid back down. "Maybe the bad people took the family."

"Dorcas, it would help a lot if you knew who the bad people are."

She looked at me for a few seconds like she wanted to tell me something, then she turned her head towards the back of the sofa.

Even though I kept talking to her until the ambulance came, Dorcas didn't know or wasn't telling where Swanson had taken the family.

Mitch stood next to me while the EMT's put Dorcas on a stretcher and carried her outside and loaded her into the ambulance. "She wouldn't tell you where he took them?"

"I don't think she knows. She still thinks Swanson has their best interest at heart, even after he left her in a coffin for who knows how long." I shivered. "I can't imagine what she went through in that coffin. It must've been horrifying."

Mitch nodded. "At least there were air vents. If there weren't, she may not have survived."

We watched as the ambulance drove away.

"Once the doctors have a chance to check her over, we'll need to talk to her again. See if she remembers anything else." Mitch said, heading towards his car. "Sheriff Walls called. Corey told her how to find the property in Washington the Swanson's own. He said if Swanson moved the family, that's probably where he's taking them."

"Is she going to go check it out?"

He nodded. His phone beeped a message, and he took it out of his pocket and glanced down. His face turned red.

"What is it?" I asked.

"Nothing."

"Is it Jenn?"

He stopped and turned to me. "Why do you think every message I get is from Jenn? I do have people who work for me, you know."

"Because she's been trying to get hold of me all afternoon. I thought maybe she'd been trying to get hold of you too."

"No. I haven't heard from her in days."

Since I told her to stay away from him? I wondered.

Mitch stalked off to his car and I went to find Enrique. I knew something besides this case bothered Mitch.

Was Mitch planning on leaving me? The thought flitted into my head. He'd acted so weird lately. Were he and Jenn having an affair? Were they planning to dump Ray and me and be together? I couldn't imagine Jenn leaving Ray's money. She might leave him, but she liked being the wife of a senator. She liked having money.

And what about Mitch?

Enrique called my name and I put my worries about my marriage out of my mind so I could work the case. "Sheriff wants us to go over this place with a magnifying glass before he calls the feds in," Enrique said.

I knew he'd have to call the feds in if Swanson had moved the children to another state. "Third times a charm?"

Enrique grinned.

After we'd searched the entire compound for the third time and didn't find any evidence except where they'd kept the children, Enrique and I left with one of the other deputies. Enrique's vehicle had been towed to town and we went back to the sheriff's office.

I was bone tired, but I wanted to check on Dorcas before I went home.

The house was cold when I got inside, so I turned up the heat. The rain had slowed down, but it was still wet outside, and it made everything feel damp and cold.

After I'd changed into sweats and a sweatshirt, I made a cup of tea and sat down on the sofa in the living room with my phone. I knew I hadn't dealt with losing my sister in such a horrible way, and the thought of telling Bella she'd been killed would bring it all to the front. I didn't know if I could handle the emotions, but it wasn't fair to not tell Bella.

I started to hit the number for her cell phone when my phone rang. For a second, I thought maybe she'd felt me thinking about her and decided to call me. That had happened so many times since she left for school. But it wasn't her number. It was Murray.

I hit the button and said, "Hello."

"Uh...Lizzie...uh...you need to come to the shop."

"Murray? What's going on? Are you okay?"

"Sure. Sure. I need you to come...uh...talk to me."

I heard a muffled "oomph," and jumped off the sofa, heading towards the bedroom to get my shoes. "I'm on my way, Murray. Hang in there, okay?"

"Just you, Lizzie. Don't bring...your husband or your son. I need to talk to you alone."

My husband and my son. I knew Murray was in trouble and trying to tell me something, but I wasn't sure what. "Okay, Murray. I'm on my way."

I slid into my tennis shoes and grabbed a rain jacket out of the hall closet. Murray hadn't sounded like himself, and I was probably walking straight into danger.

Chapter 58

The rain had come back with a vengeance as I rolled into Parkdale. I'd tried to call Mitch, but his phone had gone straight to voicemail. I left a message telling him I had a call from Murray and was headed to Parkdale to see what was going on.

I listened to an inner voice which told me to be careful and parked down the street from Murray's shop. I held my gun at my side as I walked down the street. The shop lights were off. I tried peeking in the windows, but I couldn't see anything except the shape of a couple trucks Murray was working on.

There was a light on an advertisement board which illuminated the trucks, but there wasn't any movement. I eased open the front door into Murray's office. I had a pin light and I held it up, moving it around to see if there was anyone there. The office was empty.

Where was Murray? Was he being held prisoner somewhere?

I walked around to the back of the shop to the door I'd entered a few days ago. I tried the knob and it turned under my hand. It opened inward and I eased into the room, wishing I could see.

I'd taken a step when I felt a hard metal object press against the back of my head. "Throw your gun on the floor," a deep voice growled in my ear.

I threw my gun as far away from me as I could.

"Where's Murray?" I asked, holding my hands in the air.

"He's taking a little nap." He shoved me towards the door. "You and I are going for a ride."

He pushed me outside towards a pickup. I couldn't tell what color it was in the moonlight, but it was a dark color. The man opened the passenger door and told me to get in. I finally got a look at him. He wore a face covering, but I knew who he was. Brandon Butler.

"Why are you doing this?" I asked.

"Just get in the pickup." When I hesitated, he wrenched my arm and put zip ties on me. "Don't make me tell you again."

I climbed into the truck, and he hooked my hands to the seatbelt.

"Where are we going?" My mind buzzed. Brandon Butler? What was he up to? Had he killed his mother and sister? Why?

"You'll see."

He pulled out of the parking area and headed out of Parkdale. I assumed he was taking me to the compound, but he surprised me and drove passed the turnoff.

My phone was in my pocket. I'd put it on silent mode before I left home. Now it buzzed with an incoming call. I hoped it was Mitch and he'd try to trace my phone so he could find me.

The man must've heard something because he held out his hand. "Give me your phone."

"What?" I stalled for time. I didn't want to give up my phone.

"Give it to me or I'll shoot you and leave your body on the side of the road."

I handed him the phone and watched as he rolled the window down and threw it out. He was sweating and swiped at his forehead with the sleeve of his sweatshirt.

"Why are you doing this, Brandon?"

He startled and jerked the pickup sending us into the gravel at the side of the road. "So, you know who I am?" He pulled the steering wheel and straightened out the truck, giving me a quick glance.

I nodded. His height had given him away. "Did you kill my father and sister?"

He shook his head. "Nope."

"Do you know who did? Was it Swanson?"

"You'll find out soon enough."

He pulled off the highway onto a logging road. The truck bucked and swayed over the potholes. Shivers ran down my back.

"Where are you taking me?"

He didn't answer.

At the bottom of a small hill was an old barn. There was a black pickup parked near the entrance. Brandon pulled up next to it and put the pickup in park. Then he turned off the key and opened his door, climbed out, and came around the truck to open mine.

The barn seemed abandoned. There were weeds so tall they covered the smaller door. The big door was open, and it was dark inside.

"What's going on, Brandon? Tell me what I'm walking into." I knew I was pleading, but I couldn't help it. Had he brought me here to kill me too? Was he working for Swanson?

He smirked and helped me out of the pickup. Then he pushed me towards the entrance. I drug my feet, not wanting to go inside. When I did, a scream tore through my throat.

Jeremiah Swanson sat on a stool in the middle of the old barn. Light from a hole in the roof shown down on him. His face was beaten and bloody. Standing next to him with a gun pointed at his chest was Carolyn Butler's sister, Judy.

Chapter 59

"Is he dead?" I asked, my voice a whisper. Why had they brought me here to witness this? Whatever their reason, I knew it wasn't going to end well and I hoped Mitch was searching for me.

"Not yet," Judy said, "but he will be soon if he doesn't agree to our demands."

I couldn't believe Judy was behind the killings. "You killed my father and sister?"

She gave me a look full of pity. "Of course not. Old Jeremiah here sent his goon to kill Rose and he shot your dad instead. We got that out of him before Brandon went looking for you. Sorry, Hun."

My chest filled with pain, and I glared at Jeremiah. "Why? Why did you have my sister killed?"

Jeremiah lowered his head and mumbled something.

Brandon picked up a baseball bat and moved towards him. "Tell the detective."

Jeremiah looked up at me with his good eye, no expression on his face. He could barely speak because of the mess they'd made of his face. "She wath goin to tell."

"That's right." Brandon backed off. "Rose found out about Jeremiah's little sideline business. She tried to free the children, but his goon caught her before she could leave the compound."

"How did you find out?" I asked him. It was the same thing Dorcas had told her.

"Corey told Aunt Judy. He was sick about it. He didn't want those little kids suffering like we did when we were little."

My heart broke for them, and the children Swanson had kidnapped. I wanted to take the baseball bat away from Brandon and finish the job he'd started. "What are you going to do now?" I asked. "You know I can't just let you get away with beating up Swanson even if he deserves it."

Judy laughed. "Don't you worry about us, Hun. We've got a plan. Once Swanson gives you his statement, we leave you two here. We'll call the sheriff and let him know where you are."

"And then?" I asked.

Judy shrugged. "I don't think Swanson will press charges." She pushed his shoulder with the barrel of the gun and Jeremiah groaned. "And we've got a good lawyer."

I wasn't going to argue. They'd find out soon enough that you can't take the law into your own hands. "What about Corey?"

"What about him?" Judy asked.

"He's being held for questioning in Carolyn's murder."

Brandon and Judy looked at each other. "I thought he'd gone off the grid again," Judy said. "I haven't seen him in days."

Brandon shook his head. "Why would they think Corey killed Mom? Corey loved her."

"You said yourself that she and Priscilla didn't protect him when he was little. We thought he'd let the resentment build until he couldn't stand it any longer, then he got rid of them."

I fidgeted with the zip ties on my hands. They weren't tight and I hoped I could get my hands undone. Brandon watched me with a smile on his face. I hadn't noticed it before, but he and Corey had the same look, a wildness in their eyes. I should've seen that. Maybe I could've prevented Brandon and Judy from kidnapping Swanson.

"You need to let us go." I gestured to Swanson. "You can't kidnap people and get away with it."

"Why not? This scumbag's been doing it for years." Judy waved the gun at Swanson.

"He won't be doing it any longer," I promised her. "We'll see to that." I turned to Swanson. "Where's your family? Did you have them moved to your property in Washington?"

Swanson seemed startled. "Wha' ya mean?"

"They aren't at the compound. We spent the day searching for them. Where'd you send them?"

Swanson tried to yell through his busted-up lips. He tried to stand, but Judy hit him with her gun, and he slumped over.

"Where did you find him? Did you take him from the compound?" I asked Judy.

She pointed her gun at Swanson. "We sent him a message to meet us at Carolyn's house. Told him we had something to sell him."

"Told him to come alone," Brandon said, with pride in his voice. "And nabbed him when he got there."

"He moved everyone to Washington?" Judy asked. She moved over to Swanson and hit him in the shoulder with her gun. "You lying scum. You said they were all still at the compound. Where's Dorcas? Where's my niece?"

"Dorcas is your niece?" I asked, startled.

Judy nodded. "My brother's daughter. Mariah Collins. This idiot changed her name to Dorcas."

"We found her. She's in the hospital, but she'll be okay."

Judy smiled. "Where was she?"

I looked at Swanson. "Do you want to tell her?"

He didn't lift his head.

"She was at the compound. Everyone else was gone."

"He sent everyone else away and left Mariah there?"

"No, I did." Ezekiel or Dan or whatever he was called stood in the doorway, an assault rifle pointed at Judy. "Drop your weapon."

Judy pointed at him and pulled the trigger, missing him. He shot her, blowing her body five feet away from where she'd been standing.

Brandon screamed and ran. Ezekiel shot him in the back.

I stared at him, wide eyed, waiting for him to shoot me too. Swanson chuckled. "Ith abou' tim," he said, grinning at Ezekiel. "I din't thin you makth it."

While Ezekiel went to free Swanson, I struggled with my hands, trying to get them free. I knew I only had a couple minutes to act. When they wouldn't break free, I hurled myself at Ezekiel, knocking him over.

His gun went flying and he tried to grab me. I scurried away from him, trying to get to the gun first. I'd almost reached it when his hand gripped my foot. "Drop it," he snarled.

"No, you drop it," a voice said from the doorway and Mitch, Enrique and Connolly stepped inside.

Chapter 60

Later, I told Mitch I was never so happy to see them in my life. I'd wondered how I'd get out of there alive.

"How did you know where to find me?" I asked, after I'd told Mitch what had happened to Judy and Brandon, Enrique and Connolly cuffed Jeremiah Swanson and Dan Rivers/Brother Ezekiel and led them away.

"I got your call, so I called Murray. They'd tied him up, but he managed to get free. He told me what happened. Garcia found out the cult owned this property. We traced your phone and started in this direction, not knowing if you were here, or where you were. We got lucky."

"So, did I."

Mitch drove me back to Parkdale to get my Jeep. "Go home and get some rest," he said. "We can talk this out in the morning."

I nodded, so dead tired I didn't think I could keep my eyes open much longer. The adrenaline of the last few hours had worn off. I went home and fell into bed.

When I woke up it was mid-afternoon. If Mitch had been home, he hadn't slept in our bed. His side was still made. I wondered if he was still interviewing Swanson. I stepped into the shower and washed my hair. The hot water cascading over my skin felt wonderful. My body ached from my wrestling match with Dan Rivers.

After I dressed in jeans and a bright blue sweater, I headed downstairs for coffee. I heard voices in the kitchen and recognized Jenn's. I heard her say, "We have to tell Liz."

"Tell Liz what?" I asked, walking into the kitchen with a sinking feeling in my stomach.

They both turned to me, guilt written all over their faces.

"Liz!" Jenn exclaimed. "I thought you were still asleep."

"Tell me what?" I asked, my voice quiet and deadly.

Jenn glanced at Mitch who had lowered his gaze to the floor. "We have to tell her," She said, quietly. "It's all over town."

I waited, not wanting to give them the satisfaction of not having to say the words. I gazed at my husband. "Tell me."

Mitch shook his head. When he looked up there were tears in his eyes. "I didn't want this to happen."

"What?"

"We had an affair, okay? It didn't last long and we're both sorry as hell, but Ray found out and went ballistic. He's threatening divorce and he said we either tell you or he's going to."

Even though I'd suspected, hearing her say the words filled me with so much pain I could no longer stand. I sank into a chair. Mitch sat with his head in his hands.

"I'm sorry, Liz," Jenn said. "Like Mitch said, we didn't plan it, it just sort of happened."

"Oh really? How do these things just sort of happen? You both know that you're married. You both know what you did was wrong. Explain to me how you didn't want to hurt me." My voice had risen at the end.

Mitch grimaced. "I'm sorry, Lizzie."

I started to say something, but a pounding on the door interrupted me. Through the glass I could see Travis standing there.

Mitch must've seen him too. "Great. This is all we need. I'll get rid of him." Mitch stood, but I stopped him from going to the door.

"No, let him in. I'll talk to him." I walked around Mitch, giving him a disgusted stare, and opened the door for Travis.

Travis walked in and pulled me into his arms. "I heard you'd been shot. Thank God you're okay."

I stood in the circle of his arms for a few seconds, enjoying the comfort he brought.

"We're in the middle of something here," Mitch said. "Can you come back later."

Travis looked from Mitch to Jenn and then back to me. "So, it's true. I can tell by your faces."

I stared at him. "You knew?"

He nodded. "I'd heard rumors. I tried to tell you the other day." He shook his head. "I wanted to warn you."

"This is none of your business," Mitch said, giving Travis the evil eye.

I'd stepped out of the circle of his arms and Travis smiled at me. "Well, that's where you're wrong, Mitch.

It is my business. I care deeply about Liz and don't want to see her hurt." He gazed at me with such longing for a second it took my breath away.

Mitch held the door open. "Why don't you both leave? Liz and I need to talk.'

I felt numb. My world was crumbling around me. My husband was having an affair with my best friend and if I'd read his face correctly, my neighbor was in love with me.

I reached up and hugged Travis. I cared about him, but I wasn't ready to think about how he felt about me. "I'll talk to you later."

He nodded. "Call me. Anytime. I'm always here for you." He took the door out of Mitch's hand and waved Jenn over. "Time for us to leave."

Jenn kept her eyes on Mitch, but he nodded. I could tell she wanted him to let her stay. That was Jenn, always after the thrill. She got up and walked to the door. When she came close to me, she whispered, "I'm so sorry. You have to forgive me."

In my mind, I screamed, 'I don't have to do anything!'" What came out my mouth was entirely different. "What's going on with you and the mayor?"

Jenn looked startled. "Nothing. We're just friends."

Yeah. I glanced at Mitch, but he didn't say anything. Did he know Jenn was playing around with the mayor too? Did Ray? I watched as she and Travis left. Mitch closed the door and held his hands out to me. "Please, Liz, can we talk about this?"

They say when you're dying your life passes before your eyes. I was watching the end of my life as I knew it and images of Bella, of happier times with her and Mitch passed before my eyes. Bringing her home from the hospital, first day of kindergarten, family trips to Hawaii and Disney World and seeing her off to college. *Oh, my sweet girl. What is this going to do to you?*

"Please talk to me. If you want to hit me, that's fine. I deserve it. Just say something," Mitch implored.

I hurt so much I could barely breathe. Even though I hated the thought of losing my family, I couldn't let Mitch dictate what came next. I backed up, my hands in the air. "I need time to think."

He nodded. "Okay, take all the time you need. But please, Liz, remember I love you and I never meant for this to happen."

I stared at him until he squirmed. "How can you say that? Of course, you meant it to happen, or it wouldn't have."

He cringed. "I didn't mean to hurt you."

I laughed, a sharp bitter sound. "I'm going to my dad's. When I've had some time to think, we'll talk." I turned and walked upstairs to pack.

Numbness crept over me. I knew the tears would come, along with anger and more pain than I could imagine. I had loved Mitch for so long, and he hadn't loved me as much as I thought he did.

As I threw underwear, jeans, and sweaters into a bag, I felt the first tear escape and run down my cheek. I wouldn't give in to them until I was alone. I went into the bathroom and packed my makeup and hair products. When I went back into the bedroom, Mitch sat on the bed, tears running down his face.

"I'm so sorry," he said, over and over. "Please, Liz, I don't want you to leave. Stay and let's talk this out."

I raised my hand. "I need time." I picked up my bags and headed to my car.

I'd lost so much. My dad, my sister and now my marriage. But there was one thing I knew. No matter how much I'd lost, I'd be okay. Not today, and certainly not tomorrow, or maybe not for a year. But one day, I'd be okay. I was strong. I would make it.

Mitch stood in the doorway and watched me leave. I glanced at him and wished this hadn't happened, wished I could go back in time and have what I'd had a few weeks ago. What I'd thought I had.

If wishes were horses...I remembered my mom saying that so many times when I was young. What had she wished for? Why had her life been torn inside out? I sighed, thinking I'd probably never know for sure. Then I headed my Jeep towards my dad's house. I had a lot to think about. A whole new world stretched out in front of me, and I had to figure out how to live it.

The End

Acknowledgments

I am humbled by all of the wonderful people who have helped me bring this book to life.

First, I want to thank my amazing, talented granddaughter, Kristin Fox, for doing my makeup and taking my author picture. I was remiss in not including Kristin in the acknowledgments of the last book. She has such an eye for photography and did such a great job applying my makeup and taking pictures. Thank you, my love.

My granddaughter, Haylie Fox, talked murder weapons with me and is always a great help when it comes to brainstorming ways to murder someone! Thank you, sweetie!

My son, Robert Fox, designed my website and helped me pick a cover designer. Thank you, Bob. What would I do without you?

My daughter-in-law, Andrea Fox, a 911 operator, helped walk me through how the Sheriff's Office works and answered pages of questions. If she didn't know, she knew who to ask. Thank you, Andrea! I'm sure I'll have more questions for the next book!

I'd also like to thank Sargeant Ricardo Castaneda, retired, for answering questions about police work and the Sheriff's Office. Any mistake in procedures is mine, not theirs.

I'd like to thank my sons, David and James, my daughters-in-law, Sarah K. and Sarah J., for encouraging me along the way and helping to promote my last book. Also, my grandsons, Justin and Connor, for encouraging me! I love you all!

Special thanks to my Beta readers: Mary Birk, Sharon Hoblitzell, Beverly Shackow and Datta Groover. You're the best!

And to all of you who read my first book and decided to give this one a try! Or even if this is the first book of mine you've read, thank you so much. No book will ever come to life without readers. I am so grateful for all of you!

Lana M. Fox, December 2022

About Author

Lana M. Fox is a mystery author who lives in Hood River, Oregon, where she and her family own cherry and pear orchards. When she isn't writing, Lana loves to read, travel and spend time with her family.

9 798985 042931